LENALIA

AGE OF RECREATION: BOOK ONE

BRANDON PLASTER

Edited by Lauren Buchsbaum
Book and Cover design by Brandon Plaster
Cover photograph: Hubble M31 PHAT Mosaic

ISBN: 978-0-9861244-0-2

FIRST EDITION

10 9 8 7 6 5 4 3 2 1

To mom, for always allowing me to breathe.

Twirling in a blue denim dress, she smiled. Her cheeks cracked from dried tears.
Could it be real? Was she outside?

PROLOGUE

"Did you know that behind the paint there is a world more beautiful than could ever be captured?"

Lena let out a giggle and nestled into his arms. Her dad always talked like that when he returned from working in the capital. He would fill her mind with stories of labyrinthine buildings that could change at the touch of a surface and of secret tunnels leading to forgotten cities. But he was most excited on the days when he got a glimpse of the outside.

"I don't think that's possible. Ms. Pluck told us that the murals show us what the world used to be like before us."

There was a pause, and then she felt him hug her tightly. He kissed her forehead and warmth ran down her spine. As he sighed, she knew that whatever he was going to say was important. To convey emotion through altered breathing had long since been deemed non-optimal. Forbidden.

"My little Solena. She has to tell you that. If I can teach you one thing, it's to look past the surface. Don't assume that the layer you see is the only one. There are galaxies in anthills and universes on mushrooms."

She scrunched her nose and looked up at him. His eyes were webs of soft green. "What's a mushroom?"

He smiled and ruffled her hair, and she laughed as he tickled her back into his arms. She wanted so much to see the world the way he did. When she finally settled, she peeked up over his chin. She couldn't make out the shape of his eyebrows, but he was wearing the face he got whenever he had an idea. She bit the inside of her cheek.

"I think," he paused, letting the words arrange themselves before continuing, "that I'll find a way to take you into work."

She sat up, alert, and for the first time noticed that her heart was beating perceptibly faster. She gasped. When the sound of her breathing reached her ears, she gasped again and covered her mouth. Her eyes quivered as she looked at her dad, but he only smiled and removed her hands from her face.

"Whatever people say, don't be afraid to breathe. In this house, you can take as many breaths as you want."

"But they—"

"They nothing," he cut her off. "In this house, you can have my breaths."

Her shoulders relaxed, as did her breathing. Though even as it fell back into its day-to-day, she remained aware of its persistence. "So, I'll get to see you take apart bins?" she said as she lay back down.

"Even better. You'll get to see a glimpse of the past. Mountains and mountains of relics from days gone by, from when the world you know was new, and from when the world-that-was was ending. And maybe then you'll begin to see the layers of life that exist in everything." He wrapped his arms back around her and laid his head on hers.

She curled up closer and closed her eyes. With him, she was forever safe.

PART ONE

I.

Lena sat, curled into her Safe position, her knees pushing into her lungs, restricting the volume of air that she could consume. She focused on the phrases she was taught in school, the phrases meant to reduce her breathing. "Limit to fuel; fuel to create; create to limit," she repeated to herself. "Limit to fuel; fuel to create; create to limit."

As her breathing slowed and became shallow, her mind retraced how she'd gotten here.

In front of her stood Addy, Mantha, and that bulky transfer from Racine. She could never remember her name, but her braces made her think "Railroad Mouth". They'd told Lena there was mud in the closet. Real mud! She wanted to believe it so badly. She imagined an earthy odor resonating from the metallic black of the closet's interior. Her feet jumped first, and the rest of her followed.

She saw the mud splash from beneath her feet, up onto the other girls' skirts. She saw herself giggling until she realized there was no mud, and that the other girls had stopped laughing. She saw them staring with their tiny black beads fixed on her fading grin. The door closed. Only the sound of a desk scraping against her exit followed.

She snapped back to the present. Her breathing had accelerated. She had to focus. What did the teachers say? If you're not always in the present, you'll never have a future? She pressed her knees harder into her chest, expelling any excess air in her lungs. She repeated the phrases again, "Limit to fuel; fuel to create; create to limit." Several moments passed until her breathing steadied.

There was still an hour until the air would be changed in this sector. After all, it was only meant as a transition tube between bins; it was never meant to hold breathers during inactive hours. She knew that if she was caught in here, she would be in more trouble than she was already in for missing class. Still, she had never truly fancied running out of oxygen.

Her environment was standardized, like any other school tube. Silky aluminum walls wrapped into a hallway-sized bendy-straw structure, intended for the liquid flow of children from one bin to another. But like every other tube it was unique. A thick film of dried paint lined the walls, remnants of the last Recreation Day. It was the day that marked the recycling of the world, the day where complete homeostasis was achieved, the last day that humans touched the earth. Every year on Cycle 71, at 13:00, classes across the world would take to the bins, the tubes, and even some of the containers, and they would imagine a new world, and color the walls with their creations. Most students would paint creatures with hundreds of horns, or scenes of historical battles with tiny horses, and some would even join together to build elaborate murals of mystical lands floating among the clouds. But instead each year Lena would sneak and snatch a handful of colors, primarily oranges and blacks, from unsuspecting classmates, and she would blend the paints into a muddy brown in which she would jump and splash and roll about. To her it seemed obvious. *How else*, she thought, *could I be a mud monster?*

It just so happened that she was now huddled in a dry patch of the "mud" she'd once shed. Or rather, she'd picked this spot because of that, but she liked to think things happened coincidentally. Life felt a little less controlled this way. She wished that sometimes things in her world just existed, instead of needing a purpose. Even this tube had a specific purpose, and it certainly wasn't intended for stagnation. But that's what she was doing right now, regardless: stagnating.

She was good at stagnating. *Everyone moves with a sense of purpose, without stopping. If only people would stagnate a little more, then they would appreciate the life moving around them,* she thought. It was hard to explain this to people when there were no windows to the outside. Sitting there with her hand pressed against the cold aluminum, she could feel it. Through the half inch of paint she could feel the warmth being slurped from her fingertips; she could feel the transfer, the movement of her heat to her captor.

Even without windows, even when her world wasn't following the sun, she knew that life was happening all about her. As Lena held her hand against the tube wall she felt the subtle chaotic vibrations of a slow breeze outside, just out of reach. There was a world beyond   the acrylic, one that her storybooks had only begun to describe.

The room started to hum. It wasn't like the buzzing of the ever-droning lights that lit her container at home. This sounded more like music to her. Simple. Soft. Alive. She went through the motion of pushing her hair behind her ear before remembering that she'd hacked each chestnut strand away the day before. She leaned sideways and pressed an ear against the cold metal. Settling in, she felt the tiny fluctuations dance against the even tinier hairs in her ears and she let out a snort. She wanted to feel embarrassed, but there was no one around, so she made a mental note to feel extra embarrassed about something else later. The wall began to speak to her in the ways walls normally did, when, of course, she decided to listen.

"Hmm hmm hm hmmmmm," it hummed to her.

"And to you as well," she whispered back.

"Buzz buzz buzz buzzzz," it buzzed to her.

"I know, I know, it's been so long. Nearly ninety cycles. But I'm not supposed to be here, you know that," she rebutted.

"Bhrm bhrm bhrmmmm bhrm bhrm," it bhrmed back.

She knew there was no winning with this wall; it had always seemed to have a bigger imagination than her. So instead of arguing, she apologized, and she knew immediately that it forgave her, for it became less cold to her touch. The minutes passed as she recounted all that had happened since their last acquaintance, which wasn't much, as everyone had to live by their approved schedules. Lena, though, liked to focus her attention on the little things, which made her life seem quite big.

She told the wall, whom she now dubbed Wallington the Stubborn, or Stubby for short, how she'd noticed that she could play with people's breathing. How everyone seemed to breathe at the same time as those around them, as if every person was just a single organism. Moreover, she'd found during class that she could breathe behind one column of kids and only that column would synchronize with her. And that was how it happened that one day she managed, by switching back and forth between columns, with her classmates breathing, to conduct Bach's Prelude. Or, at least the first few notes, before she was yelled at for running around the back of the classroom. In response she had just sat and grinned, for she knew that in those moments the world was her orchestra.

Stubby reverberated with delight. "Hmmm hmm hmmm hmmmm."

"Thank you," Lena replied. "It was only obvious."

"Hmm Hmm," said Stubby. "It's all clear."

Lena froze. Stubby may have been the most talkative of walls, but she had never heard him use human words. Human words were meant for humans, not for walls. She pressed her ears harder against his surface, straining not to make a noise, so she didn't miss his next words. If indeed they were his.

At first there was nothing, just silence. Even the breeze seemed to be holding its breath. And then words as if from outside: "We'll need to do a tube sweep, to verify." This was a new voice, less harsh than the first, almost feminine.

"It's C-Phase, so that tube is devoid of O_2, it'd be a waste of a sweeper." There it was again, that scratchy deep man's voice, almost bursting with wisdom. But a man? And a woman? Humans? In the outside? Beyond the domes of the cities? Nothing was making sense; Lena's heart was bashing itself against the walls of her chest.

"I thought you were supposed to be at the cabin. Not that I mind the impromptu visit, but it's nearly daybreak. What is it that couldn't wait for the meeting?"

"I won't be able to make it tonight, I had to give up Caldon. They were getting too close."

"Caldon? Damn. They won't be happy."

"It could have been much worse. I—" he started. Lena was balancing on each word and couldn't stand the pause. Then she recognized what must have stopped him. A nasally hum signaled that the fans had just started again. That meant D-Phase was about to start and students would begin flowing through the tubes again within the minute. She couldn't believe it had been an hour already. There were sounds of metal clinking outside that faded until she heard nothing. She knew that the people, if they were in fact people, had fled.

Without the time to consider what had or hadn't happened, she marked on her mental task list, right between "Feed Tulu" and "Feel embarrassed," to go over what she may have heard. She stood, inhaling the new air folding in around her, and slipped over to the side of the entrance where she knew the stream of students would begin. If she could just slide into file, she would avoid getting into trouble for "trespassing" in the tube during C-Phase. *Hah,* she thought, *trespassing, as if being here was a choice. If those jerks didn't push and lock me in that utility bin—*

"Mish Causht, how nishe of you to join shoshiety again. I hope I'm not interrupting shomething terribly important shloshing around in that thick shkull of yoursh," rasped the invading voice of a plump redheaded woman from across the corridor.

With a new silence flooding the tube, Lena's heart fell back over itself, causing a faltering thud to echo along the walls. Her eyes pulled her stare to the other door, giving her the sudden realization that she had accidentally positioned herself on the opposite side, the wrong side of the tube. Staring back at Lena was the steam-engine-shaped body of Ms. Ruebid Pluck.

Lena blinked speechlessly. She contemplated if the steam pouring from Ms. Pluck's ears was new or if she just hadn't noticed it before. The steam seemed to wrap itself into a spirally vortex of derision, quickly melting the faces off a nearby cluster of painted quadrupeds. Somewhere in the world a whistle blew and slowly Ms. Pluck's caboose accelerated forward until she was rapidly chugging towards Lena. A harsh choir of snickering crackled in the background as an audience of students gathered to witness the oncoming collision. In a last moment's effort, Lena threw up her hands to cover her ears, but to no avail. The pale flat fingers of Ms. Pluck closed upon her lobes and pulled her half a foot onto the tips of her toes. Before she could yelp, a hot starchy breath poured into her ear.

"You are to report to scheven-o-one promptly at the schtart of the nexsht Init Phache. If you're late, don't bother schowing up to classh again." Without another word, Ms. Pluck pulled and tossed Lena to the side and chugged along out of sight. A whistle reverberated from the teacher-engulfing shadows and promptly the train of students bounced along the tube into the darkness, each casting a downward glance at where Lena lay.

As the last little girl bustled out of the tube, Lena pushed her palms into the cold floor and slid her feet under her. Blood pulsed about her ear as it radiated heat and agitation. Even as the sentence of 701 scratched at her mind, and tears of pain pressed at her cheeks, Lena's body shivered with excitement. She had a secret. She was now part of a story. For all she knew, it could be her story.

II.

Lena's feet slid hard to the left as she rounded the corner. The metal ground threatened to take her balance. In front of her stood the sprawling dome-covered city of Brin: a gridded network of domino-like complexes filled with domino-like people.

She strained her little legs to push forward with all her strength. She might have been the fastest girl in the world. Thirty feet remained to the entrance to her container. Thirty long feet. She looked back quickly with eyes wide. Twenty feet. Ten feet. At five feet to the door, she dove to the ground. Her momentum carried her forward, her belly coasting across the smoothed aluminum. Just as her head was about to collide with the base of the door, a plastic flap flipped up, permitting her tiny figure entrance to her front hallway. She plunged into a mouth of pillows.

Lena lay on the ground, panting. She felt as if she had a hummingbird in her chest. She gulped the air. "Did," gulp, "you see that?" she shouted to the room. "I," gulp, "was flying!"

Lena flailed about the pillows until finally she wrestled one into submission and planted her face into its cushy cushion. Darkness flooded her eyes, which turned on the lights in her mind. She imagined the run home again. She'd run so fast that both feet left the ground. "I didn't take a breath" gulp, "for three whole tubes!" She growled with delight into her captive.

Lena was brimming with excitement. She knew running and most other forms of strenuous activity were forbidden, but she also knew that they were only forbidden because of the extra air that people used while doing them. *Well*, she figured, *if I don't breathe when doing it, then I'm not breakin' no laws.* A proud smile rested on her lips. She uncovered her face to take another sip of the sweet air.

After letting her breathing settle, Lena flapped her arms to standing and walked backwards to the door to seal the entrance flap. As her hand released the gate, a memory washed over her. *She was walking home from school, her feet dragging along the cold metal ground. Ms. Pluck had forbidden Lena from bringing in Tulu as show-and-tell. She'd said it was "too dangerous". Ms. Pluck was a pansy. As Lena rounded the corner with an overdramatic storm cloud above her head, she saw her dad in the distance. He had one of those smiles on his face, one of the ones he always had when he was proud of himself. She pointed up to her cloud, but he pointed down to the base of the door. She squinted to try and see what he was signaling. What once had been a solid door now contained a small hole, a hole slightly larger than her circumference. She squealed and sprinted forward, leaving the dark nimbus to cry itself out of existence. As she'd done each day since, she leapt onto her belly and slid through the hole into an embrace of pillows. She laughed herself to tears.*

Lena opened her eyes; small watery beads balanced on the acmes of her cheeks. She crinkled her nose and forehead and swatted away the memory. "I'm busy, come back later," she asserted. Her tears fell to the ground, defeated.

Back in the present, Lena jumped, realizing whom she'd forgotten. "TULU! TULU, I'm home!" she shouted. The steps disappeared under Lena's feet as fast as her legs could move. Up she went past the second floor with the bathroom, through the third floor containing the kitchen, around the fourth-floor playroom, and finally stopped in front of a small oak door on the fifth floor. The door was twisted and crooked, and snuggled its way into the frame, trying to appear like it belonged. Its stained surface was littered with engravings of initials faded by time. A fresh set of letters revealed the door's younger layers. Lena traced them with her fingers. L-E-N-A. She fought back another memory.

At Lena's touch, the door made a surprised creak. Instantly, a whirring and burring and spurring sounded from inside the room. Lena pursed her lips, and dimples formed on her cheeks. She stamped her feet giddily, and from behind the door emitted a "bararhrarhrahrah!" Gripping the brass handle, she pushed the door open. From the shallow depths of the room zoomed Tulu. It planted its mop hair into Lena's shin, and spun its head in circles. Lena giggled as its dreadlocked bristles whipped about, tickling her calves. Grasping him in her arms, Lena picked him up and walked through the doorway. Tulu's wheels spun in delight.

The little robot had been Lena's best friend and cohort since its creation. Tulu was born from Lena's belief that life existed in everything. Just three years ago, when Lena was nine, she had visited her dad's workplace for the first time. As a bin-recycler, he would deconstruct outdated and abandoned bins, oftentimes finding unique relics that hinted towards what the initial years of the Recreation were like. When Lena discovered his collection of history, she knew that life was crying to come out again. She had always seen jewels when others saw junk. Climbing through the mounds of treasure, she pulled out the base of an autonomous vacuum, the neck of a blender, and the head of a mop. And thus, Tulu had come to life. He had always been there, though, really. He'd just been waiting for a friend to pick up his pieces.

Dangerous, she thought. "You're not dangerous, are you?" she teased.

His motor growled his most vicious "varoooooom vroom vroom!" Tulu set his spin on high and drove in circles around his master, patrolling her perimeter. The centrifugal forces caused his hair to stand on end.

Lena laughed. "You're a monster! A terrifying monster!" At this, the monster hummed. "Well Mr. Monster, if you please, you must be terribly hungry." Lena stepped over the sputtering robot and picked up a box from the top of her dresser. Tulu stopped spinning and faced Lena, his circuits vibrating in anticipation. His bristles fell with a flop. "Sit!" Lena commanded.

Tulu bhrmed impatiently.

"Roll over" Lena continued, smugly.

Tulu anxiously glared back.

"Paw!"

At this Tulu rumbled forward over Lena's feet, causing her to toss the box into the air in surprise. Hundreds of tiny specks of reflective paper rained from the sky in a rainbow of color. As the squares of confetti hit the ground, Tulu lunged on top of them. He gobbled the tiny flakes, and they were sucked up into his belly, only to be shot out the top of his head again. The resultant confetti continued to rain down in a vibrant cycle. His master spun and danced with glee about the room. She, too, was a cyclone of confetti.

A coating of reds, greens, and blues blanketed the room as the two finally settled. They lay exhausted, panting. Lena felt safe. She knew that her house was the only place she could breathe freely, without the concern of running out of air. Her father had made sure of that.

"Tulu," she sighed. "Can you keep a secret?"

Tulu snuggled in closer to her.

"Tulu, I heard something outside today. I think it was people. And they were talking. But they were talking about the inside. I think they were people from the inside that made their way out. Just think: if we could find them, and have them take us with them, then we could be free. We could see the sky, and the grass, and the earth. Tulu, I could roll in the mud! I could run and run and run until it was me that was out of breath, and not the room!"

Lena looked down at the now-sleeping robot. She frowned. He did not seem to share her enthusiasm. It might not have been his dream to explore the world, but it had been hers ever since she had learned to remember. People weren't meant to live in floating prisons. *Though,* she thought, *people weren't meant to break the earth either.*

Slowly, careful not to wake him, Lena got up and went to the door. She turned back and watched what used to be the indent of her body reshape into the flat surface of her bed, as if she was never there. Descending the steps, she made her way back to the front hallway at the base of her container. She pushed the pillows away, revealing a metal panel on the side of the staircase. At the base sat four screws, reminding her that she hadn't resealed the panel since her last visit. She pried back the sheet of aluminum. The soft whirring of hover engines emanated from the darkness. After pulling on a string, the darkness resolved into a yellow flickering. She made a mental note to replace the bulb, but she knew she wouldn't, at least not until its heart stopped beating. Lena crawled through the opening. She went down past the ducts and wires and pipes that sustained her little home. She reached a point where she knew she couldn't go any further and she lay down against the floor. The purring of the engine was louder here. It rumbled and warmed her. Here was the closest she could be to the earth.

Her father had shown her this place. He had shown her that in every bin and container there were secret places like these, if you knew where to look. Once he'd even told her that on the outside of these structures were railings and platforms for the mechanics to walk along if they needed to work outside. He couldn't show her though. He said that they didn't have a small enough exosuit for her to wear. "Anybody who goes outside is required to wear an exosuit," he had said, "so they don't share the same breath with the earth." She didn't care, but when did that ever change anything?

As the engine sang her to sleep, a memory soon became her dream. It was the day she had learned that her father had died. *She had gotten out of school a phase early and was excited to tell him about how she'd played music with the students' breaths.* Had it really only been sixty cycles? *She had not been as excited to tell him that she had been sent home early because of misbehaving, but she'd figured that since she had never "missed behaving," he would find this amusing. She sat with Tulu at the base of the steps, waiting to surprise her dad. As the hours passed, she began to worry. Every so often she would stick her head out of the door flap to look for him, but he never came home. As she was putting Tulu to bed, she heard the abrasive thud of the mail tube. This was a sound that she never wanted to hear. To get a paper letter meant something horrible had happened.*

The slow walk to the bottom floor was agonizing. Every sigh of the steps resonated through the soles of her feet, constricted the beat of her heart, and pounded violently in her ears. By the time she made it to the door the house interior was blinking yellow, and her vision was swirling in a liquid blur. She ignored the low O_2 warning and pulled out the envelope from the slot.

It read:

Recipient: Lenalia Caust

We regret to inform the recipient that Arthur Caust, listed as the recipient's father, is deceased.

A notice will be issued as to the cause of death after investigation. As requested, the remains of the deceased have been Recycled. We honor the deceased for this contribution.

The deceased leaves to the recipient all possessions not owned by the capital. This includes, but is not limited to:

Residence located at: A364 Sector 4, Brin.

The deceased's policy is insured for 9000 O_2 Credits, taxable.

Please continue with standard schedules.

The Office of President Durin

It was not until three weeks later that Lena was informed of the cause of her father's death. According to the official statement, he had been working in an old bin with first generation O_2 tanks. Back in the first gen days, the concentrations in the mixing system had been imbalanced, and this had resulted in high levels of pure oxygen. The report stated that an accidental spark was caused in the bin, incinerating the crew. No survivors. It had said that they didn't feel pain, but Lena didn't think they could know this.

She didn't really care about going back to school, but eventually a man from the Council patrol found her and forced her to go. She figured it was something to do for now, so she didn't put up too much of a fuss. He'll probably have those bite marks for a while, though.

As the night went on, the memory repeated several more times in Lena's dream. In the end she just kept walking down the steps until finally she opened the door and flew away.

III.

The stale air of eighty-six recycled breaths warmed the room. Circ, the wrinkled tube driver from Deloy, tapped his fingers. Four angry pistons hit the table in succession. He was getting too old to be babysitting. Someone towards the back shifted her hips. The soft creak that stressed from her chair caught everyone's attention.

It was 23:09. Nine minutes ago the meeting of the Outcry should have started. Nine minutes ago the meeting hadn't started.

A darkened tin table slouched at the front of the room, a warped relic that had escaped The Recreation. Behind it sat Circ, a young writer known as Lin, and an empty three-legged chair without a back. A small radio quietly gurgled from atop the table; each person kept one ear on it and one ear on the door.

The crowd breathed in unison, but separately each member glanced about the room, scrubbing over every detail. A cluster of thoughts permeated the bin.

Something must have gone wrong. Is that time right? Can that Racine filth be trusted? This chair is making too much noise. He keeps looking at me. Why haven't we started? Why hasn't Sado spoken? The nearest exit is in the northeast corner, but that could lead anywhere. Is this a setup?

At the stroke of a quarter past, breathing stopped and everyone focused on the radio. A moment passed, but the gurgle persisted.

"We need to start!" erupted a voice from the crowd. "The longer we wait, the more chance we'll be found."

Murmurs upon murmurs upset the silence. Assent and dissent modulated through the crowd.

"And who would lead us?" retorted a Mother from Brin. The tap-tap-tap of Lin's tap-pad mimicked the woman's tone.

A man from Kardel nominated himself by standing but was quickly laughed to his chair. The sharp chin of a woman from Racine pierced upwards through the air, but she in turn was hissed to her seat. Three more members stood and three more members were sequentially opposed. The radio looked out onto a mass of disorder. Everyone was yelling and nothing was changing.

The O_2 sensor on the wall faded from green to yellow. That was changing.

Five pasty tendons wrapped around the brick-like radio. Five twangy bangs resonated through the bin as the radio and table furiously kissed. Eighty-four rabblers hushed and turned their attention to the front.

Circ set down the radio. It babbled happily, blissfully unaware of the high tension and low oxygen blanketing the room. *Lousy schmucks. No respect.* With a gristly cough, Circ cleared his throat and stared at his audience. "Talia has arrived," he stated. He promptly sat.

A crisp woman now sat in the three-legged chair. Long black hair spiraled from her head down around her shoulders in a tight helix. Her black-and-red-streaked lips pursed. Talia lay her hands face up on the table, her cherry oak skin blossoming against the grey. "As you know," tap-tap-tap, "we are gathered here today to discuss change." She took a pause.

Lead it in slowly, Tal. Remember, people follow the calm. She could hear Sado's words. "We are a people that come from the soil, and the mountains, and the oceans that surround us. Yet, for the last two hundred years, fear has decoupled us from our origins. We live in floating cages, imprisoned by society's claim that we are saving ourselves from disease and that we are bettering the earth. An earth that we cannot touch, or see, or savor. Who here has felt the breath of an autumn breeze? Or has tasted the fragrance of lavender? Please speak if you have hummed to the buzz of the honeybee."

The room breathed in her poetry.

Talia continued. "Each cycle we fight for a chance to breathe, when outside these walls exists a vast sphere of life-giving air. President Durin and his Council spread his lies that the earth cannot heal itself with our presence, that the air is still toxic with man-made poison. He claims that our loved ones must be Recycled for a self-sustaining society to be realized. But I have been outside. I have seen the trees. I have breathed the air. I have witnessed that after two centuries the earth is not only healed, but it craves our attention!" tap-TAP! "Let us break apart these barriers and join the cycle of life once again!"

The rigid chair legs scraped the container floor as Talia's audience jumped to the air in applause. In this moment they were all brothers and sisters. Talia pulled her hands together and allowed herself a moment of hope. *There is still life left inside this box,* she thought as the crowd continued to hum to the buzz of their honeybee.

Next to her, Lin beamed. Her script had been given life. This was not a meaningless editorial on a new brushless toothbrush, or a Councilman's speech for increased walking taxes. The words meant change.

Talia gave a quick smile to Lin, then nodded and the crowd settled. She was amazed.

To think, just a few years ago Sado and I prevented them from tearing apart the city. Foolish breathers without focus. Even now their momentary calm is volatile.

Talia kept her face impassive. "Thank you, my friends, for sharing this day with me," she began. "I also thank you for your patience. I know many of you are wondering about my lack of," she paused, "punctuality." The bin chuckled. "And more so, I am sure you question why Sado has not yet spoken." Anxiety hushed the room.

"Late last night, Caldon received word that there would be a massive shipment of O_2 tanks occurring at 23:00 hours, from Brin to the capital at Racine. Caldon and Sado went to intercept the transport but their communication link shorted and they were separated.

When Sado came upon the transport, he found Caldon captured and the shipment crawling with Council patrol. Caldon sacrificed his cover to protect Sado, and for that Caldon will likely be Recycled. He was a leader, our brother, and our friend. Let this serve as an example of what the Council will do to keep their fleeting control. Let us have a moment of silence for Caldon's sacrifice to help free us."

As her words sank in, muffled cries came from the crowd, and Talia prayed that Caldon's death would help unite the fragmented Outcry. It had been a struggle to convince each member that they truly fought for the same cause. More than once someone had broken from rank and lashed out upon the streets of Racine, only to be quickly Recycled. Those moments were fruitless. Even if someone caught word of aggression it was quickly brushed off as an isolated case. A person without an army was just a person, after all. Now that their numbers had grown large enough there stood a real chance for change. *If only we can keep them together,* Talia thought.

Caldon's moment passed. The man from Kardel stood slowly. This time his neighbors remained silent. Talia's gaze washed over him, smoothing the sharp grey bristles lining his face. She had seen him before. He wasn't a regular, but he'd been around since before they'd called themselves the Outcry. She knew years ago his wife had been taken for protesting the Council, and that it still burned inside him. But she didn't know if he was stable, if he had control over his anger. He waited for her approval to speak while she decided whether to permit him. At last the man bowed his head and Talia nodded. He spoke in a fatigued tenor. "Talia, it's not that I wish to abandon Caldon's memory, but please, what has happened to Sado? Does the Council now know of the Outcry? Are we safe here?"

"What is your name, sir?" Talia asked gently.

"Joseph."

"Joseph, you needn't worry. Sado is safe. He has not spoken today because he was called to testify. When found by the transport's guards, Sado claimed ignorance, but as is routine, he was required to appear in front of a court official for government record. As for Caldon, he was dedicated to the Outcry and would not have revealed us. He was well aware of his mission's risk and knew what he must do to protect our secrets."

Joseph exhaled with the rest of the room. "Then we're still a secret?"

"To our knowledge, yes. Our sources in Racine say that the incident was marked as just another outlier in a happy consensus. Soon, however," she paused, unsure of how the crowd would respond. "Soon, we will make ourselves known."

Before the crowd could react to this, the lights in the bin shut off and were replaced by flashing red and an aggressive siren. The crowd's panic sounded over the last few taps of the stenographer's tap-pad. Talia stood quickly but signaled the audience to remain seated. She strode over to the side of the room where the agitated screeching emanated. On the wall was a dusty screen littered with dead pixels. As the screen blinked from black to red, Talia read the words *Low Oxygen Levels. Replace Oxygen Tank Immediately*. She smirked. *These old bins and their last-minute alerts.*

With a restored calm, she walked to the table and pulled out a silver canister from underneath. *All our lives exist in this can. We work each day for just enough life to work tomorrow.* As she slid the tank into the wall, the words on its side shined yellow to the audience. On it was printed "Caution: Pressurized Gas." It might as well have said, "Be Afraid: Life."

With a last click of the canister, the flashing and the sirens ceased. Half the crowd was crammed against the east side of the room in an undulating blob. The other half of the crowd had remained seated, now smug at their lack of panic.

Talia took to her seat, and the crowd followed her lead. Even with the Outcry's present obedience, in the back of Talia's mind lingered the knowledge that in a moment of pressure they would still fold. She did not trust them, for they did not trust her yet. If they were to succeed, this had to change.

This time the Mother from Brin stood. Caldon's Mother. She wiped tears from her eyes. In a voice short of breath, she introduced herself as Esta Amell. "You talk of making our presence known, but are we ready? You saw just now that when the oxygen runs out, we only want to save ourselves. What chance do we have to convince the world that we are a unified front when we can't even convince ourselves?" The crowd nodded in consent.

"Esta, you are a Mother, correct?"

"I am," Esta replied warily.

"And so, as a Mother, you give birth to a new child once every two years, correct?"

"I do, but I don't see how—"

Talia interrupted. "You are a generator of individuals, each of which has the power to evoke change. Do you not see the power in what you create? Yes, without a fire we cannot burn down the house, but without a spark, we cannot start a fire. I agree that before we make ourselves public we must learn to work together. But the longer we wait, the more likely it is that we will be discovered, and as we wait, we give more chances to those who would quell our fire one spark at a time.

"Keep in mind that we do not do this for ourselves, but for future generations so that they may live freely outside these walls and breathe freely as they were meant to do. We are unjustly confined; is this not reason enough to work as one?"

Esta still stood; parallel lines indented across her brow. Even with the newly replenished air, the bin felt stale. There had always been tension between the two of them, ever since they had first met. Talia had always seemed to be hiding something. Everyone had secrets, Esta accepted that, but it was something else. It didn't appear that there was anyone Talia cared about more than herself. *The way she brushed over Caldon's death. She isn't a mother, so how can she be a leader?* "Talia, you speak of greater causes but what are *you* risking? As always, your word weaving shows your capital origin. While we would die in your war, you would hide safe in your shadows. As for future generations, why would the world fight for them? The blood that flows in today's children is mine, mine and the blood of thousands of other Mothers. Why would I believe that you would fight for someone who is not truly your own? No, I will not go public. Not until I hear Sado say we are ready."

With that, Esta made her way to the door. The crowd parted, giving her eight-month belly room to stride. As the door slid open, Esta paused and turned to look back at the meeting of the Outcry. "When my children feel the earth at their feet, and they will, if you have stayed to the shadows until that day, I will make sure that you are confined to the shadows." Esta took a step into the tube and the door slid shut, engulfing her in darkness and the Outcry in unrest.

The tap-tap-tap went unheard.

IV.

At 00:00, the automated district of Brin reset. The silence of the darkness was replaced by the slow fade-in hum of the overhead lights. To those awake, the noise was pollution, reminding them that the world was still asleep. To most others though, it went unnoticed. By 01:00, the beginning of the Init-Phase, it would be constant. The droning would be their silence.

Down below the lights of Sector 4, beneath the grid of six-story pencil-like apartments, in the underbelly of container A364, laid the sleeping body of Lena Caust. As the nasally droning surpassed the low tones of the engines, it prodded at Lena's temple, pushing its way into her dream.

A fruit fly frolicked about Lena's ears. Its tarsal hairs brushed her inner helix. She swatted and flailed with a hundred arms, but still the fly chasséd to safety. As she and the fly danced atop an ocean of verdant clouds, its buzzing resonated in her tiny bones. Realizing that her fly-catching attempts were fruitless, Lena dreamed a change in strategy. She pressed her pause button and floated motionless in the infinity of space; she closed her eyes and was made of sugared gelatin. A moment passed and the fly, desiring the taste of maraschino, went in for a tasteful landing. As its hairy legs contacted Lena's wiggly cheek, Lena knew that this was her trigger. With the might of a falling star, she swung her open hand at the fly's location.

Thwap!

Lena woke with a start. The side of her face throbbed with the color of cherries. Her hand felt full of needles. She scrunched her eyes at the district lamps that still buzzed somewhere in the distance. As she rubbed her cheek, her eyes adjusted to the scattered light of the crawlspace. *Where am...* she glanced around, groggily. *Oh, I guess I fell asleep down here again. Well, what time is—* she froze. Lena's eyes widened as her pupils dilated and her lungs inflated with a quick inhale. "Oh my gosh! I'm going to be late for 701!" she shouted. Tumbling over wires and ducts, she pushed her way up through the crawl space until she flopped out into the hall and, without taking the moment to dry-clean or change, flailed out the front door flap.

Even at this hour when the sector seemed barren, Lena knew she had to be careful with her breathing. The air in every public space was strictly allocated based on a scheduled number of breathers. In some newer areas it varied based on the current cycle's starting capacity, but Sector 4 was old. Brin was old. As a result, if someone were out of place, then one of two things would happen. Sometimes an alarm would go off, and the person that didn't belong would get into a heap of trouble. Most times, though, no alarm would go off, and everyone would be in a heap of trouble. For this, Brin had long since been written off as an example of technological progress. In its time, it had been one of the first cities to be updated and was marveled at for its innovation. But, as always, technology moved faster than people. So, while Brin was still paying for its own reconstruction, updates came to Kardel, Deloy, Racine, and to all the other cities.

As Lena shuffled towards the transport tubes, she remembered years ago the field of people curled into balls, compressed into their Safe positions, lining the streets. A field of dandelions caused by someone out of place. She wanted to pick them all and blow in their faces, so they could break away and fly into the world. Instead, she too had been a dandelion, repeating to herself meaningless words as her dad held her. *Limit to fuel; fuel to create; create to limit,* her mind echoed.

As she got to the transport she wondered if she would ever see a real dandelion. *I certainly wouldn't put a dandelion in a jar,* she thought. *I might put it in my hair though.*

A moment after Lena stepped into the tube the transport's doors slid closed and the hollow cylinder bulleted forward. The canister hurtled around the outer ring of the district, levitating in its vacuum-sealed tunnel. The only way its passengers knew the windowless compartment was actually moving was the invisible force that pinned them against the wall. Years ago, a persistent blinking light would illuminate the passing sector's number, but now the display just flickered a pixelated gibberish. When people complained about the defunct screen, Lena would cover her face with her hands to hide her grin. Her ability to translate the seemingly dead language was one of her little secrets. At this early hour though, no one complained, for Lena was alone. She sat, tapping her feet nervously, and pulling at the wrinkles that covered her green-and-white-checkered pants.

After twenty-six minutes the transport decelerated and stopped at Sector 13. The thwunk of the airlock cued the door to open, and Lena hustled out of the tube and down along the path to her school. When the segmented classrooms came into view, she breathed a sigh of relief, and quickly checked around her to see if anyone had noticed. She walked up to a sterling door. Across its front were the numbers 7-0-1. They appeared to be scratched into the metal. With three minutes to spare, Lena stood staring at the numbers until at last she pushed her hand on the tap-pad. It glared green and the door slid right, letting out a starchy odor. Her nostrils flared. She hated the scent, but it wasn't often that places had a smell, so she took it in by the noseful.

"Get out of the doorway and take your scheat, Mish Causht," rasped the mucus-heavy voice of Ms. Pluck. Lena blushed as the other students in the room giggled. *Ugh, my face just stopped being red from earlier,* she thought as she shuffled to her chair. As she sat, it dawned on her that her entire class was there. Their eyes were fixed on her with a concentration that tried to bore into her skin. A metal smack brought their attention back to the front of the room, where Ms. Pluck stood gripping a silver ruler in her hands. As the door slid closed with a click, Lena took a last glance outside and saw that the lights had just reached ambience. The humming persisted now, unchanging.

"You are all here becaush you have mishbehaved. Shome of you, I have sheen before," she glanced toward Lena, "and for shome of you, thish ish your firsht time. Shadly, shincsh beating hash been banned, due to itsh effect of acshellerating breathing, you are to activate your tap-pad and type the following shentence five hundred timesh. I will not repeat the shentence, sho you had better pay attention."

Ms. Pluck paused as the students hurriedly got out their tap-pads. Before they were settled, she continued, "The shentence ish: I will reshtrict my actionsh sho that the world doesh not shuffer on my behalf." She grinned as the students hesitantly typed the sentence, unsure if they had heard properly. Whispers spread throughout the room, questioning what had been said.

"Quiet! There schall be no talking!" Ms. Pluck interrupted the clamor. "You have one hour to complete your punischment. If you do not complete it, you will return tomorrow to do it again. And sho on and sho forth. Now begin."

On cue, the room became a chorus of clicks. Lena listened as the typing synchronized. Thirty-three children with 330 fingers all danced at the same time. *Amateurs,* she thought. She reached down and took out her tap-pad. The screen purred at her touch. She typed out the sentence with a single finger, making sure that she accurately translated Ms. Pluck's spit-filled statement to

English. She spread out her pointer finger and thumb over the screen. The sentence glowed blue. With a few swipes, a keypad appeared. Lena typed in the number 500, and the sentence replicated itself. Her assignment was complete. Lena turned her head to check that her autonomous neighbors were still following their instructions. A subtle note of pity made her eyes widen, but she shook it off, not understanding why their behavior made her sad.

Half an hour passed. Still the tap-tap-tapping, but it was now just a piece of the ambience blending with the lights. Lena's mind ruminated on the voices she'd heard. *"...Had to give up Caldon...They won't be happy..."* Who was Caldon? Who won't be happy? Would anyone believe her if she asked? Did she believe her?

She scanned the room again. Not a soul to be trusted with a secret like this. Still, its heaviness pulled down on her jaw, pleading to escape. *Maybe one of the girls,* her mind bargained, *it couldn't hurt to tell one person.* She bit her lip. Ms. Pluck was certainly out of the question. She wouldn't believe Lena, and she'd probably report her directly to the Council. Lena didn't fancy being mulched. Not even if that meant being with the flowers. Lena leaned to the right, toward a girl from Sector 8. "Psst. Molly." The girl ignored her. "Psssst! Molllly! I've got something to tell you," Lena continued.

Molly's head turned slightly sideways, but her fingers kept typing. "What do *you* want?" Molly snapped.

"Are you mad at me?" Lena's eyebrows quivered.

"Of course I am. You're the reason I'm here. You're the reason we're all here. Why can't you just get to class on time? Why can't you just be normal?" She hissed in response.

Lena faltered. She hadn't come prepared for a battle. She was getting ready to share her secret, but now all she could do was stare forward and pinch hard at her thigh so that her eyes didn't well up. Her knees threatened to rise to her chest to her Safe position. Her jaw quivered.

Several sentence iterations passed before Molly became aware that Lena hadn't responded. She had been expecting some sort of loud retort, or even hands lunging at her face, as Lena seemed to always look for an excuse to quarrel. Even though Molly would watch other kids mock her, she had always admired Lena for not backing down. Lena's silence worried her. Molly stretched her peripheral vision as far as she dared, and she saw that Lena just stared blankly forward. Her eyes were glassy. Molly's ring finger trembled and she hit the wrong key. She quickly deleted the mistake and resynchronized with the resonant typing. The event unsettled her.

"Lena," Molly said in a softer tone. "Lena, I didn't mean... I'm... What did you want to tell me?"

Lena's grip on her leg loosened. The stinging in her skin dissolved, and she found herself back in 701. Her blurred vision refocused on the black braided hair in front of her. She felt foolish for trying to confide in a random person, let alone a classmate. *Don't assume,* she scolded herself. It occurred to her that Molly had said something, but her hearing was just now unmuffling. "What?" she asked as she turned her head.

"I...um...what did you want to tell me?" Molly asked, perplexed at the abrupt shift in composure.

"Oh!" Her mind told her to reassess if she should tell, but her lips were already speaking. "I heard people outside!" Lena whispered as she gripped her chair to stop from jumping out of the seat.

"Um... yeah, they were probably going to work. So?"

"No, I mean *outside*-outside." She was committed. "Yesterday, outside the tube." She winced. She might *get* committed.

Molly scrunched her face and raised an eyebrow. "But there's nothing outside." She turned back to her desk and strained to avoid eye contact. This, she hoped, would end the conversation.

"There is. That's what I'm saying. There were people outside. They were talking, and saying things like 'tube sweep', and uhm... 'getting too close', and things about a meeting. They knew about the tubes not having air in them!"

"Lena, I think, maybe, because you were running out of air... I mean, you may have thought you heard something."

Lena's brow scrunched as her eyes opened wider. "I'm not crazy!" she said in as loud of a whisper that could still be called a whisper.

From the front of the room echoed Ms. Pluck's chalkboard-scratching voice. "No talking! Fifty more shentencshes from everyone!" The room groaned in response. Lena turned to Molly to apologize, but she would no longer meet her gaze. The girl in front of Molly glared at Lena. To Lena, it looked like she had just eaten something sour, or perhaps rotten. *Perhaps a rotten lemon,* she thought.

"Nice going," the girl scathed. "Why don't you shut up for once, noma? Or should it be nopa?"

Lena's brain hadn't had time to react before her hands were removing the obstacle that was her desk from between her and the girl. She felt the muscles in her calves clench and spring her body forward, her arms now flailing wildly. She watched her claws wrap around and tug at the bouncy golden curls connected to a now-startled face. A scream. It reminded her of Tulu's first dry-cleaning experience. She hadn't actually meant to smile at that thought, but the girl's scared eyes told her that she had. So close to her face, she noticed a lone hair on the girl's dimpled chin. *Odd,* she thought, as she was pulled away by a set of jagged pincers. Her gaze followed them up to see that they were connected to the bulging arms of Ms. Pluck. When Lena's mind had finally caught up to her actions, she took in the silent room with its students huddled against the front wall, clutching their tap-pads.

"Mish Toma, are you all right?" Ms. Pluck inquired to Addy, the girl that Lena had attacked.

Addy took a moment to respond. The room shuddered. "Uhm...yeah. I think," she answered, still bewildered.

A bell sounded, and the door of 701 slid open. Init-Phase had ended. Ms. Pluck nodded her head, signaling for everyone but Lena to leave. The students scurried out of the room, keeping their distance from where Lena stood. Before the last one had left, Lena heard Molly say to the group, "She's crazy! She hears voices, and she says they're from outside. Like, *outside*-outside." The students laughed a low and concerned laugh.

Lena stood in the now-empty room with Ms. Pluck breathing hot starchy air down her neck. "Can I—" Lena started.

"Schhh." Ms. Pluck quieted her. "What am I going to do with you? You don't behave. You don't follow rulesh. You don't even follow the law. By exsherting yourshelf, you not only put your life at shtake, but you put everyone elshes livesh at shtake ash well."

Lena could see the water starting to boil in Ms. Pluck's expression and wondered if soon her ears would begin to whistle. "Why did you attack Mish Toma?"

"I don't know," Lena said to herself, but loud enough for the teacher to hear.

Words, she thought. *Express emotion through words, and pictures, and creativity,* she could hear the old recordings fizzling in her mind. *Not through physicality. Never act physically. We live through discourse and die by physical force.* She wanted to spit at that lesson. *What good was a body, then?*

Ms. Pluck cleared her throat, still waiting for a response.

"She called me a bad name," Lena stated, still lost in her head.

"And what wasch that?"

Lena hesitated. *Is this a trap? Does she just want me to say a bad word, and get me in more trouble?* "I don't remember."

"Mish Causht..."

Lena sighed. "She called me a... noma. And then she called me a..." Lena bit down on the inside of her cheek. "A nopa."

The room swallowed the word like a dry pill. A capsule wedged in a throat, resistant to leave. "I schee." A note of sadness resonated in the teacher's voice, a tone that Lena hadn't thought her capable of. Ms. Pluck's grasp on Lena loosened, and Lena found herself standing in 701 with Ms. Pluck's hand resting on her shoulder. "You know, there is no schame that you don't have a mother." She spoke slowly. "You will find that being the daughter of a profeshional Mother will schoon be the norm. And that it will be normal for shingle parentsh to be having children. It ish often that cruelty ish directed towardzh change. But people are schtarting to schee that it ish more effischient to produsch children from optimizched Mother'sh." She glanced down at her student, her bulbous lips attempting a smile. "It makesh you a better breather, you know."

By now, Lena's cheeks had flooded with hot tears. She tasted salt on her lips and felt nails in her palms. "I don't care that I don't have a mom..." The words fell from her mouth. "I miss daddy," she cried out. Lena pulled away from Ms. Pluck's hand and ran from the room, not caring if anyone saw. The room's shoulders drooped.

Ms. Pluck stood watching Lena push her way through the crowds outside: a little person pushing away the world. She inhaled deeply and let out a somber sigh. It was the first time in years that she had fully filled her lungs.

V.

Esta made her way around the perimeter of Brin with each beat of the clock. She planted her right foot slowly, and on the third tick she placed her left. She knew the sound of the clock wouldn't cover her pregnant steps. She knew the sound was only there to synchronize the city. But knowing didn't mean she could change. Some little mechanism in her mind only progressed her body every two counts. She wondered if the child inside her would walk to the same rhythm. A toy soldier infinitely wound.

The dimmed lights overhead signaled that it was somewhere between 21:00 and 23:00. But she knew that it was 21:37. Everyone knew that. Was it possible to not know the time?

Even under the cover of the grey night-lights, beads of worried blue blossomed on her forehead. Their meeting had convened just three cycles ago and had not ended on a positive note.

Is Sado hurt? Does the capital know? Her mind wandered as her hand ran along the outer wall, searching for a forgotten thumbprint. Looking into the blackness, an empty cloud of winged fangs flashed in and out. She shook away the imagery as her fingers found the cold edge of the entrance. Would her child's mind also be filled with fear? *Flood the world with emotions so that the body no longer reacts to stimulus,* she remembered. *Reduce the intake of oxygen.*

She pressed her thumb to the translucent pad. The door didn't greet her, but it slid open to show she was welcome. *Maybe that's why I joined them. To feel alive.* Gripping the frame, she took a deep breath and pulled herself into the tube. She wobbled forward into the numbness. A tuft of air signaled that the door had closed behind her.

***

Outside, in a speckled darkness, a forest of pines sat together and watched the life-filled jungle gym swim across the sky. The earth exhaled its evergreen breath and the structure creaked and moaned but did not inhale. The earth tickled the maze's silver underbelly with emerald brushes, but it did not laugh. The earth spat soft dew upon the web's curved cheeks, but still it did not react. It drifted dead upon the grainy dark with blind eyes turned.

Deep in its hollowed veins, in a bin marked "Recycled", pulsed the steady blood of the Outcry. Though the walls swayed with the playful gust, its inhabitants' nerves flared with an ingrained fear of natural entropy. The shadow of a faded voice surfaced in their minds, embedded from childhood, *"In the same way that our walls protect nature from our order, they protect us from nature's disorder. Though we rely on her to shelter us from the cruelty of space, she makes no point to protect us from herself. For this we must hide our existence."*

As the memory slithered back into some neuronal crevice, the quiet of the container filled with the scratchy rattle of a pill tube falling to the ground. The collective quiet of their minds was interrupted with images of melodic serpents luring victims to desert graves. Even when the noise settled, the quiet flashed images of the protracted descent of a dark arachnid. Its weightless legs kissed the backs of their necks, and a hopeless cold cascaded up their spines. Still, they felt numb. With constant fear, their vitals remained stable. Only when the radio spoke did their hearts flicker faster.

"It's nice to see you again," emitted a worn voice amidst the static. The audience replied with their customary laugh, warmed by the air of subtle waves.

"You, too, are a sound for sore eyes," Joseph replied to the black box, a soft grin of relief balanced on his face. His reply passed through the microphone; a million-billion air molecules converted to little electric carriers, extra excited to swim down this current. On the other end, Sado responded with a hearty laugh.

How he does it, I will never understand, Talia thought as she watched the crowd focus solely on the radio. Their grips on their seats loosened and their shoulders sank below their ears. A lively pink was now painted atop the white of their knuckles. *To fully trust in a voice alone... He told me it could be done,* she smiled. *Am I the fool?*

Sado's laughter descended to silence and he began again, slowly. "I know you must have a lot of questions, and I will answer them as best I can."

As he paused, the box whispered a pop and crackle. The radio dial glowed a mellow amber. Even now, his silence warmed the room.

"First though, I want to thank you." He cleared his throat with three short coughs. "In all my life, and I'm old, I have never seen such a desire to be alive. I walk the tubes and everyone is as lifeless as the walls around them. Everyone paints in bright colors, but they're colorblind. You paint in black and white and see rainbows. Does that mean we're crazy?" He paused. "Sure, probably." They shared a laugh. "But at least it means we bleed red. So thank you. Thank you for letting your heart beat at its own pace." The radio continued to hush the room with its insistent "shhhh."

Talia rested in her backless chair, her spine making a sharp right angle with the floor. *Is he talking to just me?* she thought. Her mind processed his words, filtered them, rewound them, cut them to bits, crumpled, encoded, modulated, and alphabetized them. A sapphire fingernail glided up and down her palm, pressing slightly deeper with each iteration. As she felt the first layer of skin give way to an etched white, she looked down and smiled again. *He's talking to everyone, and everyone thinks "Is he talking to just me?"*

"So, as it hasn't even been a week since the last meeting, I assume your first question is "why are we meeting again so soon?" The short answer is that there have been recent events that need to be addressed. But before I let everyone digress to an outcry," he paused. The group simmered for a moment, and then bubbled to laughter. "I want to calm your worries from last week, but I must also acknowledge that this comes with an inherent sadness. It is true that Caldon and I went to intercept a large O_2 shipment. We understood the risk, but such an opportunity comes once in a Recreation, so we decided to take it."

The heavy confirmation of unwanted news pulled the crowds' heads down. The floor felt the bleak stare of the Outcry. "It is unfortunate that Caldon's source of information turned out to be misguided, as the shipment was crawling with patrol. Our brother has been Recycled." A sigh billowed among the static. "Something that is becoming more common these days."

Esta watched from the back of the bin as the crowd leaned onto itself. Each body pressed against its neighbor with a uniform sadness. She leaned to her right and felt her arm mold around the knobby shoulder of a lightly freckled boy, who was also supported by the crowd. On a normal day, her first thought would have been to scold this skinny stranger for needing to eat more, but today she just rested. She felt her toes unscrunch and the sole of her foot loosen from the grip it seemed to have on nothing. She breathed in unison with her neighbor, and her neighbor's neighbor, and with every person in the world she knew and didn't know. Even with every muscle relaxed, she was immovable. For an instant, the Outcry was immovable.

Talia slowly stood from her perch as she surveyed the crowd. With everyone's head bowed towards the ground, no one seemed to notice her. She floated softly to the side of the bin, a silver canister in her hand. Long before the O$_2$ alarm had a chance to sound, she replaced its contents and drifted back to her seat. As she grinned, the round outline of her cheekbones extruded her face.

With unspoken consent, the Outcry sat up, ready to hear Sado once more. When he began, he spoke with a relaxed haste. "As Talia stated, I was brought in on account that I was found outside of my home at such a late hour. With a bit of luck, and the fact that my beard grows lower than roots, I was confirmed as senile and sent home.

"Now, with this event, there is no reason to believe the Council will have connected Caldon with an organized group. However," Sado paused. He inhaled the chatter of the speakers for just a moment. "There has been word that a child has heard people on the outside."

Half a world away sat a koa-wood table whose ingrained knots danced in an intricate samba of motionless streaks. Atop its surface stood a proud radio, readied in attention to echo the Outcry's response. Still, with a foundation of ebb and flow, the relic set murmured its Gaussian gurgle. The sound of static released an ounce of tension in Sado's forehead, and what was four wrinkles became three. He continued. "As to what she has heard, it is uncertain. But it can be assumed that since we have learned of this, it is only a matter of time until the capital finds out, if they haven't already. As is their way, they will begin an investigation, though how much attention they will give is unclear, since the words of a child are less than meaningful."

Back in Old Brin, the crowd sat fixated on their box. They leaned forward, waiting for Sado's next message to resonate, to instruct them on what to do, but their concentration fractured as Talia's voice pushed through their ears. "I think I speak for most when I say that we need to interrogate this child to learn what she knows and then make sure she doesn't reveal anything again."

Before the small room could flood with a barrage of opinions, Esta was on her feet, supported again by her deceptively stable neighbor. "You speak for yourself. If you're suggesting we kill this child to satisfy your sick need to have control, you will find your pretty little fingers packaged in a pretty little box."

The room remained unphased. Only Sado seemed to physically react, and his short chortle was masked by the radio's ambience.

Talia exhaled, her patience cracking. "If you have a better idea, by all means, but don't act like a martyr when you're just part of the problem. You pretend that your birthing of children is so noble, but you're just allowing the capital to use your body to plant their seeds and in return growing the roots for this corrupt society to have a perpetual foundation. You want to have a real impact? Get every Mother to abandon their projects."

"How dare you. You sit on your pedestal pretending to know why any of us are here, but—"

The radio fizzled, letting the room know that it was time for silence. "I understand that you both have different views, but please try to remember that we are all here, whatever the reason, for the final objective to be free. To live again on the outside. Let's not diverge to pettiness. Now, this child, this small girl, may know more than she should. Whatever her fate was, she has now stepped in our path and something must be done. I will hear anyone's opinion but know that the last word will be mine."

Esta spoke again. "Sado, please, to kill this child who has accidentally overheard us is not what our new world should stand for. Our foundation should not be laid with blood. There are other ways. Couldn't we just Restore her? Surely that is more reasonable than death."

Talia refuted. "A Restoration is not foolproof. The mind can heal, and there is no guarantee that something will not trigger the memories. Or if she is put in the hands of the capital, there may be ways they can extract the information, no matter how obfuscated it is. The only real guarantee is if she is Recycled."

"But what if she's already told others? There is no way to contain the spread of gossip among children. Would you suggest we kill them all, like some disease?"

"If that is what is necessary to preserve the hope for a better society, then yes."

No one made eye contact. The floor felt a heavy stare, waiting for Sado's voice to carry the burden. "I have heard enough. The night grows old and we have more matters to discuss. I will let you know my decision, and that will be that." Silence chilled the thin air of the room. "Now, though this may be sooner than anticipated, this possible leak that we exist may be the perfect reason for us to act quickly and to make ourselves known, so that we are not caught off-guard."

This time Joseph's tenor nulled the void. "Not to contest with you, Sado, but do you really think we're ready?"

"It is often the case that when the world is ready for you, you must be ready. Since the first day we met, I have known that you were ready. But what I think doesn't matter. Do you think you are ready, now? That is for you to decide."

"What would you have us do?"

"I have ideas, but first I want to hear what you think. I am all ears."

The room permitted itself a short laugh and embraced the last moment of silence that it would hold that night.

Miles below, a cricket stopped rubbing its wings to watch the work of two centuries of engineering pass over a once-Brazilian sky. In its momentary pause, the cricket's body was whisked into the air by a nearby bat.

VI.

"A giant gooey Snarglops, its pores oozing platterpaste, with eyes of lumin–, luminescent green, glared down at Lady Adele. With an angry pounce, it pinned her against the scalding sand, its mangled claws clashed flush against her steel blade. She felt her exosuit radiate heat onto her skin. Sweat ran from her forehead into her eyes, causing her to squint in pain. As her body sank deeper into the suffocating surface, the Snarglops hissed and growled and slashed, igniting sparks on her sword. Lady Adele could feel her last moments before her, as the earth swallowed her into its... its... per...nic..." Lena scowled. Her lips rounded and her tongue pushed but all that came from her mouth was a bubble of spit. "Tulu, how do you say that word?" She lowered the tap-pad to Tulu's height.

Tulu paused for a moment. He moved closer and his blonde strands pressed against the screen. "Per... per... perbrrbrrbrrrrrrrr," he exclaimed as he spun about, cleaning the device with a whirlwind of mop.

She pulled back the pad as she let out a pitter-patter of silvery giggles. "You're incorrigible!" She paused, as her own words touched her ears. Stooping over slightly, she raised her bottom lip in a pout and lowered her left eyebrow in skepticism. She cleared her throat halfway, and let out her raspiest, "You're incorrigible!" Her warped mirror reflected her contorted image, and Lena fell to the ground as she tried to catch her breath. The spot-on impression of Ms. Pluck kept her laughing while Tulu puttered and whirred into her side, making sure it didn't split.

When Lena finally caught up to her breath, she rolled over and picked up her fallen tap-pad. Tulu whirred sleepily as his little motors wobbled him to his corner of the room. He crinkled into his nest of confetti just as his nose faded from yellow to red. Lena smiled at him as she watched the tones of red rise and fall, knowing that he'd wake up in the morning full of energy. She knew her bed would do the same for her, but she'd always wondered if her nose also blinked as she slept. She made a note to try and check that.

"Lady Adele could feel her last moments before her," she continued in a whisper. "As the earth swallowed her into its perbrrbrrbrrr jowls. In her final breath, she thrust Excalibur upwards and let out a muffled cry, lost quickly to the shhh of the sand. The Snarglops's howl of triumph was quickly disrupted as the blade pierced its belly and it too was pulled deeper into the unforgiving surface. It whimpered and struggled as the ground closed in around it and the Snarglops was no more."

Lena stopped. Her body shook. The tap-pad strained in her scrunch. In a momentary silence, she propelled herself off the ground. "That was," she exhaled. "So clutch! If I were the earth, I would eat up everything that fought, and only spit them back out when they stopped. And then, I would grumble when people ignored me, and sneeze lava at their toes if they stopped dancing."

Lena spun in circles, jumping up and down to avoid the liquid rock attempting to tickle her feet. As she sprang up upon her blanketed mattress, she found the covers anxious to cover her. They gobbled at her ankles, causing her to pivot into the cloudy folds of her bed. Her thump wobbled the ground.

And then she felt still. She felt the sand build a wall around her, one grain at a time. The wall became a coat became a castle became a sculpture that would remind a future era of her likeness. She felt the stares of a curious city, and heard words like "hero", "legend", and "masterpiece". As the city and its people crumbled into forgotten relics, she felt the wind wash away her golden shell. She was clean. She felt unpopulated.

***

Lena opened her eyes to an empty bin. The sound of another morning buzzed around her. The time projected on her ceiling signified that the weekend was over. Lena closed her eyes for a moment longer and opened them again to make sure that the time was accurate.

Getting ready was a hurdle. Her body drifted about like a tumbling bag of sand. The idea of seeing Ms. Pluck and the rest of her class again made Lena's stomach want to hurt. Her semi-regulated diet prohibited such a thing though, so she just continued to flump about instead.

She tried to gag at the idea of eating more of the school's recommended multicolored multivitamin wafers, but she caught a look at herself in the mirror and laughed at her fishlike lip dance. She hoped she looked like a fish, at least. Seeing them in movies was hardly a basis for reality. *Maybe it was all just a dream,* her mind splashed back, letting her thoughts of fish swim away. *Yeah, a dream!* She smiled. *People on the outside, what a crazy thought!* As she made her way to school she repeated this over and over, oblivious to the stares she received because of her intense concentration.

For once, Lena arrived early to class. Instead of going in, however, she paced in small circles outside the door. She finally shuffled into the class bin just as the door slid and sealed shut. Keeping her head down, she made her way around to a desk in the back. As she loaded her tap-pad for the day's lesson, the sound of laughter made her pause. She slowly raised her head, bracing herself to take on the beady eyes of the room.

Lena raised an eyebrow. No one had noticed her. No one had even looked back at her. More so, everything seemed normal. She glanced around and saw that the source of the laughter was just a group of girls watching some old video of a polar bear walking backwards. She looked about to find Addy and had to double take when she finally did. There was Addy, unscratched, unphased, and unbelievably giddy as she digipassed notes back and forth with a boy across the room. A shining example of someone that had never experienced hardship in her life. A whole twelve years of life in a box, and Lena couldn't find a single wrinkle on her. She even thought she noticed a naive glaze in her eyes, albeit faint. Searching the room, there wasn't a wrinkle in sight. Was she the only one with a wrinkle? Her hand started to reach up to start pulling at her own hair when Ms. Pluck entered from the side room, complete with more than forty years of wrinkles. Lena felt a momentary calm.

"Pip pip," Ms. Pluck said in a slightly wavering voice. The room ceased its babble. She cleared her voice in three coughs and continued more solidly. "Today, we schall continue our schtudy of the Hishtory of Fight or Flight. And why do we schtudy our pasht?"

"We study the past to be objective in our future," the class replied in one voice, with extra emphasis on each "S".

"Correct. We schtudy the pasht, becaush we each control our future, and the pasht tellsh ush how to objectively act to each shircumshtansh. And when we control the preshent, we control the future." A faint skepticism was barely audible over her lisp. She continued. "We musht..."

Lena's mind drifted up above the class as Ms. Pluck continued about the importance of understanding the complex relationship between humans and nature. How, at first, people had fought and tried to control nature, but realized that through controlling nature, nature was then destroyed. And how nature had evolved to be dangerous and existed to limit existence. And with this limitation, it fueled its own creation, in a cycle of perfect stability.

She continued by likening this to the generation of early impressionist painters and writers and, Ms. Pluck's favorite topic, musicians. But by then Lena had noticed something that had been bothering her. Not something that had happened, but something that hadn't happened. Typically, when the class mocked Ms. Pluck's speech, she would scowl, and sputter, much to the class's delight. Today though, she'd just moved on. It was like it had never happened. *It was like*, Lena paused in thought. *It never happened.*

She focused in on Ms. Pluck. She drifted about, circling her, sizing her up, floating an inch in front of her nose, gazing into her unglazed eyes. Her rugged starchiness still petrified the air, so that hadn't changed. Her pleated forehead could still grate cheese, so it wasn't that. No, it must be something else. The concrete foundation on which her voice used to bellow seemed to have fractured. The resolute focus that could splinter paint, now just flickered in between sentences, with momentary hesitations on unspoken words. *What's plucking your nerves?*

Her heavy confusion pulled Lena back to her seat. She looked at the tap-pad in front of her, which now showed the day's historical nature video. The screen flickered as a mischievous string dancer lowered itself on its crystalline thread. The exotic splash of red on black, its eight slender legs gently caressing the darkness. Lena allowed herself a momentary smile and squirm of excitement. *Everything is deadly*, she thought, *but nature makes things beautiful.* She watched as the tiny ballerina stroked a man's neck and touched his skin with a sweet kiss. His eyes faded into blackness. *Probably intruding in her territory,* she reasoned. The wails and squeals around her let her know that her classmates disagreed.

She drifted off again as her screen began to show something new called a "bat". It fluttered its wings with a passion and sang into the night, but her vision defocused from the tap-pad. It was all right though, as she knew they would show it at least a dozen more times. When her eyes refocused, Lena watched as all the heads of the class turned to look at the clock just two moments before the lunch chime sounded. Their pulses ticked with the clock.

Lena paused at the door before she left the room. She looked back at her distracted teacher and had the sudden urge to tell her about the people outside. Something stopped her. Maybe pride, maybe embarrassment, or maybe just that she knew she wouldn't be believed. She sighed, and simultaneously heard Ms. Pluck sigh. They made eye contact. In an instant they poured out a hundred silent thoughts, but before a word was spoken, Lena darted away.

The cafeteria container's walls were splotched with the dusty pastels and glossy fluorescents of creative freedom. Every oddly accented chair and table appeared so out of place that it was easy to tell that it was right where it belonged. No one really knew who had painted what first or when, but ever since then the room had been in a constant state of flux. Blue-indigo-violet plates sat atop red-yellow-vermillion counters, which were held up by orange-orange-orange legs. The ventilation ducts, yesterday a chartreuse-beige-burgundy, were today a bubblegum-buttercup-tan. Even the digital server's hair appeared to be made of cotton candy and watermelon taffy, more than likely correlated to the flavor of the day.

Lena wanted to hurl. Again and again and again. Something about the room, the colors, the tastes, felt off. What was strawberry-bratwurst-polenta and why had she never just tasted straw, or berries? Why was every color every other color, and why couldn't it just be itself? Did green exist as green and only green? Or did it feel necessary to disguise itself as burnt sienna when it felt self-conscious? Lena sighed the same sigh she sighed each day at this time. She walked to the server screen, which jumped to life with a "How can I brighten your day?"

Lena frowned. "I would like a green wafer, please."

The screen thought for a second. "I'm sorry, did you mean 'green-orange-purple', 'green-cardamom-burgundy', 'green—'"

"I said green, just green."

"Thank you. Your order of 'green-rust-green' will be ready momentarily. Create a beautiful day!" The server screen shut off and out slid Lena's multicolored wafer. She shook her head and carried her meal off to a corner table with three legs of different lengths. In five large bites and five large gulps, she downed the wafer, bypassing the optimized texture and taste. She didn't have time to be paralyzed by a mouthful of oversaturated sensations.

Standing up, Lena then walked over to the table where Addy and a group of girls sat, absorbed in both their food and conversation. The girls paused as they noticed Lena standing behind them.

"Hi," Addy smiled.

Lena just stared, mouth open.

"Is everything all right, Lena?"

"Oh, I, uh, wanted to apologize. For what happened. In 701."

"Oh no, did you get sent to 701 again? I'm sorry. What for?"

Lena hesitated, a bit puzzled. "No, I mean, when we were in 701 the other day."

The other girls giggled. "Addy, you didn't tell us you were sent to 701," poked another girl at the table. The girls started to snicker again.

"Hush, I wasn't. Lena, is this a joke?"

Lena's breathing rapidly climbed and cascaded. Her knees trembled and her head lightened. "But, you were all there. Just, just three days ago. We were all, you were all, I told Molly, and I hit Addy, and I'm sorry, I..." She stopped. The girls just stared at her, specks of bewildered concern in their black beady eyes. The same eyes that had pierced at Lena the day she was pushed into the closet. Lena felt her body turn and propel forward, just as the chime sounded and the doors opened. As she got to the door, a sound made her stop. She listened. It was the same sound that had been bothering all day, but she hadn't been able to isolate it. As the clock struck its next second, she heard it again. And then she recognized it. It was the synchronized breathing of the room; the persistent, rhythmic inhale and exhale. But it was different. It was a moment late. A moment off.

She ran from the room.

Lena spent the rest of the week listening. She got to class early, hid in the back, and was always the last to leave. As the week went on, the girls' breathing resynchronized with Ms. Pluck, and Lena questioned whether she had really heard a difference in the first place. *Maybe it was a dream. Maybe I am broken.* The only notion that kept Lena focused was Ms. Pluck's lack of focus.

On the last day of class that week, Lena sat and watched the other students leave the room. She cleared her throat and Ms. Pluck looked up.

"Mish Causht, are you planning on shtaying the weekend in shchool?"

Lena remained seated. "Ms. Pluck. I heard people on the outside."

Ms. Pluck blinked, one eyelid trailing the other by half an instant. "Mish Causht, I haven't the time for your shtories. Pleash go and enjoy your weekend."

"It's not a story." She could sense nervousness in the teacher. Her body seemed rigid and when she spoke, her teeth clenched.

"Thish ish not shomething to joke about. Go home," she snapped.

"Can I ask one question, then I promise I'll go?"

Ms. Pluck lowered her shoulders. "Jusht one."

"Did the entire class go to 701 last week?"

The teacher's face relaxed into a quizzical gaze. "Why yesh, of coursh. What a shilly queshtion, you were there. Now off with you."

Lena jumped up and exited, leaving both her and the teacher a little more confused than before.

VII.

Ceiling boots? Check. Oxygen mask? Check. Pointy, turny, opener thing? Fire-sword? Hair band? Marker-marker? Assorted gummy shapes? Twine? Check. Lena placed the last item, a small wooden horse three times the size of a peanut, in her bag. As Brin's clock chimed the 24th hour, the small girl slid out the flap of A364, bypassing the counter that tracked the world's movement. The sector continued believing the home of Lenalia Caust was occupied.

It had been almost a year since she'd been to the hidden tunnels, more formally called Old Brin. She remembered when her dad had first showed her the entrance, forgotten along the outskirts. The gateway to an entire city of tunnels thought to be recycled, drifting on the edge of suffocation. She hoped the invisible markers her and her dad had placed were still visible. She only had five hours to explore, blinked the digits on her oxygen mask, so there was no use in visiting places she had already been.

Getting to the old city's entrance was by far the easiest part of the journey, but it being out in the open also made it the riskiest. While the late hour meant that the walkways from Brin's center to the outer dome were clear, it also meant that, as darkness does, any slight noise would amplify all the way to Racine. Lena sneaked and snuck and snacked a bit, too. She pivoted about corners, and tiptoed past doorways. Had there been alley cats prowling about, they surely would have welcomed her as she pounced on top of trash bins and scurried behind boxes. Lena made her way as noiselessly as she could to Brin's perimeter, past the inside world filled with inside people.

As the air got colder and her arms became textured with tasteless taste buds, she pulled out her fire-sword. Its checkered-black aluminum body mimicked that of a flashlight. With a push, she painted the wall with a white luster. With a twist, it glowed a deep violet. Lena traced the fireless flame along the outer wall. Her pace accelerated as the wall glimmered back monotonously. *Where is it, where is it, where is it?* Just as her mask beeped "4 hours", a nibble of faded yellow touched the corner of her eye. She turned and coated the spot in purple. Within the bruised radius, the light excited a weak outline of the forgotten doorway. She grinned. Next to the doorframe glowed a smaller frame, which encompassed the thumbprint scanner. Next to that, in an even fainter yellow glowed a small handprint. A Lena-sized handprint. She started towards it and hesitated. A soft stream of remembrance flooded her vision.

It must have been her third or fourth time to Old Brin, because she was leading her dad there, instead of the other way around. He had let it slip earlier that day that there was a surprise for her at the entrance, so she'd insisted on going as soon the last lights went out. When they arrived she searched about the glowing doorway, but turned back confused. He smiled his "Let me help you" smile. He took her tiny hand in his and used the marker to paint it in entirety with an invisible glow. The cold dampness gave her chills, but his warm hands calmed her. Taking her coated palm, he centered it a foot to the left of the glowing thumbprint and pressed it gently and fully against the wall. She scrunched her forehead, but before she could scowl the entrance slid open and a familiar voice whispered, "Good evening, my little Solena."

Lena opened her eyes. Her hand had made its way to the handprint and hovered just aloft, shaking lightly. She pushed forward.

"Good evening, my little Solena."

She shivered.

As the door slid open she shined her light into the welcoming dark. The slight pull of positive pressure tickled the back of her neck, and she shivered again. She could feel herself riding the flow of O_2 for but a moment, and then there was equilibrium. The walls glowed with dim arrows; yellow wandering into the black and orange guiding out. Her feet brought her forward as her heart dragged back.

Lena made her way through the abandoned world, all the while decorating the walls with fresh directions. She pushed through empty class bins, old stores, and stumbled upon what appeared to be the old City Hall. The absence of oxygen had preserved the ruins in a pristine eeriness. Anything that was left locked remained locked, as the power had been shut off a long time ago. Twice, Lena found herself having to unscrew panels to get through doors. Her dad had once told her about the complexity it entailed to rewire the solar generators. "Something has to keep the engines going to keep the relics afloat," he'd said. But those were just words to her.

At the sight of a toppled snow globe, Lena crystallized. A small child in baby blue held a snowball in his mitten, frozen in time. A girl in pink crouched unaware rolling a mound into a snowman. Their world existed sideways and snow fell left. Or would have, had time not abandoned it. Lena crouched down and cupped the tiny world in her hands. A snowflake shifted at the base of the glass. *I am the master of time.*

With a balletic twist, Lena and the world became a flurry of motion, and the room stopped what it was doing just to watch the snowfall one more time. As it settled, she placed the glass in her bag, and left in its place her tiny wooden horse. *One cannot just take, after all. It's an even trade.*

She pressed on, searching through the remnants, not entirely sure what she was looking for. Something had led her feet through the tunnels, some inkling that forced her to deny the suspicion that she was crazy. That it wasn't all a dream, and that she really had heard voices on the outside. It didn't make sense that she was crazy, because she knew the rest of the world was crazy. If it wasn't, then she'd be sitting at home, curled up in her father's arms, listening to him read Lady Adele's monolog in his scratchy falsetto.

Instead, as her mind grappled playfully with her sanity, her body climbed over warped wooden desks and her fingers crinkled mounds of parched paper. She was so preoccupied that she missed the first words. Before her ears received the next few, her body had melted and she was a puddle on the floor. She pressed her ear against the ground, unsure of the direction of the sounds. Sure enough, the muffled voices emitted again from below her.

"...still hasn't been found."

"Then all the others were Restored for nothing?"

"I'm not saying they were right in what they did, but I get their logic. It was a necessary precaution. But still," she paused. "They were just kids. A Memory Restore can really screw with a developing mind. Gets them all fuzzy, ya know?"

"What do you think they'll do when they find her? I hope Sado listens to what I said. She's just a little girl, after all."

Lena's eyes widened. Her mask blinked that she had an hour left. She could feel the blood pulsing heat from her ear as it pressed against the floor. She ignored the ache. Out of the corner of her eye was a hesitant movement. Looking up, she saw the stack of papers she'd touched quivering with mischievous excitement. She mouthed "no" but the papers couldn't see because of her mask. Like a flurry of guillotines, the documents plunged towards Lena.

At first, there was no sound. The world stopped to let the sheets dance through its nothingness. But as the first fibers embraced Lena's wintry skin, the world again became a waterfall. The papers crashed and tumbled, banged and boomed, all the while burying Lena in a mound of lament.

When the last page was balanced nimbly atop the clutter, Lena listened again. The voices were long gone, as was her hope of discovering about whom they were talking. Even so, she felt a slight sense of peace. Even if these people were just on the floor below her, she knew that there were people out there, separate from her world, living in secret. And if they were willing to risk being outside the city, then they were willing to risk being *outside*-outside. Or so she reasoned.

As she crumpled her way to standing, she then realized the invading darkness. She frowned. Somewhere buried in the thick flood of papers was her light. She waded through the mess, kicking and flailing, hoping that a purple hue would give up its hider's location.

"Come on out, little guy. You can't hide forever. Are you there?" She kicked high. Just a snowfall of agendas. "Darn, what about here?" She swiped her arms. A stack of lunch forms scattered about. "Gah. Hmm, where can..." She paused.

A faint petal of lavender glowed five feet in front of her. "Ahah! There you are!" Stepping forward, her foot caught on a thick envelope and a tearing sound filled the room. She let the sound settle. And then she felt it. Her stomach grasping at the walls of her throat. A phantom touch crawling up the ridges of her back. The void pulling at every hair on her body. She knew that something – or someone – else occupied the darkness. She took in a long breath. "Hello?"

"Hello, Lenalia."

And then nothing.

She thought she remembered the bite of a lonely fire ant kissing her neck. Her body drifted on the inside winds, possibly on the firm breath of an angry furnace, or the fleeting exhale of shadowed whispers, for how long she didn't know. She didn't know she didn't know. For some time, her speckled memory consisted of darkness, and movement, and her questioning of how her body swam upon an empty ocean.

Eyes closed. Eyes open. Yes eyes. No eyes. The world was without its candle. Her hands paddled about her, without her, and moved in swirls and stars and all shapes that wax can melt. Perhaps she was the world's candle? Had the idea caught flame, she would have dripped to a puddle, her fingers and toes molded together on the back of an envelope, pressed into the shape of an L, for Lena. But she evolved. First, into a gaseous lamp without fuel, then into a light bulb without filament, then to a flashlight without batteries. Each new embodiment caused her body to take a new shape. Twice she felt the weightlessness of free fall, but just as quick she was three times as heavy, being gripped tighter to her obscured source of motion. Her entire history seemed to exist in captivity. Now that she was light, she lamented ever attempting to control herself.

More time passed. She was a diode. Her blood was a particulate flow, directed. Her breath was a false sun. A wannabe. Water fell from her eyes, because she was artificial. Man-made. A feeble attempt at nature. Soon she was plasma, and fire, and the atomic bomb, and hate, and war and forever a beacon. Prometheus held her hand for a moment before he too was struck down. Now she was too real. No one would touch her. No one would look at her. She looked down upon her neighbors, or her captors, for she now held them all in place. She gave them warmth, and love, and inhaled night and exhaled day. Some died from too much love, some died from too little. Only one lived on. She spoke softly, "What do you see when you look at me?" and it was replied, "I see only red."

A cold hand of water slapped Lena across the face and her eyelids shot up with a start. A liquid white filled her vision and she felt her damp face drip down her chin. She was in a room that seemed to wiggle in circles, but that might have just been her vision. She squinted. She could make out the silhouette of relaxed shoulders.

"You have caused quite the dilemma, Ms. Caust."

Lena felt her body stiffen at the sound of the scratchy tenor that resonated from the shadows. Something about that voice echoed familiarity, but as hard as she tried to focus, her memories frolicked away in an orchard of labyrinths.

"Not only have you spread your knowledge of the existence of the Outcry, but you have seemingly stumbled upon one of their meeting places. As I'm sure you could imagine, this information could prove detrimental in the wrong hands."

Lena's head drifted back and forth, dancing to the charm of this funny talking shadow. He was speaking with reason, but something about his words seemed hidden. Like two snakes trying to dance in the same basket, or maybe one snake trying to dance in two baskets. She laughed.

"Is something funny?"

Lena wasn't sure she could speak, but she let her mouth open, in case it had something to say. "I can't tell if you're happy or angry. Are you angry I found out, and happy to have caught me, or are you happy I found out, and angry to have caught me?"

Something about the man shifted. Lena couldn't help but feel that he now wore a slight smile. "You're speaking gibberish." He raised his hand and spoke into his cuff. "How much did you hit her with?" There was a silence. "Only 30 milligrams. You're sure?" Another silence. "I don't think she'll be responsive to questioning. You'll have to isolate and scrub the memories manually. On my leave you may enter." He dropped his hand to his side. "Ms. Caust. What did you hear outside of the tunnels?"

Her mind swirled. Still more clouds. "I heard..." She closed her eyes. From a stone maze hopped a small bunny. In its mind hung the word she knew was the truth. *You.* She wanted to shout *I heard you,* but something stopped her. This was her secret, and if he didn't know she knew, then she had a power over him. And so, she didn't say it.

She buried the word back into the bunny's mind, and the bunny hopped away deep into the network of twists and turns that was her own mind. "I heard the wall."

His face no longer smiled. "And what did the wall say?"

She cleared her throat. "It said, buzz buzz buzz buzz, and bhrm bhrm bhrm bhrm, and one or two hmm hmms." She giggled but stopped quite seriously. "I expect you to keep that in confidence. Stubby doesn't like gossipers."

The room stared blankly at Lena, but she just smiled back. Next to her, a machine that she had not yet noticed beeped and scribbled consistently, unchanged by her words. The man, dumbfounded, crossed the shadows and left the room.

As Lena drifted back into the clouds, tired of all her mental exertion, another door opened. This time, two men in white coats walked into the light and surrounded Lena, speaking words longer than she was old. They pointed and prodded at her, and they tugged at little suction cups that she just realized were attached to her head.

"You're sure everything is secured?" asked the one with stonewashed hair.

A younger man with white-rimmed glasses responded. "Of course. Look here, you can see the pattern of the conversation that just happened. And here are the words we're speaking now." He pointed to a screen at

Lena's side, but when she tried to turn to see, she realized that she was strapped down.

"How odd. There seems to be no discernable structure to the model selected memories. Either they don't exist, or they're hidden in some other isolated recollection."

"Are you saying she could hide her memory?"

"I'm saying nothing of the sort. It's more likely that she's suffered some sort of trauma that has induced hallucinations. I'm just theorizing the possibility of transitional memory storage through self-stimulated internal processes."

The younger man laughed. "Let's keep your research topics for research-worthy subjects. We just need to Restore her and make sure she gets home in one piece."

Lena's eyes widened as she felt a heavy cold press into her veins. Her vision faded to a dreamless dark, just as her mind felt the prodding shock of an intrusion. Somewhere, past a hundred or so left turns, up a thousand and one steps, back behind a dusty vase, sat a scared bunny with a secret, hoping that no one would find him.

VIII.

The morning alarm chirped. Below the city, atop the snowy fluff of a nearby cloud, a high-flying sparrow spun about, searching for the source of the mating call.

Tulu woke with a start. His rotating torso mimicked the sparrow's circles. The threaded braids attached to his core orbited his body as he crept silently to the base of Lena's bed. The girl lay asleep, oblivious to the bird's call and the robot's intent. Tulu turned his wheels ever so slightly, just enough for his yarn-like hair to graze the bottom of Lena's feet. In half a heartbeat she pulled her feet to her chest and giggled herself awake.

Lena lay smiling at the ceiling as the alarm chirped and her best friend danced his morning routine. A fuzzy warmth embraced her head like a soft hug. Something about the day made her feel wonderful. At the thought of seeing her class, she jumped out of bed. An overwhelming sensation washed over her. Surely they would be apologetic for locking her in the closet. And knowing that she had to go to 701, that meant them treating her kindly for at least a week. What a splendid week it would be. Lena clapped twice and the chirping alarm ceased. Somewhere below, a sparrow sighed and continued his morning routine, never having found his mate.

The next few cycles passed in a haze. Lena went to school, ate her technicolor wafers, was frightened by and screamed at her worldly lessons in all the right places, and came back to her bin to sleep. The same smile she'd awoken with was sprawled across her face all the while. Life was normal. And just as she had expected, the class apologized and welcomed her to their tables. They even laughed and looked in awe when Lena nonchalantly said that she couldn't remember 701.

When the week ended and a new week began, Lena found herself closer than ever with her classmates. As she pulled in her next breath, she listened to the silence that followed. *This is what it's like to fit in. For everyone to breathe at the same time.* She exhaled and the room exhaled and the entire world exhaled. She swore she could feel the subtle breeze of the thirty boys and girls ebbing and flowing.

"Lena." Molly whispered. "Is everything okay?"

Lena stared back, confused. The sudden realization that she was standing came over her. Her cheeks burned crimson as she sat back down, hoping that only Molly had noticed.

Lena hesitated. "I was just wondering; do you think everyone in the world breathes at the same time? Both inside and outside?"

As she finished her sentence a sharp pain flared above her right eye. Her teeth gritted and her vision blurred for but a moment, and then it was over. Out of the corner of her eye she thought she spied a bunny, but that was physically impossible. She shook her head to clear the image. "I mean, inside and outside of this bin. Like all of Brin, and Racine, and all the other cities."

"What else would you have meant?"

Lena hesitated. "I...I don't know. Well, do you think so?"

"I guess so. I've never really thought about it. Does everyone in here do that?"

The two girls' eyes met in a glazed gaze two worlds apart. The two feet separating them contained an ocean, but neither had learned to swim. So they sat, and they stared.

Lena's face twitched. She could feel the crinkles in her cheeks forming from her week-old smile. A question brewed in her mind: was her widened jaw pulling her temple taut, or was her temple pushing out her jaw into an unfounded grin? Either way, it felt as though the two halves of her brain no longer enjoyed each other's company and were attempting to go their separate ways. The divorce was excruciating. Still, she couldn't seem to drop eye contact.

Something told her that a connection was missing in her mind. Something was hidden somewhere and somehow latching on to the black of Molly's pupils let her balance on a strand of focus. Lena bit down hard on her new molars and, squinting her eyes, she willed her two hemispheres to squeeze into one. Molly smiled back, content to wait for an answer. In a silhouette of red, the ripples of voices appeared in Lena's vision. What was at first muffled began to resemble the voice of a man, and then a woman, and then a party. *A party?* The red vanished and Lena looked up to see Molly standing in what was once the endless ocean.

"I said, I'm having a party this weekend. Do you want to come?"

Lena blinked. Her head no longer throbbed, but her face beat red. "Oh. Me? Uhm. Sure."

Molly grinned and walked off. The bell must have sounded, as the rest of the class was heading for the door. Lena began to stand but her legs shook her back to her seat. She didn't know if they were just anxious about being invited to a party for the first time, or if they were tired from balancing on such a delicate thread of memory. Either way, she let them calm down before she forced them to take her home.

The walk to Brin felt new, different somehow. She mounted each step in time to the ticking of the clock. She felt like a heartbeat.

Lena rounded the corner. Her apartment came into view. A wave of butterflies emitted from her stomach and blanketed her body. She sprinted without hesitation, without breath, and without understanding. As she slid on her belly through the door flap, she screamed with excitement. "Daddy! I'm home! And I got invited to a party!"

The apartment replied with an unbroken silence.

"Daddy! Did you hear?"

Still, the apartment just sighed, not knowing what to say. Its walls looked down softly on the girl.

Lena waited. Her smile wavered. Something wasn't right. The stairs remained motionless. Her body shook. The tingling that had resonated from her stomach moved up past her chest and wrapped itself tightly around her throat. She struggled to breathe. She was suffocating, but the O_2 sensor remained calm. Hot tears touched her cheeks and glimpses of a forgotten life trembled in her eyes.

A letter. An endless walk down the stairs. Her inheritance. How could she have forgotten that he was gone? She curled into a ball as her body shook and moaned and inhaled the same hopelessness she'd felt the day he died. Her eyes squinted, trying to picture his face, but it had been so long since she'd seen it. The memories washed through her fingers as she tried to grasp them. They were too far away now. All she wanted was to imagine his face, but more images relentlessly pushed him back.

She sat curled up in a tube. She could feel the wall, and then it was talking. Not from its exterior, but from the wall's interior, which was the world's exterior. A man, older, scratchy, and a woman talked. They were outside. Then there was 701. And everyone was there. And then Addy's hair was in her hands. Then it was just her and Ms. Pluck. Then crying. Walking in the hidden tunnels. A globe of specks. A storm of paper. More people talking. About a girl. Then nothing. More nothing. Then now.

Lena opened her eyes. The O_2 sensor blinked yellow. She'd been hyperventilating. Her head felt clearer, like only a haze was left of the fog. She couldn't make sense of how she'd gotten back from Old Brin that night, but then again, she wasn't entirely sure she'd even gone there in the first place. How could she have forgotten? Eyes widened, she jumped up, changed the tanks, and took to the stairs two at a time.

"If it's there, I went. If it's not, I'm crazy. If it's there, I went. If it's not, I'm crazy. If it's..." she repeated as she made her way to her room.

Before Tulu had a chance to pounce, the door burst open and Lena leapt for her closet. It exhaled with a procedural grace, overflowing the room with mounds and pounds of socks and shoes, dresses, hats and crowns, bottles new and old, clocks oblong and an hour short, smoothed pieces of wood and stone, fuzzy things, squishy things, and stringy mangled shiny things, every bit and bob, knick and knack, and spring and bolt worthy of collection. A tattered shirt, made before regulated diets, advertised "BBTol: The Beta way to Block." A similarly faded Aspirin poster read "Breathe thinner with Blood Thinners." Lena pushed through the timeless puddle, with no time to envision herself as an alligator in a swamp or a fawn in a thicket.

"Where is it? Where is it? Let it be real!"

Lena sifted through every member of the pile, avoiding the myriad associated memories, allowing things to be things just this once. At first, items gently skipped across the room to leave the collection of possibility, but soon the gentle skip turned to a frantic tumble turned to a desperate clatter. Tulu became buried in panic.

Five minutes later, Lena slumped in her emptied closet. The room looked in on her with a new skin of old relics. "It's not here." She could hear her heartbeat in her ears. Each thump made her head constrict like it was being chewed on by a mouthful of pillows. She could sense the colors slipping away from her surroundings, and her mouth started to taste of tongue. Lena pinched at her thighs and held onto them tightly. The sharp twists brought her eyes back into focus, and her legs told her to stand.

"Maybe I dropped it. I'll just have to go back to the hidden tunnels." She pushed through the fabric sludge and opened the first drawer of her dresser, but all that was left of her fire-sword was its indent. Her brain lifted as her heart plummeted. It should have been there.

From somewhere beneath a denim dress, mumbled a muffled "vroom." Lena's heart sank further as she went about excavating her entombed companion. Before she could apologize, Tulu ruffled his head and the remaining sea of debris parted. He balanced triumphantly atop a backpack; his overflowing hubris made Lena laugh.

"And what are you so proud about?" A sense of calm was restored into her voice.

Tulu wheeled down from his pedestal with a slight hint of swagger.

"What's in the bag, mister?" Lena picked up the empty backpack, with an unexpected strain. Its weight was not so empty. She zipped it open and pulled out a pair of boots, a spindle of twine, a marker-marker, and then her hand touched the glassy edge of an unfamiliar sphere. Her heart hesitated between beats and as time picked up its normal pace, she found herself holding a cold world in her hands. Tiny crystalline flakes dusted the airless sky of a boy and girl in mid-quarrel.

The snow globe was real!

She fell to the floor, defeated in her victory. Somewhere in her mind, a bunny emerged as a rabbit. The daunting possibility of madness retreated if but for a moment.

***

When Lena returned to school the next day, it was with a resumed hint of sadness, and with a finer grasp of reality. The class breathed as one, and she breathed as another. Wallington the Stubborn greeted her with delight.

As she settled in, she made a note to celebrate her return to normalcy some other day, as now her eyes locked on a slender man of marble skin who towered next to Ms. Pluck. His spine shot up like an arrow aimed at the sky. The adjacent desk slouched to his right and seemed to blush at his touch. His fingers danced in a controlled chaos atop the surface's integrated tap-pad. When viewed from an angle, his black suit reflected a misty gold.

"Classh." Ms. Pluck gazed wide-eyed out on her students, one arm firmly gripping her tap-pad, the other hidden at her side picking at her fingernails. "Thish ish Mishter Hulten, from Rascheen, and he hash a very schpecial announchment for you."

The class oscillated with the rumbling tenor.

"Brin Class 633. You've been selected for a unique opportunity. You will take the test that is now being transferred to your devices. One of you will have the opportunity to accompany me to tour the capitol in Racine and to meet President Durin." He moved his eyes to Lena. "The rest of you will not. Now begin."

The class became a blur of arms as each student pulled out their tap-pad and clattered away fixedly at the silent keys.

"Yes, Ms. Caust?" His stolid face looked down at Lena's raised hand. Beside him, Ms. Pluck shook her head.

Lena flinched at the sound of her name. It was a common enough occurrence for the Council to send some pencil pusher to check up on the school's curriculum, but a prize? A visit to the capital? A visit with the President? Something tasted grey-green-fishy. "How come you picked this class?"

He blinked. "Random."

"Then why do we have to take a test? Why can't you random up one of us?"

"Mish Causht. Thatsh enough. Now take the tesht, thish ish a wonderful opportunity."

The quiver of desperation in the teacher's voice stopped Lena from continuing her inquisition. *Maybe this is what has been distracting Ms. Pluck. Did she know someone would be coming?*

Lena scowled as she read through the questions. Why people bothered to test her she'd never understood. Any test she'd ever taken once, she'd had to take again. And again. She could even hear Ms. Pluck saying "*Jusht try and do your besht.*" *Well Ms. Pluck, my best gets me a 10 percent and guessing gets me a 25.*

After poking her tap-pad randomly through the series of questions, Lena sat back to watch the rest of the class squirm away, pressing, unpressing, and pressing each answer over and over. Mr. Hulten continued to loom over the class. He positioned himself next to the wall, which, Lena noticed, was appearing quite self-conscious about its own posture. *What's your deal, Mister capital Man?* His eyes darted towards Lena again, and she felt the instant budding of sweat across her brow.

"That's enough." At the sudden boom, the tests vanished from the student's screens and the room burst into a chorus of groans.

"Classh!" Ms. Pluck's face bloomed a livid scarlet. "You'll schow reschpect to our guesht!"

As the class silenced, the teacher's desk blurted out three harmonic bleeps. Ms. Pluck's forehead ruffled at the name that filled the screen.

"Lenalia Caust. Congratulations." His monotone was masked by the barrels of eyes that now glared at Lena.

"You'll collect what you need from home during B and C phases and meet me at the Brin Tube Central Station promptly at the start of D-phase." He paused. "Do you have any questions?"

Time took a few steps forward before Lena realized she was being addressed. How was it possible that she had the best grade? She had always assumed most of the class had heads full of starch, but to be outsmarted by probability was just improbable. She wished she had looked at what answers she had guessed. Then, at least, she might be able to justify the system's mistake, but for all she knew, maybe luck was her companion. *Or maybe...*

"Ms. Caust. I said do you have any questions?"

"Oh. Um. Mr. Hulten?"

"Yes?"

"What's your first name?"

Ms. Pluck's eyes grew three sizes too large. The world muted and in its silence Lena thought she could hear a lonely bird searching for a mate somewhere below.

"Mister," he said.

Lena sighed. *How tedious.*

IX.

Talia's eyes dilated at the ebony sea suspended above her. Upon its surface, countless fireflies danced alone in static motion. Her chest ached. How many times had she seen the night sky? She knew she could count if she tried. Her world spent so much time chasing the sun that the only nighttime most knew was artificial. It had been just her and Sado that first time almost a decade ago. She couldn't remember if it had made her feel as empty as it did now. Her hand grazed across her stomach as she let out a sigh.

"Shhhh," snapped a voice from behind her.

Talia's glare shot back to the shortest of the three young men she'd brought with her. Like her and the others, his matte black outfit cast all but his eyes into the shadows. Even with his minute visibility, he flinched as she met his stare.

The four drifted with noiseless steps to the center of the room. The fresh taste of untouched, unprocessed air touched their lips and in unison they took an extra breath. The plants that breathed this sweet existence stretched in concentric circles about them. Above them, a dome of green glass looked up in longing. The eye of a fallen titan.

At the tap of her palm, the tips of Talia's gloves glowed a soft etched yellow. Talia motioned left and then right, and the two tallest figures slipped off into the caged forest. Her fingers beckoned, and her remaining companion moved closer. His slight hesitation made her grin.

"Now listen closely," her lips moved. Near silent words slithered into his ears. "I'll only say this once. You question me again and I'll have you Recycled. It wouldn't cause me a second thought. So, if you'd like your organs unabashedly borrowed, your veins emptied, and your carcass dried, please test me. I would be happy to breathe the air produced by the plant that is grown in your decomposed remains. Tell me, please, I know you've got something to say. Just tell me. What is it that is so important you felt it necessary to question me?"

The man gulped. He couldn't tell if it was late enough that the exterior glass was just coated in dew, or if the walls had broken out into a sweat. "Nothing," was all that managed to escape his mouth.

"Then take the northeast quadrant of the room and wait for the signal."

As the last consonant snaked into the open air, he sprinted off, the noise of his footsteps caught by the pillowy rubber of his soles. Talia's spine stretched a little taller. It was refreshing to smell the salty tenderness of fear. So often she'd questioned the reason for her nose, since odors had been eliminated even before she'd begun.

Talia glanced back out at the blackened abyss that was the outside to her outside. How many people had actually seen the world for which they'd shaped their lives to protect? How many fools had felt real warmth through the film of paint and light-breathing membranes? How would they react if they did?

From the corner of her eye dashed a powdered blue in a soft smudge. By the time she fixed her stare on the spot in the sky, its luminescence had been eaten by darkness. An uncaught falling star.

We could still be that way, she let her thoughts pine. *We could still disappear into the night sky, uncatchable, and leave this prison behind.* But she knew that argument had ended when the Outcry began. Her lips pursed and she turned back. These plants weren't going to steal themselves after all, and if people were going to follow her, she had to be seen as someone willing to risk her own life.

While the world slept, Talia and the others filled the synthetic pouches around their waists with handfuls of seeds. Mutations whose ancestors once wrecked society now supported it. Even through her gloves, she could feel the dormant flora sifting between her fingers, mocking her with manufactured fertility. The spherical nursery, like a translucent stadium-sized marble, was a monument to man playing god. Thousands of modified plants, the lifeblood of society, were fixed with struts on both sides of the plane that bisected the sphere. While one side would bask in sunlight, the other would hold on for dear life.

She shook her head just as a delicate tremor on her wrist signaled that it was time. Talia backed into the southwest corner of the room and felt her back shiver against the glass. Her hand twisted and pressed into her wristlet to stop the vibration. From the bag on her back, she pulled a reflective sphere. The dilated optic in its center glared out at Talia as she secured it to the base of the glass dome. Her wrist buzzed again and her heart skipped. As she searched through her bag, she felt the floor begin to rotate up. It was time for the greenhouse to invert in order to give sunlight to the plants on the bottom side of the sphere. When the angle of the room hit a five-degree incline, Talia's feet began to slide towards the center. She turned and leaned towards the glass, still sorting through her bag. At ten degrees, her thighs burned. She pressed as far forward as she could to keep from toppling into the forest behind her. Just as her hair lifted from her back and pointed towards the dome's center, Talia pulled out a black handle and thrust it onto the glass siding. The suction cup on the other end stuck to the windowed wall and as the room inclined fifty degrees, Talia's feet left the floor and dangled in the air. Her ears perked up for a moment, but nothing was heard. The others must have secured themselves too.

An audible click let Talia know that the room had finished its flip. The world felt entirely new. On the opposite side of the sphere, the now-upright plants were preparing for the sun. Her feet still hung, so she pressed them back to feel the cool glass now below her. She looked out across the room at the sea of plants suspended upside down. Dim lights on the encircling engines cast a scattered glow.

The strain on Talia's arms became noticeable just as her wrist hummed for a third time. She took an opportunely scheduled breath and pressed the release on her handle. She felt a sense of weightlessness as air rushed past her. All too soon, her body made contact with the glass dome and she slid with the curve of what was now a bowl. Still, silence as her silky exterior helped funnel her towards the earth below.

When Talia finally slowed, she found herself at the acme of the dome, suspended alone. Below her, moonlit clouds floated, their haze lit at the soles of her feet. A half minute later another dark figure slipped down the glass. As he slowed, Talia walked over and helped him up. They nodded at each other. After another half minute, a shorter figure came, and then when the last finally slid down, they took a moment to inhale their momentary success. They hoped the others were having as much luck on their missions.

"We have two minutes before the rays start tracing the perimeter. Everyone, take a corner and split the glass clockwise along the seam." Talia began to walk to a corner, then stopped and looked back. "Oh, and don't stand towards the middle of the circle."

The others let out a whispered chuckle as they pulled out pen-shaped tools and stepped onto the outside of the fused ring of glass. In unison, their tools emitted a flickering blue and white, piercing through the carbon joints in a slow precision. A minute passed. A half-minute. A quarter-minute. And then silently the circular peak loosed from the dome and disappeared into the midnight clouds; somewhere far below it shattered into history.

Just as they stood back up, the two-minute mark passed and their wrists vibrated. Above them, on what once was the floor, glowed two orthogonal beams of vibrant indigo. Together they rotated, taking time to score every intersecting obstacle. In an instant, the sky was full of potted plants.

"Go, go, go!"

Talia and the others each pulled two handles from their packs and rushed carefully to the incised hole. The thin air outside pulsed like an angry drum. Its music was a chaotic ebb and flow. Talia dangled her legs into the nothingness and slid her handle onto the dome's exterior as the wind lashed her thighs. *Let it hold.* As the first plant collided with the side of the sphere and slid towards them, Talia swung around the opening and gripped tightly onto her single lifeline. Her body swayed and jolted but the suction cup remained sealed to the surface. The others hung adjacent to her and the four dared to smile at each other. While she secured her second handle, from the hole poured a stream of leafy green. Achillea millefolium, Cirsium vulgare, pines and thistles, ferns and chrysanthemums all funneled out into the milky heavens, headed back to a home they'd never known. Born in captivity and returning to the wild. The clouds became splotched with verdant defectors.

Nearly twenty minutes passed before the last piece of straggling bamboo rolled out towards the earth. Sweat dripped from Talia's brow and licked her eye with a salty pinch. She winced. Even with her months of training, the tendons in her hands pleaded with her to let go. Had people really been this accustomed to physicality before? Every moment that her thoughts lingered on her arms merely served to increase the pain.

One by one, the four members of the Outcry pulled themselves back into the vacated nursery. They pushed out a few remaining pots that teetered along the edge, and after a quick sigh they began the long climb back up the side of the dome, one hand after the other. By the time they'd reached the top, a crimson blush peeked over the horizon. They made their way up through a drainage shaft and crawled out onto the floor of the second half of the sphere, glad to be working with gravity again. The plants in this dome mirrored those lost to their makeshift well. It would be seven hours until the room rotated again. Seven hours until the Outcry's existence was truly known. *Plenty of time,* Talia thought, *to disappear.*

X.

Day-lights cast a gentle pearl glow over the countless ceiling scrapers of Racine. The giant carbon pillars intermingled in grid-like precision; a steady flow of human traffic meandered motionless on fluid sidewalks between their bases. Stained murals hugged every side, top, in, out, crevice and crack, culminating in a landscape of living pastels. Lena's eyes squiggled up and down, but her vision fractured into shards of focus. As soon as she'd find herself in a crystal ocean of painted urchins, a sparkle would pull her back through the collage of a living library, or maybe the portrait of a three-story giraffoclops. *Even,* she thought, *if everyone were to be quiet, the city would still be too loud.* And still the metropolis echoed with the chatter of a world awake.

Lena sat with her jaw plopped down in her hands, her face smudged into a squishy frown. *Wait outside, they said. Sit on these steps, they said. Don't move, they said.* She looked back and saw the capitol looking down at her with one eyebrow raised. Even with a population bustling in and out, no one glanced towards her. Upon the only expansive walkway around the city stretched a vibrant plastic marketplace, muddled with every knick and knack she could and couldn't imagine. Breathers cluttered the stalls; their hands were an ebb and flow of give and take. Lena gave a final assessment of the overlooking building, and then trotted off.

"Shine your shoes for a credit?"

Lena's eyes shot left to a scruffy man with pockets full of tarnished rags.

"Genuine watermelon! Modified to stimulate your taste buds! Only six credits!"

Lena looked right to a chubby woman holding a melon with a clear rind. She'd never seen real fruit before. She guessed she still hadn't.

All about her the marketplace breathed with exchange. Vendors offered exotic foods, wafers that promised to improve your eyesight or excite your love life, automatic toothbrushes powered by emerald toothpaste, bottled odors, tiny music boxes, dustless chalk, earthless clay, and even, it was whispered, birdless feathers. All, she heard over and over, for the "low low price" of just a few O_2 credits. Most seemed to relish the opportunity to give their precious breaths away for frivolities. Some, however, held tight to their plastic cards, swiping away their earnings for tidbits of wafers, in hopes to feed their families.

Lena's arm brushed against a tattered pant leg and she looked up to see a grey man clutching a grey canister. A scrap of plastic in his left hand read, "Can you sp-air?" Lena smiled and pulled out her card.

"Sir? Sir, can I help you?"

A long, sunken face glanced down and gave Lena a subtle grin. He reached his hand towards her, but, before he could speak, a nasally squeal rattled from behind Lena, and a twig-like figure rushed towards them. She swatted and flailed.

"You get away from that little girl at once." With the tip of a skeletal umbrella, the lady poked and prodded until all that was left of the man was his wilted silhouette fading into an alley.

"There, there, girl. Nothing to worry your sweet little cheeks about. How about you come over to Auntie Cran's and we'll get you some replacements for those unfortunate clothes?" Before Lena could respond, a bony paw wrapped about her wrist and pulled her towards a stall that had enough sequins to blind a bat. A hundred million sparkles all winked at once, and Lena had to close her eyes to see.

"Now you'll be needing a sash, and a scarf, and something to bring out those petite ears of yours, oh, and skin polish, we can't forget that." She ploughed through a heap of cloth and fabric, tossing bits and pieces this way and that, occasionally wrapping an article around Lena in a slowly weaved web. "Now, you look a three, but I bet you'll soon be a four, and we'll need to make room for your hips, they'll grow in quite nicely with these boots. And I take it, you'll be paying with credits?"

"I wouldn't advise that." The words came from the doorway.

Lena peeked through her pile of accessories at the new voice that filled the booth. It made her think of lavender. "Now now, we've got nothing in your size, miss, so please leave my other customers alone."

"Girl," replied the soft voice, disregarding Cran. "Haven't you heard there's an oxygen shortage? You should hold on to what you've got. Don't waste it on such petty accessories."

Cran's face boiled a dark berry. "I won't have you preaching your nonsense in my shop. You get out now, or I'll call the Council."

Lena shook and tossed until all of Cran's pieces were littered about her shop. "You look like a fish," she said. And with that, she strutted out into the market.

A soft tap on the shoulder let her know that even in this faceless crowd, she still wasn't alone. Lena looked back to see the same woman from the shop, her face more golden than the pasty sea around them, and her robe a simple violet. Her thin face betrayed her swollen belly, and Lena realized that what she thought was a tap, was actually the woman's attempt to stabilize her unbalance. Lena stood firm and touched her hand as she breathed in relief.

"You know, I wasn't going to buy those things. I was just pulled in there and she kept tossing clothes at me and I–"

"I know."

Lena paused. "You know?"

"You're not from around here, are you?"

She brimmed. "Nope. Brin girl, born 'n raised. Just here for..." She thought briefly. "You know, I don't really know why I'm here. I just took a test, and now I get to meet the President."

The woman looked as if she were about to laugh before she stifled it. Lena had the familiar sensation that she was missing something fundamental. When the woman spoke again, her tone was softer. "I'm from Brin, myself. Maybe I know your parents, are they around?" She turned her head in search of a familiar face. "You actually remind me of someone I once knew."

"No. Why were you going to laugh?" Lena could feel her ears getting hot.

"What's that?"

"When I said I was going to meet the President. You wanted to laugh."

She grinned. "Well aren't you perceptive, dear. You must know?"

Lena raised an eyebrow.

"Really? Well, no one ever meets the President."

"But they said—"

"Do you see that face up there?" She pointed to the large dimpled visage of President Durin, sprawled on a canvas hugging the capitol. It was a beautifully androgynous blend of high cheekbones and a square jaw. Below it read *Limit to fuel; fuel to create; create to limit* in an engraved translucence. "That face hasn't changed in a hundred years. Maybe more."

"He doesn't look that old." Lena squinted her eyes and tried to imagine the portrait with wrinkles.

"Aw sweetie, he's not. A long time ago the Council chose a face. One they determined would be the face of the perfect leader. And since then, no matter who the leader is, they hide behind that face."

"But then who is the leader?"

"Secrets of the capital," she smiled. "The Council chooses him or her from some unknown batch. Even they don't know what the President really looks like. He's just a blood sample to them."

Her eyes widened. "You mean it doesn't matter who's President?"

The woman's gaze shifted left and right for a moment, as though in search of someone, before she resolved her focus back on Lena. "Quite the contrary. Durin has the final say. But no one seems to know who he is or where he comes from."

Lena's eyes drifted toward the clock that crowned the capitol, unable to make sense of such a strange place. The second hand swiveled past thirteen. Something was missing here, but what? She furrowed her forehead; well aware of the prodding glance she was being given. The crowd around them began to thin, and, even through the lingered haggling, the quiet penetrated.

"I don't hear them." She leaned her head back and frowned at the faraway ceiling.

"Who don't you hear?"

"Not who. What. The lights. They're not all buzzly. Like at home."

Now both of them stared up, but Lena could see from the corner of her eye that she was being examined. This woman was searching over her for some clue of crazy. She wouldn't be the first person to report her for odd behavior. Lena's record seemed to grow faster than she did.

"You're special, you know that."

Upon hearing these words, Lena felt the small pinch of her tear ducts, pushing back the possibility of unfiltered emotion. *Special,* she thought. Images of her dad threatened to surface. It was the first time since his death that that word had been said about her without a taste of sarcasm. Who was this strange lady? Something about her voice resonated in her ears, like it had been there before.

"It's strange. You're just a little girl, after all, but you already have such a profound view of the world. Is there anything else you notice?"

Lena gasped. The words crept into her mind. *What do you think they'll do when they find her? I hope Sado listens to what I said. She's just a little girl, after all.* Her knees began to feel soft. This woman had certainly been in Brin. In Old Brin.

"Dear heart, did you hear me?" Her face was warm with a smile. Ripples of soft skin lined her cheeks.

Lena's face was hot. She could feel her pulse behind her eyes. "Your baby breathes at the same time you do."

Then silence. Most of the marketplace had cleared, except for the few vendors packing up their carts. Lena's legs urged her to turn, but her stare remained fixed. This woman could be the door to the outside. She certainly didn't look threatening. She didn't look like a criminal. But somehow, even with this tiny creature inside her, she had managed to make her way into the depths of the hidden tunnels. Lena watched as the woman's face turned from curiosity to caution. Was she afraid of Lena?

"What did you say your name was?" Her feet backed away like a lilac current.

Lena opened her mouth, but before she could speak, a firm hand grasped her shoulder. "Lenalia Caust." The smooth bellow permeated like jazz. "We're ready for you now." She turned to look back at the woman, but the market was empty. The urge to sigh filled her, but the hand on her shoulder reminded her of where she was, so she resolved to save it for later.

"What happened to Mr. Hulten?" She turned to the capitol.

"We've all got our place." He smiled. "His job is to intimidate others. Mine is to persuade them. I'm Paxton."

As their eyes met, shivers rippled from the top of her head. He let out a hearty laugh, which shook his buoyant belly, and Lena couldn't help but giggle as well.

They walked over to the capitol building and with Paxton's touch the doors breathed open a crisp air that tickled the roof of Lena's mouth. Her face contorted in preparation to sneeze, but Paxton touched the bridge of her nose and the need went away.

"Not in the capitol, Ms. Caust."

Inside, there were doors within doors, rooms within rooms, chambers, tunnels, tubes, bins, and even the occasional container that snaked about and sprawled in and out of sight, presumably without end. The people here seemed to move in a planned procession, and Lena wondered if their sole purpose was to assemble and stand in line all day. She watched as a door slid open, let out a person, closed, and when it opened again, it led to a different room. She looked to Paxton and pointed, but he just nodded and grinned.

"Wouldn't want to get separated in this place. Near impossible to find the way out. From what I hear, no one person knows all the complexities of the capitol. Its secrets are contained by the collective minds of all those who work and live here."

When they reached a small lobby that glowed a gentle emerald, Paxton told her to have a seat and excused himself. *So, this is the capitol?* She thought. Her eyes floated about and pressed against each divot and dent. *Not much more than at home. Squishy carpet, desk, lamp, tap-pad, picture of a window, more squishy carpet, firm cushion, a—* Lena's brain twisted left as her head twisted right. And as soon as her legs caught up, she was thrown out of her chair towards the only other living thing in the room: a lily.

Color poured from its yellow veins, so much so that any voice it could have had stayed quiet in Lena's mind. Its bulb looked down towards its toes, which lay hidden beneath a refined soil. Whatever youth it once possessed was veiled by its arched stem.

Lena's finger stroked its honeyed flesh as she lifted its chin, but its petal pushed her away and its head drooped lower. *Something with so much life, planted in a cage.*

"Beautiful, isn't it?" Paxton's voice hummed softly from behind her.

"Yes, he is."

"You seem disappointed."

"Aren't you, Pax?"

Paxton's russet tones wrinkled into a worn grin. "No one's called me that since my mother passed away. You know, you remind me of her."

"Was she disappointed too?"

"She paid more attention to the rest of the world than she did herself."

Lena turned to Paxton as he held out his hand to her. Their gazes met. Somewhere deep in his eyes flickered a hurt covered by a world of denial. Was it this pain that made her feel like she could trust him? She wanted to peel back every layer of his existence to understand him, to comfort him. Who'd broken his beautiful soul? She reached for his hand and hers was immediately engulfed. She held onto three of his doughy fingers, and he squeezed her hand with the tenderness of an old friend.

"Why am I here?"

Paxton turned to lead Lena out of the room. She glanced back to see the lily, holding out his petal, reaching for her, but her feet shepherded her away. She wondered if she'd ever see him again.

When they finally stopped, Lena found herself in a room whose brightness defied her eyes. As her pupils adjusted, she questioned the point of eyelids if they were so useless. When the world finally revealed itself, Lena gasped. Thousands of feet in the air, drifting atop a Siberian tundra in a translucent bubble, Lenalia Caust saw the world for the first time. She fell to her knees.

The earth lay crusted in a blanket of white frost. Barren and pure. An afternoon sun painted the surface with a splotched brilliance as clouds soared in dreamless slumber.

"Sad, isn't it?" Paxton sighed as he sat down and placed his hand on a small silver table.

"It's beautiful. The most beautiful thing I've ever seen. Like a thousand million ideas, all at once. It's what paintings want to be, but it's an empty canvas." A tear slipped down her cheek. And another.

"It wasn't always like this. Two centuries ago, before we saw the error of our ways, this snowy white was thick clots of grey. Humans stripped the land without understanding, and when they finally recognized their impact, it was too late. There were too many people making too many mistakes. Some say we ran from disease," he rubbed his eyes. "We were the disease. The earth couldn't heal itself with us there."

Lena's lip quivered. "So, what did they do?"

"What would you do?"

She hesitated, though she knew the answer he wanted. "I would leave."

"And now, after two hundred years of healing, the earth lives in peace, as do we. No more pollution, no more need to pillage its crust for minerals, and no more need to fear the dangers of its wilderness. Wouldn't it be a shame for someone to destroy it again? To destroy the balance we've created?"

And there it was. Lena finally understood why she'd been brought to the capital, why she was the one to pass the test.

"What is it that you want?"

Paxton's composure remained. "I want to protect your empty canvas. And I want to make sure that you want that too."

The frosted landscape still flowed beneath them, but in the vastness of white, Lena saw specks of verdant green. Thick with snow, pines reached from the bitten surface, beckoning to her. Her body ached to be among them.

"Couldn't we live together now? Now that we've learned to live apart?"

A defeated breath escaped Paxton's lips. "I wish it could be true, Lena, but history tells us differently. Maybe at first it would seem to work, but people don't change. Slowly, we would forget what damage we could cause. Just a building here and there, we would say, that couldn't hurt. A hundred trees, we would say, just cut down one for a desk, that couldn't hurt. And why not dig a well here, there's water underground that isn't being used, how could that hurt? Humans are predictable. We puncture and tear and steal, and we continue to do so until there is no easier way than the hard way. And when finally we've done our damage, and the only path to take is that of giving and healing, it's too late. It's always too late."

"But, how can you be sure?" There had to be a way. Her dad had believed it so.

Paxton sat in silence for a moment while a chill wiped the glass with a thick condensation. As the sun broke through the clouds again, the moisture evaporated into clear ringlets. "We can't know the future unless we keep control of the present. And if we don't control the present, then there is no guarantee. Would you trust the world to those risking its destruction?"

Lena lifted herself off the floor and sat in the chair next to Paxton's. "Then you already know about them?"

"We've believed there to be a few stragglers here and there whose selfish ways may lead them to crave the past, but only recently have we discovered that they are organized and preparing to challenge our way of life."

"Then what do you want with me?"

"Just to know what you know."

"And what would you do to them?"

Paxton smoothed the wrinkles of his pant leg. "Whatever is necessary to ensure the earth remains as it's meant to be."

Lena's mouth opened to speak but the table promptly interrupted her. They both looked down to see a reporter in a checkered brown shirt appear across the screen.

"This just in," the woman read. "There have been reports that a terrorist organization, calling themselves the Outcry, have attacked three government establishments throughout the city of Racine during the early hours of the present cycle. These include the destruction of an O_2 production nursery, a chemical research facility, and a robotics assembly plant. Here is a quick word from President Durin."

The screen flickered to the still face of their ageless leader. A smoothed tenor resonated from the table in a slow pronouncement. "These are sad times that some of our own brethren have felt the need to bring violence upon us. It is unfortunate that they have felt that they could not address their concerns openly. I give you this one chance at forgiveness. Turn yourselves in, and you will not be harmed."

The surface flashed back to the reporter. "Members of the group are considered extremely dangerous. If you suspect someone to be a member of this terrorist organization, do not approach them. Report them immediately." She paused for a moment and touched her ear. "I'm getting word that there are a number of casualties that are being reported from the attacks. Please stay tuned for a list of names and faces of the victims."

Lena watched as one by one, faces flicked on and off the screen. A man from Kardel leaving behind a wife and two girls. A woman from Deloy leaving behind her husband of thirty years. The list seemed to go on forever. She wondered if any of these people were Paxton's friends. As she was about to question him, something caught her eye. The picture of a familiar face came onto the screen. It was labeled "Beloved Mother from Brin, leaving behind three generations of children." The pregnant woman standing in the picture reminded her of lavender. Lena's head pulsed and she felt the vein on her temple sear. The name on the screen read Esta Amell.

XI.

Damp salt dripped onto Joseph's lips and he knew he would dream of the ocean that night.

It had been three days without end since the Outcry had been told to seal off Old Brin. Three days since the world had learned their name. Nearly six hundred people sought to join them, and over a hundred thousand sought to destroy them. So Joseph worked, and the Outcry worked, to keep their hidden city a secret.

Over a hundred different tubes and tunnels connected Old Brin to other sectors. Each one was deemed a liability. The cities were designed to connect and disconnect from each other, but that didn't make it easy. Joseph pushed hard against the wall; his hands wrapped tightly around the oversized wrench. He could sense the blood pushing away from where the tool indented his palms, a wrinkled white depression awaiting relief. As the bolt he was working with squealed a sigh of release, the first sight of day splintered through the tube's walls. In his momentary triumph, the wrench slipped and splayed him flat on his bottom in a loud "humph!" *One day you're repairing the tubes,* his mind reminisced, *the next, you're taking them apart. Arthur would have been proud.*

"What are you doing sitting on the job?"

Joseph turned in the direction of the dulcet voice. "Well you're a sight for sore eyes. Aren't you supposed to be dead?" He grinned. She made him feel safe.

Esta's round face scowled back at him. "You know, you and the rest of those declared dead seem to be missing the point. There's a reason we were declared dead, and it wasn't because we're all in hell."

Joseph chuckled, picking the wrench and himself back up.

"I'm serious, Joe. It was a threat. Somehow, they found out about some of us and put out the warning that if we're found we'll be Recycled, seeing how in the system we already have been."

"Maybe, maybe not. The way I see it, they've gone and tried to make us all martyrs. They figure if the whole world knows that such great people," Joe gestured to Esta, "have been killed by a bunch of rabble-rousers, then they'll solidify the position that the Outcry is indeed just a bunch of no good rabble-rousers."

"Then why are you so chipper about it all? You and I, along with the others declared dead, we won't be able to reintegrate. Not until this is all over. So what use are we?"

Joe locked the wrench back onto the bolt and turned, this time without strain. "It's what Sado said yesterday. 'A hurdle is just a low arch.' We might not be able to show our faces in the cities, but the people that come to us will see that we're alive. It'll solidify their feelings towards the

Council and Durin. And that's how it all starts. The Council might as well be working for us."

A sudden kick inside Esta made her flinch a weak smile. She gently rubbed her swollen body and leaned against the tube's inner wall.

"You okay?"

Before she could answer, Joe gave a final twist and the bolt let loose. A widening seam of light pierced through the perimeter and from the opposite side of the platform the giant metallic straw retracted into the adjacent city, leaving Old Brin's tube looking out onto a pillowy expanse. Where once was silence now pulsed a scraping wind.

"Just..." Dimples of sand freckled the earth far below the now-breaking cloud line. "...a kick." Esta slumped against the tube's side, her eyes darting around as she inhaled the foreign backdrop.

An unspoken agreement brought them both to be sitting on the tube's edge with their feet swinging above a bottomless sky. Esta's body shivered and her chest fluttered while her mind writhed to comprehend this unnatural feeling of fear. She'd been born above the clouds, but a fear of falling, a fear of heights made her feel foolish right now. And yet, in all her life, her feet had never truly left the ground. She pinched hard against the lip of her world; its biting metallic flesh comforted her.

"For thirty years," Joe spoke out to the trembling dunes, "I maintained these tubes so breathers could travel. It's funny to think that I wasn't really letting them go anywhere."

Esta squeezed his hand. "You made sure people could go where they needed to go; you brought people together. There's something to be said about that."

"I helped turn the wheels on a society that exists only to tell me to turn its wheels. How am I better, how are any of us better, than the world that created us? What right do we have to live out the rest of our cycles on a world that we've abandoned?"

"We don't, Joe. But you said it yourself. We're already dead. I'd imagine our dust would blend in rather nicely with the sands down there."

"So you don't think that there is any truth in what Durin said? How we're all just a bunch of terrorists."

Down below the winds kicked up with a frenzied passion and died down just as quickly. A faint blemish of green wandered motionlessly through the desert, seemingly aware that it didn't belong.

"I think perspective is a dangerous thing. The only difference between revolution and terrorism is who writes the history book in a hundred years."

Joseph's eyes refocused on his knee and his mind once again existed behind his forehead. "How do you think they found out about us?"

"Talia."

A loud clank sounded from behind them and their heads shot back. The wrench that Joe had propped against the wall had clattered to the ground. He turned back to Esta, his face a somber inquisition. "Why would you think that?"

"Have you seen her since then?" She snapped, taken aback by her own aggression. "How can she expect us to trust our lives in her hands?"

Joseph's shoulders fell forward as his chest sunk into himself. His eyes felt old. "I don't pretend to know Talia, but Sado trusts her and so must I." He scratched the side of his head. "You told me once that if you let doubt play with your world, then you'll quickly find that doubt will be all that's left."

Her feet swayed atop thin air. "I don't...that is, I'm not saying Sado hasn't led us well so far, but to just trust in him blindly? First that he was willing to Restore those children, and now this vague plan of his to ground Kardel? And Talia. How quick she was to suggest Recycling. Don't you—"

"Esta," he said, so firmly that it scared them both. Esta retreated into herself. "We're all scared. Until now, we've always known when to take the next breath. But really, we've always had to trust our lives in other people's hands. Just as society has acted the way it did for a reason, so does Sado. So does Talia. This is no different. If we have not seen her, then perhaps we are not meant to have seen her."

They looked out over the crystalline horizon, on which the sun now rested its tired chin. The hills seemed to quiver under its weight, but the earth stood. They watched until the last ray was held in the edge's bounds, and until the onyx sky tittered and tattered in speckled conversation. Esta felt the warm life inside her lift her from her shelter. *He's already so strong. Let him not have to fight for his world. No child should feel as if they are a threat.* Her eyes sunk. The girl from the market materialized in her thoughts as the moon awoke from behind a cloud.

"Got something on your mind, Es?"

Esta looked up. Her face blushed when she realized how hard she had been grasping his fingers. "I met the girl."

"What's that?"

"Lena. The girl who heard us. I met her in the market of Racine. She was being taken in by the Council."

"Must have been how they found out about some of us." He paused, then his eyes widened. "She saw your face?"

"I don't know, Joe. There was something about her. I don't think she would have said anything."

"Es," he looked to her with profound sadness. "I know you don't want to think about this, but she might not have needed to say anything. If they wanted information, she could only do so much." With slowness, he pushed himself away from the ledge, and gathered his tools. "I should start heading to the next tunnel. I think there are still four more to go, and we're supposed to disconnect all but one before the end of the cycle."

Esta sat looking down over the ridge. "Joe?"

"Yeah?" he paused; the zipper halfway shut on his bag.

"I think she's Arthur's daughter."

He stopped. The sound of his heartbeat threatened to be heard. "Caust?"

She nodded. "It didn't click at first, but the way she talked, the way she saw the world. It was him. Somehow he managed to keep her hidden."

"Why wouldn't Sado have told us?" His head was beginning to hurt from its racing thoughts and the sound of the wind beating against the open tube. *Damn it, Arthur. Even in your death, you are changing this world.* He ached for his lost friend.

"Maybe he didn't know." She rested her forehead in her hands. "Could we help her? If we brought her in, could we help her?"

He walked over and rested his hand on her shoulder. "That's going to be up to Sado. Now that the Council knows about us and her, something must be done. We'll bring her in, but there's no guarantee that we'll be able to help her." He squeezed her shoulder. "We don't think she could remember much, but we'll need to know what she's given them."

"If they haven't torn that from her as well." She sneered.

"No, I don't think they would risk that. Sado thinks that it would be more logical to try and convince her to tell them. To use her as a seed for the rest of the schools."

"Well, I..." She stopped. Esta felt her body churn with a sharp twist, and her hand clenched down hard on the rim of the tube. Inside her, it felt like a new reality was pushing and pulling itself into existence. Where once was a dormant child, now clawed a suffocating energy. Esta screamed and Joseph tumbled backwards, his feet caught on his bag. She pushed herself away from the opening as every muscle in her body tangoed in dissonance. Fourteen children had come and gone like harmonious clockwork, but this inkling of a being now fought to see the light of a real day.

And on the edge of two worlds, a boy was born.

XII.

"And we pieced him together from parts of a vacuum cleaner, a blender, and a mop!"

Paxton smiled as he watched Lena's eyes flair and her grin blaze. She'd been speaking for the better part of the ride about her robot. *No,* he thought, *Not her robot. Her friend.* There was something compelling about the vivacity of her words, the origin of her tones, and the way no sentence was crafted and refined. Maybe it was that, that everything about her was raw and unfiltered. Whatever it was, he could feel his heart reacting towards her unabashed care for this creature. He chuckled.

The body is a funny thing, his mind prodded. *To be so manipulated by words.* He shook his head slightly; curious how he felt so impacted by Lena. She was intoxicating. Dangerously so.

He was uncertain if her visit to the capital had produced the desired results. Over the three cycles of his lecturing, she had appeared receptive of the ideas that he planted, but her apparent lack of knowledge of the Outcry had been suspect. Though it was never apparent that she was lying, he could tell that she had managed to hide something from both him and herself. *An odd patient, indeed.*

A bell chimed and Paxton looked up, taken aback. He had become so internalized that he had lost track of where they were. He noticed his own breathing for the first time in sixty years.

"This is my stop," she said with a foot out the door.

His eyes groomed her with a wordless inquiry. He wondered of what she had silently convinced him. Him: the convincer and word-weaver. Him: the reverse psychologist. *She will either go far, or she will find herself falling short. A mind like hers,* he squinted at her, *is not one to stay unnoticed.* "I'll—"

"I'll dream you a head of hair." He winced at her words and, before he could reply, the tube slid closed and propelled him away, staring at his own glassy reflection.

***

When she was sure he was gone, Lena collapsed to the ground by the tubes into a lump of fatigue. The world was bigger than she had thought, and it was trapped in a smaller bubble than she ever could have imagined. Bits and pieces of her wanted to keep this collection of life enclosed, confined, and limited. It was similar to how Paxton had described the early painters. Only when people are limited will they create something new. Impressionism was fueled by confinement. Without society's strict definition of what art was, people like Monet and Renoir would never have pushed the envelope to see what art *could* be. And the only way to fuel further progress was the creation of limitations.

Lena's stomach churned. So much talk of circles made her dizzy.

It had taken all her energy to summon up wells of childish ignorance while Paxton took needle and thread to her brain. And still, she could tell patches of his woven mental fabric managed to blanket layers of her previous beliefs. She scratched at her scalp and shook like a wet robot, but nothing seemed to fall from her ears. His words continued to linger.

Around her, Brin felt blank. Quiet. Buildings stood grey in the humming fluorescence. The faded pastel backdrop of the outer dome fractured at the thought of the loudness of the capital. A few days ago, Brin had felt overwhelming. *Perspective,* she exhaled. *How odd that a picture becomes empty next to a movie.*

She picked herself up. She felt like a dirty nose rag, and she held her body as far away from herself as she could manage. The walk home took three thousand heartbeats, and with each thump people around Lena scattered further away. At times the floor even sunk away from her footsteps, shying away from persistent contact with her. There was some kind of visible odor that the capital left on people. It made her feel like she was just a breather. She remembered the few times that her dad had gone to Racine, how he'd always dry-cleaned as soon as he'd gotten home.

When she got to the door, it slid away from her touch.

"Not you too, Bernie!"

The house didn't bother to reply, and Lena's torso slumped lower, almost to the floor, had the floor not also been avoiding her.

She made her way through the house, dragging her body behind her, making a note of the locations she'd have to clean later. As she turned to a new page in her mental notebook, the room filled with a whizz, a burr, and a bang bang bang. Down the stairs, three steps at a time, thumped an over-anxious Tulu, like a ten-pound tumbleweed. Lena's body tried to dig itself deeper, knowing that Tulu would attempt to tumble right back up the stairs as soon as he saw her contaminated aura.

She turned away as his last thud resounded at the bottom step, but in an instant she found herself tackled on the floor with a twisting and flailing mop stationed on top of her. He stopped turning and nuzzled into her as his motor purred. The warmth of his lifeless body filled her chest with a trembling happiness and her eyes with a warm tear. She held him tightly until the room blinked with a dull yellow warning, and even longer still, until for a moment they both existed breathless.

After her lungs were again filled with oxygen, and her body was buffeted with solvents, Lena made her way about the house, no longer with the fear of scornful observers.

"No time now, Bernie, but you can bet your silver siding we'll talk about how you acted when I get back!" Lena scowled as she filled her bag with an assortment of odds and ends. The house drooped in reply. She knew his silence betrayed his nervousness.

"Tulu, I trust you'll take care of the place. I don't know how long I'll be gone, but I've got to get answers, and that could take hours!" She flung her hands up in the air. "I can't find it." She eyed Tulu. "Have you seen my fire-sword?"

He shook his head left and right, and then in full circles to get the point across.

"Gah! Okay, well, I guess I'll just have to take a regular flashlight. Do you know where we keep them?"

He spun in circles and vroomed.

"Useless!"

Tulu danced smugly.

By the time Lena was ready to leave, the lights over Brin flicked and faded, leaving the city silent and shadowless. She heard Tulu whimper as she slipped through the flap in the door and out towards the hidden city of Old Brin.

The night was a lagoon. As she journeyed forward, Lena's pupils drank until they drowned and she could no longer hope to see. She removed her shoes to muffle her passage, then placed them in her bag. As she dipped her toes into the first metal street, a liquid chill rippled through her. The world gave her silence for her warmth, and in symbiosis she swam through the black, guided only by the memory of footsteps past.

Twice she was forced to tread, as the calm was stirred by figures with floating green eyes. *Either a Snarglops or the Council on patrol*, she thought in a whisper. *Probably a Snarglops.* It didn't surprise her that the urchins would be active, as the attacks had put most of the cities in lockdown. All the more reason to avoid their sting.

When Lena finally found the outer wall, it was with a thud. As a thank you for her warmth, the night gobbled up the noise, and Lena gave it a nod and a shiver.

Finding the entrance turned out to be no more difficult than on her previous trips, as a hidden doorway in the dark is no different than a hidden doorway in the light. As always it opened and greeted her, and she paused for a moment to confirm that the quiet stayed quiet. No green eyes, she checked, and so she let the door slide closed as she secured her O_2 mask.

Tunnels and tubes passed undiscovered as Lena felt her way down the narrow corridors. On occasion a door would act more like a wall and she would need to retrace her steps until some new path would appear and continue her spiral into the sightless city. She let herself be led by her sense of touch, as subtleties became blatancies in lingering pockets of heat against her skin.

Lena stopped and absorbed the space about her. It was less stale and seemed to vibrate with a welcoming greeting. Either she had been here before or this place mistook her for someone else. She thought to ask it, but her mind became a puddle when she noticed a gradient in her line of sight. Lena's eyes shot open, or at least she assumed they did, as nothing about her vision changed. Her ears strained but only took in the patter of her heart.

Somewhere a source of light mocked her blindness, just as her fading heart mocked her deafness.

Behind what she thought was the beating of her heart fluttered a subtler pattern that matched the rhythm of her chest. *If that's my heart, then what was...?* Lena sprinted forward, or left, or right, or in whatever direction it was that got her closer to the source of the senses. She heard the pitter-patter noise again, like a leaky faucet. If only the world contained leaks. Or faucets.

Footsteps! She pushed towards the sound. She ran through the black and through the grey. Somewhere in front of her, the footsteps hastened. The tunnel echoed a clip-clap-clop. Fabric seemed to whisper as it slipped on and off itself. She began to make out the silhouette of a shuffling figure with perhaps a cane, or maybe a third leg. "Stop!" She started but never finished. As her mouth opened, Lena's foot caught a hard edge disguised as a shadow. A wince of pain. A wave of arms. It took only a moment for the floor to embrace her face like a rotten lover.

***

If she had passed out, she couldn't tell. The world was dark again when she opened her eyes, and if time had passed, only someone with the sense of it could say. She'd given that up for her memories. She pushed herself up in hopes that she could find some hint towards the direction of her pursuant. A faint gushing filled her ears, like a thousand whispered secrets. Whatever it was, it was close. She reached her arms out in front of her, but she grasped at nothing. The hushing continued, and as she turned her head, it followed her, always in front of her. She swung out again but was met without resistance. Lena sat down slowly as her head began to feel light. And still the sound followed.

Had there been light in the room, she would have noticed it spinning, and it wasn't until purple spots floated in the darkness that Lena began to shake. She brought her hands to her face but they were stopped by a mesh of rubber and metal. *How strange*, she thought. *I don't remember my face feeling like this.* Her heart gave a loud thud, and she could feel it pushing harder than it had ever done before. She felt her face again and traced the rubber ridges up over her nose, leading down to a cold metal cylinder. And then she felt an involuntary breath of air pushing slowly away from her face without remembering ever having exhaled. The breath flowed and flowed, and while it flowed Lena understood.

All this time in the dark, she'd forgotten she was wearing an oxygen mask. When she'd fallen it had split the tube, rendering it useless. She wished she could see her life glide away from her on a lifeless current, but all she could see was a liquid purple dancing about her. A splatter of lavender fireworks igniting somewhere in her mind. Her body lay down as the last wisp of air was breathed in by the old city, and she felt her body writhe as it inhaled breath after breath of nothing.

XIII.

A tiny ball of fire a million miles wide cast hard shadows on the four seated at a table of broken wood. Five, if the figure whose silhouette was the size of a tiny melon counted. Had the room contained wind, a subtle whoosh would have been heard over the silence. The four stared with unbroken concentration at folds of paper in front of them, their edges touched with an aged russet. As if on cue, their eyes darted towards each other in an accusatorial dance as nostrils flared and fingers tapped.

Joseph grinned with hesitation as he splayed out his five pieces of imaged parchment. "Seven, Eight, Nine, Ten, and Jay. All paws."

Esta groaned and slapped her cards down, changing her focus to the baby in her arms.

Circ gripped his cane and knocked it twice on the ground. "Hah!" He laid out his hand. "Two, Three, Five, Seven, and Kay."

Lin scowled, her smooth Racinian forehead erupted in wrinkles. "What's that supposed to be?"

Circ smiled wide. "All primes!"

"Kay isn't a prime!"

"Sure it is. It's the eleventh letter. Eleven is prime."

A chirpy giggle emitted from Esta's arms, and wordlessly the room agreed to bask in its music. Small bubbles formed and the giggles became gurgles as the boy squirmed in amusement. He then promptly fell asleep.

"And what have you got?" nudged Circ in a whisper.

Lin whipped her glare towards him, her lips in a sharp vee. She flipped over each card with a prolonged twist, until six ladies with crowns lay smug and astute. "Six ques, thank you very much." She reached for the pile of antiquities at the table's center, her eyes fixated on a bristled stick.

"Wait a breath." With the foot of his cane, Circ pushed Lin and her chair away from her lost prize.

The others wide-eyed him.

He grimaced. "Just because I can barely hobble away from a little girl doesn't mean I don't have the arms of a buffalo."

Joseph coughed a snort and covered his mouth. "What does that even mean?"

If Circ's cheeks weren't a permanent cherry, his blush would have lit the room. "I don't know. I just assumed, what with their big bodies, they prolly had strong arms," he mumbled. "Anyhow, I'm asking the questions. How come you have six cards, and they're all the same? I thought there were only four of each."

Lin scooted back towards the table. "Maybe we're just missing two of all the other cards. Can't assume what we think we know about the past is really how it was. Not these days. Besides, the last creatures to play with these ground them from trees. We can't really give them much credit for being logical."

Everyone nodded in agreement and Circ grumbled as Lin pulled towards herself the odds and ends of another time.

Around them, a speckled, splotched green accented the massive hemispherical nursery that they were occupying. Thick film coated the glass walls from decades of not being cleaned, cared for, or even known to still exist. Clay pots lay distraught about the room, disconnected and shattered, remnants of a time before containers could invert themselves for space efficiency.

In this bone yard of flowers, scattered about in recently-uprighted vases, a plethora of stolen seeds had awoken beneath layers of freshly engineered soil substitute. In a day they would be saplings, in a week they would be trees, ferns, or some variety of modified organism spawned to breathe life into a world without sun. But today they took their time waking up from their prolonged dormancy.

When the cards were shuffled again and the baby slept, Joseph's concerned tenor broke the silence.

"Not to cover up the light of this beautiful day, but I've got to ask. What do you think happened to the girl?"

Esta cleared her throat and accompanied it with a stern glance. "Lena, you mean? She's got a name."

The others looked back at Joseph, whose expression now slumped disheveled. "Now Esta, I didn't mean anything by it. It's just, we don't know if she is—"

"I won't have such a thought filling this place. Talk of," she looked from side to side and exhaled a whisper, "Dee-Eee-Ayy-Tee-Aych, could cause the seeds to get depressed, and not come out of their shells." She glimpsed down at the tiny creature in her arms, his chest fluttering slowly, rhythmically, and yet separately from his Mother's. *No*, she smiled, *his mother's*. "Life shouldn't know of such things before they have learned to live."

"I'm sorry, Es."

"Es," Circ began. "Something bad had to have happened to her, because you know, with my knee, I couldn't dream to outrun her, but when I turned back to check, she wasn't there."

"Well how did she find you? You know we're supposed to be watching out for this sort of thing."

Circ sat up, his patchy hair looking considerably more ruffled than usual. "She was walking around with no light, no nothing, and not making a single sound with no shoes or anything, and there's only one tunnel connecting to Brin, so, how can you expect me to have any idea, I mean, really—"

"Circ," Lin cut him off. "Take a chill pill. It's not your fault. We're all just trying to understand."

He loosened his grip on his cane, noticing the bloodless white that was his fist. Before he continued, he slipped his hand into his pocket and pulled out a small tube. "She must have fallen and gotten hurt. There are tons of things she could have tripped on. Stupid kid running around in the dark." The tube rattled as he opened it and he took a small pill from inside. He swallowed it dry.

When silence settled, Lin stood. "I'm going to go check on her and see if there's anything I can do."

"She could be a spy! Es, you yourself said she was taken in by the capital. If she's de—" Esta scrunched her eyebrows at Circ. He paused. "If she's not alive, then maybe that's the way her story goes. Can't go changing what you ain't the writer of."

The three got up and walked away from the table, leaving Circ mumbling himself to stand and hobbling to catch up.

When they stopped walking, their feet teetered along the edge of a square plot of fabricated soil. Lin glanced towards a beige cot in the distance. "We did leave her on the stretcher when we brought her in, right?"

Esta looked down at Lena as she swam her arms and legs up and down, imprinting her body like a ringing bell. "Looks like she found her way to the daffodils."

Lena looked up at the four silhouettes surrounding her garden oasis; five, if she counted the swaddled melon. Their faces wore masks of emerald stars, cast down by an endless ceiling. She squinted without resolve, for the darkness had left her pupils wide and the light had swallowed them whole. Until the world became clear, she would just have to enjoy the blend and confusion of a colored blur.

"Am I dead?" she let out, almost quizzically chipper.

If anyone smiled, Lena couldn't see, but the playfulness in their voices, the rise and fall from throat to stomach, hinted that some of their tension had been dissolved.

"Not today, dear heart." Esta spoke softly as the swaddled boy nestled closer to her resonating chest.

Lena's ears perked up as a cascade of electrical signals in her brain lit to the familiar sound. Through the blur, she could make out a lavender glow radiating from the woman with the melon.

"You sound familiar. Did you recently have a tiny person inside of you?"

Esta chortled. "Yes," she motioned towards her arms, "this is Lume."

Lena squinted harder until her eyes were almost shut. *Oh*, she thought, *that melon is a baby.*

By the time Lena could finally see normally again, they were sitting around the table drinking in the last sips of a fading sunlight. They'd spent the last hour trying to convince her that she was a spy, and that she must have told the Council something. Lena spent the time dreaming that she was a spy, and pretending she was a spy who was denying their accusation. In the end, her lack of conviction gave her ruse away and it was decided that she was just a girl pretending to be a spy pretending to be just a girl.

"Then how did you get here?" shook Circ.

"Where?"

"Old Brin."

"You brought me here, silly."

Circ's ears sizzled, and Lin hid her laughter behind a cough.

"What I mean," he ruffled slowly, "is how did you get into Old Brin in the first place?"

"The first time? Years ago?"

His false teeth ground together, sounding like chiseled concrete. On cue he inhaled and exhaled, but for once he noticed that it was with a deep intention. "Right now. This cycle."

"Oh." She scrunched her lips to the right. "I'm confused. Did you not bring me here, then?"

Somewhere behind his eyes an image of youth ignited in a tantrum. It flailed and wailed and when his eyes focused, his hands were covering his face and his head was shaking. Lin patted him on the back.

"Lena, how did you find us?" A hint of awe was imprinted on Esta's words. *She's just like her father.*

Lena brimmed. "I was a ghost, but I didn't glow. I just floated through Brin like a word on the tip of your tongue. And when I got to the hidden tunnels, I swam through the dark until I saw a three-legged light bulb, and I would have caught it if I didn't fall. Then I died. And I woke in a room where hundreds of lives have just been planted and I seem to be trapped on the border of the bright green heavens and a world of metal and false hope. I can only imagine the four," she paused, "four-and-a-half of you are my jury, deciding what my final verdict will be." Her eyes opened wide in expectation. "I vote heaven."

The four sat, gazing into Lena like a starry night. Something about her both terrified them and filled them with wonder. Her words lingered in Esta's ears like a bedtime story promising a happily ever after. Even Circ felt a warmth churn inside him without his consent.

"It's okay, kid," the tenderness in his voice caused the others to turn. "You're okay. You're not dead, and we're not here to judge you." He hesitated but for a moment. "Whatever you may have heard about us in the capital is undoubtedly false, and I think that needs to be set straight. We're not terrorists. We're just a group of people that wish to be free of this place." He gestured all around.

"Did you destroy those factories and steal all these plants?" She mocked his gesture.

Lin pushed up her sleeve. A grid of unnatural charcoal squares was imprinted along the inside of her arm in code-like precision. Lena flinched.

"I know you think you understand, but there's a lot that goes unpublished. The Council hoards our breath and mulches our friends. They confine us, they control us, and if they see fit, they label us. They're no better."

"Lena," Esta started. "I know it's difficult to see, but when you're grown up, you'll—"

Lena slapped her hand on the table, effectively hushing the room. She wondered if this was what it felt like to be a ballerina. To spin, and twist, and to be on her toes. To be able to silence a crowd. She raised her arms above her head in fifth position. "Look!" She bellowed, not quite sure what she was pointing to. The others focused intently on the sky. "Just because someone locks you in a closet, doesn't mean you should lock them in a closet. Sometimes," she wrinkled her forehead in thought, "in order to get out of a locked closet, you've got to be locked in it first, because otherwise, you wouldn't know what the difference is between being inside and outside of a closet. Specifically, one that is locked."

She nodded her head as she brought her arms down and crossed them for emphasis. *Nailed it!*

Esta opened her mouth to speak, but wordlessness engulfed her as they continued to stare into the night sky. The black seemed to flicker like a heartbeat, at moments igniting the underbelly of a vaporous grey. Esta had initially dismissed these flickers as exterior tube lights. And yet there was an inherent wildness in the crimson haze. She stood and walked to the glass, where beyond was another world. Miles below, a forest was engulfed in passion. Orange silk caressed charred pines whose once-verdant branches now glowed with anguish.

"I've never seen real fire before."

Esta turned to see Lena pressed against the glass, her nose and forehead smooshed in an attempt to better see over the edge. "It's dangerous and unrestrained. Just think, if we were down there, we could stop it and protect the forest."

Lena sighed, and a thick fog coated the window, fizzling her breath into and out of existence. "No. It's beautiful. And it's protecting the forest. Their branches grow high so that the fire can destroy the bottom-feeders. So that it can scare away those that would steal the nutrients from the true rulers of the forest. And when the soil is fresh with the ash of the intruders, the trees release their children into the world so that a new generation of life can thrive." She looked at Lume. "You would do the same to protect him."

Esta turned back to the world outside, her eyes heavier. She clutched the infant in her arms closer. "How old are you?"

Lena pressed her hand against the glass and let the liquid chill wash over her. It felt good to not just be regarded as a child. "How old are *you*?" she cast back. The words simmered. She had been hoping the Outcry would convince her. Tell her that they had it all figured out, and that they would be able to live outside as part of nature. Tell her how wrong the capital was about them. Tell her that she was making the right choice. But they couldn't. They were just like Paxton had described. *"People trying to control something they don't understand."* That's all it was ever about with adults. Control. *Well,* she thought, *I guess I'll just have to teach them.*

The three generations stood together, watching the earth consume itself so that it could grow stronger. When Joseph and Lin finally joined them, the inferno was just another part of the world, a gradient of earth, tree, and fire.

"Hey Es," Joseph touched her shoulder. "We should probably get her home. It's getting early, and she'll be expected at school in a few phases."

Lena felt the words knock the wind out of her, and she felt her mind regress back to the child that she was.

"But I want to stay with you guys. I want to go outside and be a bat, or a butterfly, or the shell of a turtle." Her face pleaded to her judges, but her sentence was three patronizing smiles.

"Now Lena," Joseph looked down at her, "you're still young, and you've got a lot of growing up to do. There's no sense in making your life harder by hanging around with us."

"But I can help! I'm really good at ideas, and thinking on my toes, and faking accents. And I wouldn't get in the way, I'll be invisible, like air, and you won't even hear me, because I won't wear shoes."

"Lena," Lin patted her head. "You can help by not telling anyone anything about us. If you want to be able to join us later, we've got to still exist, so don't tell anyone what you've seen."

She bit her lip. Something about their tones told her she was losing this argument. "Why can't we just leave and go to the surface now? Then you don't have to worry about me telling anyone. We can be part of nature."

"Dear heart, you've made me realize more than ever that that won't work. If we went off without the ability to sustain ourselves, then we would just begin interfering with nature again. I'm sorry, but Lin's right. Maybe someday you can join us, but right now it's too dangerous."

"But, but, but... Circ what do you...?" She turned her head, but Circ wasn't there. "Where's Circ?"

As she heard his name resonate in her ear, she felt a cold metal thread sew into the back of her neck. She saw Esta mouth apologetic words, but before the sound touched her again, a swift darkness overlapped her vision and she lost consciousness.

Joseph caught her as she slid to the ground, her body wilted. "I wish it didn't have to be this way." He lifted her onto his shoulder, feeling a profound heaviness weighing down her small body. "Make sure to keep her mask," he called to Lin. "We can't have her sneaking around Old Brin again."

***

The trip to her container was thankfully uneventful. Twice, Joseph nearly dropped Lena, but at the last moment Esta swooped in and caught them both. How she managed to juggle both Lena and the napping Lume, he was never quite sure, but still the world slept. When they'd finally laid Lena down in her bed, the day-lights were beginning to warm up, so they made a point to hustle back. Not without, Joseph noted, Esta tucking her in and giving her brow a soft kiss. "Sweet dreams, dear heart," she whispered goodbye.

"There's something special about her," Joseph spoke as they approached the nursery that they now called home. "She really is Arthur's daughter."

Esta just smiled as her eyes said, *I told you so*. "I'm sure she would appreciate hearing that."

"Wait." Lin let out a loud snort and Joseph paused before the door. "Did she say she was going to be the shell of a turtle?"

The tube filled with a laughter that began but did not end in whispers. Circ could feel his stomach strain, and they looked to the tunnel's sensors out of concern of wasting air, but no light blinked. They wondered if they'd ever laughed so hard, or if they'd ever have the chance to do so again. The four, Esta glanced down, four-and-a-half continued to giggle until Joseph took the moment to touch his hand to the reader, and only then did the tube grow still.

"Hi," a sharp voice greeted them. In the light, the garden now overflowed with hundreds of the Outcry.

Esta stepped into the room. "Hi, Talia."

Her crisp lips smiled in a point. "It's time to suit up, Es. We strike tonight."

XIV.

Lena woke floating on a garnet cloud above her sleeping body. She reached down and touched her face and ruffled her hair, only to feel her own face touched and her own hair ruffled. When her cloud grew restless, it soared away with her rolling in its tufts. It brought her through an endless desert in the blink of two eyes, one of hers and one of its. It dived low to a waterless ocean, and Lena dipped her toes in the cold salt. She shivered, and it shivered, and like the changing of reels, the whole world shivered. And just before she was too cold to stay floating in the placidity of reverie, it swaddled her projection in a fluff. It purred, like clouds do, and she held onto him like it was part of her.

In the distance a small flame flickered on a migrating puzzle, and so they soared as one to its source. Atop an erector set of dilated pupils grew a field of violet red. Lavender and rose intertwined in a thicket whose petals glowed in tumult. Lena was herself, and the cloud, and the thicket, and when she cried, the cloud rained and the thicket grew. She embraced the rose, and its thorns broke her skin, and she embraced the lavenders and its bees licked her wounds. She knew, though, that she was both of them and that they were she, and that in an instant, petals were barbs, and stings were kisses. When she pulled back, there remained only a spatter of her blood speckled on a field of contracted eyes, and beneath them ten million people could see for the first time.

Lena awoke three cities away from the Outcry as ten of them carried aluminum tanks up the outer dome of Kardel, sweat blossoming on their brows in the cool autumn twilight.

"How much further do we have?" Talia gasped in between gulps of thin air, her voice fizzling through her oxygen mask.

The sun continued to fall behind the earth, smearing the sky with cherry hues. For the last three hours, ten of them had meandered their way along the city's exterior, following seldom-used maintenance paths. From the inside, the walls were a canvas for two centuries of artists, each building upon its predecessors. From the outside, they were an engineering marvel, where hundreds of thousands of blackened solar cells stared at the sun, collecting the power to fuel a civilization.

"Not too far," eased Joseph. "By the looks of it, we've got two levels to go before we hit the peak, and then we'll get to the city's master central air duct. Just don't look down." He forced a laugh in an attempt to deceive his own fear.

Esta glanced over the rusty barrier that was the only divider between them and the open air. She leaned against the city's shell and clutched the railing.

"Careful not," Talia panted, "to fall." She smirked.

Joseph held up his hand to stop them, motioning for everyone to be quiet. He checked his watch just as it began to blink for the changing of the phases. Below them, the world suddenly flickered and hummed as the early risers getting ready for Init-Phase took their chance to change containers. Only the wind reverberating against their chests dared to make noise, and it went unnoticed by the rest of society. When ten minutes had passed, Joseph's watch illuminated again, and he motioned forward.

As the walkway leveled out, their breathing resynchronized with the world, and Talia straightened up, her back sore from the canister's weight. She couldn't imagine being more exhausted. Yet in front of her, Esta carried herself with ease. *Everything comes so easy to her*, her head pounded.

"Esta," she said softly so that no one else could hear. "I heard that you had a boy. You must be happy that you get to keep this one."

The words themselves were sincere enough, but to Esta, Talia's tone sounded scathing. Esta bit back a tear. "I've had fifteen beautiful children, and I've loved them dearly. Every one of them has gone to wonderful parents that I have chosen, and now that Lume is in my life, he is my light in the darkness."

"But why did you do it? Why were you willing to give them away? Why were you okay with perpetuating the system like a...farm?"

And at that Esta heard something that she hadn't noticed before. It was subtle, that was sure. An intonation in Talia's voice hinted at something that was hidden. Some sentiment buried deep in the ridges of her criticism. *Is she jealous?*

"You seem to have heard a lot for someone who hasn't shown her face since the news about us first came out."

"Where I was the last few cycles is none of your business," Talia snapped back. "If I didn't keep my position secure, the Outcry would have a lot more issues than it does now."

Esta's eyebrows narrowed. It had always been speculated what Talia's position was in society, but never was it supposed that it was one of importance. Maybe, they thought, a hair stylist or someone's secretary, but nothing that was indispensable. *Maybe she's bluffing. But something about her voice is on edge. Some strange hint of pain, like she'd lost something. Or...* Esta thought. *Something she'd never had.*

"I'm sorry, Talia." Esta peered into her eyes and her heart scolded her for not having seen it before. "It's none of my business where you were. If Sado trusts you, then I trust you."

Esta gave her a short smile, turned, and continued forward, leaving Talia speechless in her wake. It wasn't friendship, but the optimist in Esta marked it as progress. *Everyone has a story. Nothing is just black and white.* Her neck carried her head a little higher.

As they rounded a wide corner, the sun tucked its final rays behind the horizon and the world became lit by a crescent moon. Joseph called out that the peak was in sight, but his announcement was muffled by a dangerous creak. Corroded alloy let out a contorted shrill as a piece of paneling snapped.

Esta turned back just in time to see Talia disappear over the side of a newly formed crevasse. Her shriek was masked by the metal twangs of the departing sidewalk tumbling down the dome's side. She froze, gazing at the space that Talia's body had once occupied. A cool gust of air left bitterness on the tongues of the nine members of the Outcry who stood breathless.

Each subsequent ring of the falling panel strained at their ears until the final rung slid past the floating city and faded into the chasm of the world. If their plans succeeded, then maybe in a hundred years, when they came upon the fallen pathway, it would be memorialized as part of the struggle faced while freeing society.

Esta rushed towards the edge, her body acting before her mind could catch itself in fear. The remaining jagged rungs jutted out, leaving a wide gap with rotted teeth lining its lips. Down its gaping throat a city awoke from the pounding of a platform crying for help, now long lost.

Esta's heart throbbed as she peeked over the edge. Beads of moonlit crimson intertwined with a braided wire rope that swayed precariously. Six feet below swung Talia, who was now the pendulum ticking away at her own life. Her hands quivered as metal threads embedded themselves into her palms and fingers, the warmth of blood contrasting against the chill of the air. Her body shivered and she was left without words to cry out. An alarm sounded in the distance.

"Talia, it's going to be okay. Just hold on." Esta looked back, but the others were out of sight. Her arms shook in expectation of pain. She wrapped the bottom of her shirt around her hands and gripped the cable, linking their two lives with a single strand. As she saw Talia's body apex away from her, Esta pulled and felt the clothed barbs cut into her. The cable tugged as Talia swung underneath the platform and Esta screamed as it dug deeper into her skin. Her teeth clenched and her vision blurred with tears, but still she pulled as Talia reached the outer peak. When Joseph and the others finally approached, Talia's fingers could be seen cresting the rift. He latched onto her arms and pulled her up, prying the cable from her hands with a slow tenderness.

"Talia," he held her. "Can you hear me?"

She stared up at the sky, realizing it was the first time she'd even bothered to look at it that night. Her body sat up as her mind drifted to her savior, the one person she wished *hadn't* saved her. Talia watched as Esta sat against the railing, pressing her hands into her stomach, letting the tears trickle down her tired face. *Would I have done the same? Would her baby be motherless had it been her, and not me?* She looked down, noticing a shift in the numbness of her tattered hands, and watched Joseph wrap his torn shirt around them.

Her voice began weak and leveled out into a quiver. "We need to keep going. By now, maintenance personnel will be suiting up to check for damages, and with the heightened security, they'll be sure to send guards." She tried to stand but her legs shook. Her hair had come undone from her pristine braids, and threads of it hung in front of her face. She didn't ask for help, but it was given to her as she stood, supported by Joseph and the short bulky man that had accompanied her to the nursery. He just nodded. Esta trailed behind, keeping watch over her flock.

When they reached the city's summit, Talia forced herself to walk again and led several steps in front of her pack. At the crest of the dome was the maintenance room where all the city's filtering systems led. Every public duct embedded in the city's maze-like vents eventually journeyed through the main filtration system. There, any excess O_2 was pumped back through the system and combined with the stores of fresh supply down the chain. Talia pressed in a code to the door panel and it slid open. The pressure on her wounded fingertips made her wince.

"Go in, hook up your tanks to the station that reads "Cleaning Vessels," and come back out here. When they're all attached, I'll insert the code to activate them." She looked around at everyone, but she could hardly tell them apart. They blended in with the night sky, outlined only by a violet-red hue cast down by the moon behind the clouds. "Now go."

As the others followed her orders, she looked over to Esta. Both of them listened carefully as the faint grumbling of maintenance workers came drifting on the wind. From the sound, they wouldn't have much more than ten minutes to complete their task.

"Es," Talia mustered as the Outcry began to disperse. "Can I talk with you? Inside."

Joseph glanced at Esta with worried eyes as their limited time ticked away, but her smile soothed him. It was that same smile she'd given him when they first met.

Both of them frightened, their lives being given a second chance by the stranger they would come to know as Sado. There were only twenty people in the room then, long before they would be called the Outcry. Just a year after Joseph had lost his wife, Isabel, he sat, giving out his heart, his story, hoping that they would cast the judgment that he need not carry on.

And then there was Esta. Her body was swollen with a girl, hardly six months conceived. She walked over to him, this stranger in a room of strangers, and she took his hand, and placed it on her stomach. He remembered the heartbeat, the warmth, that smile. And Esta saying that there will always be lives out there that needed him.

He smiled back at her and mouthed, "Thank you," as she and Talia disappeared into the room.

The walls were a dull grey, a stark contrast to the painted canvas they'd grown accustomed to. Talia connected her canister to an empty socket and walked to a dimly lit panel where she began typing. "Just insert yours over there," she motioned towards the wall opposite the door. A single slot remained vacant next to those that the others had filled.

Esta took her container out but stopped halfway. The weight on her bandaged hands made them shake. "What is it that you wanted to say, Talia?" Her lips struggled to remain steady as her words came out unsteadily.

"I," she turned and hesitated. "I wanted to thank you. For," she struggled, "for saving my life. And..." She took a breath. "I'm sorry."

Esta smiled and turned back towards the wall. She began to slide her tank in, then stopped and pulled it back.

"Talia, what are these?" Her eyes widened as she read "Caution" on the tank's side.

Talia kept typing. "They're the reason we risked breaking into the research lab. They're the first step."

"And how is it they're supposed to bring this city to the earth?" She turned towards Talia.

"It's just like Sado said. We're going get the people out of Kardel. It's a type of compressed chlorine gas that is going to force the Council to either ground the city and let people outside or risk all of Kardel flooding into the other cities."

Esta could feel her heartbeat quicken and began to feel dizzy. All this time, following them blindly, they'd never bothered to question the plan. Sado's instructions were absolute.

"Talia, what if they don't? What if Durin locks off Kardel from the rest of the cities?"

Talia turned to face her. "That's not going to happen. Durin will push to ground the city, and the Council won't have another option."

"But, how do you know? Hundreds of thousands of innocent people could die, but for what? So a few thousand might see the light of day?"

"Es, this isn't the time to question the plan. It's what Sado knows is best. Durin will see reason. But even if Kardel fails, it will amplify the cruelness of the Council. People will flock to us afterwards, and by then we've won."

"No. No, I can't let you do this." Numbness stilled her hands as she thought of her children. *Mel, Aden, Jal.* "It's like what Lena said. Only when the soil is fresh with the ash of the invasive will the trees release their children among the world." *Hon, Corli, Veil.* Their images flickered before her eyes. "If we burn the people, we burn the forest. We need to burn the structure instead, so the forest can grow."

"Lena? You mean that little Brin girl? Esta, it's too late. Put the last tank in, and let's go."

Esta no longer met Talia's eyes. *Eris, Eera, Prin.* She fought back the burning in her throat. "No." She stood firm, the canister in between her bleeding hands. Her fingers wrapped around the tank's valve. "Leave, or we both go." She took a step towards Talia. *Fen, Author, Serh. It's the only way to stop it.*

"You wouldn't." A strike of panic infiltrated her voice. "Think about your son."

Esta winced, turning the knob slightly; a faint hissing invaded the air along with a lavender mist. *My beautiful Lume.* "That's what I'm doing. I'm thinking of my son, and all of my other children, and what will be my children's children. I'm thinking that even if this is my last cycle, my boy will grow up knowing life and not death."

She took another step forward and made another turn. Talia could feel her lungs craving more oxygen, pleading for it. "I'm thinking of how two of my boys have already died, without a final breath. How every breath I take, I thank them for providing me and the rest of the world with another chance to breathe." *You had so much ahead of you, Guere.* "I'm thinking of how my foolishness has led me to seek revenge on people instead of society, and how it took an odd little girl to make things clear."

A shallow breath. *I'm sorry, Caldon.* She twisted the canister one last time and the hiss faded into a silent flow.

Talia opened the door and ran out in the night coughing, her body retching. Behind her the door slid closed. A loud smash and the thud of a bolt echoed across the metal exterior of Kardel. Talia looked back at the room, but the flickering of the panel let her know that it couldn't be entered again. In a shroud of chlorine, Esta had sealed the door.

Three cities away, in a cedar cradle, Lume cried.

PART TWO

XV.

In a field littered with dead pixels, a woman in a digital suit flickered from sweater to dress to mesh and settled on an aqua suede halter-top. Her smile stretched across the width of the screen in a close-up. "And today's lucky numbers are 32, 51, 1009, 4, and…"

Ms. Pluck flicked off the monitor. The class bloomed into a bouquet of sighs. "Now now," she echoed, "It'sh not like anyone ever winsh. Thatsh enough for the daily newsh. Time to schtart working thoshe nogginsh!" Her voice resonated with defeat.

Lena sighed again, her voice trumpeting over the class. "Turn it back on, there could be breaking news!"

Ms. Pluck let out a faint groan. "And what could there be breaking newsh about, Mish Causht?" She said in routine. "There'sh never any breaking newsh."

Lena squirmed. Every cycle for the last five months had been set on rinse and repeat. As if scripted, Ms. Pluck would turn the screen off as soon as she knew she didn't have the winning numbers. Lena would tell her there could be breaking news, to which the teacher would ask what it could be about. And Lena would say with hesitation, "I dunno. But we won't know unless you keep it on."

Lena's insistence had worked the first few times, but now she was just shrugged off until the next day. The Outcry never appeared. Not only that, but people seemed to act as if they had never existed in the first place. Immediately after Lena had met them, there were whisperings that the capital had foiled some terrorist plot and Recycled its leader, though she never saw it confirmed. But now, even the whispers had died down.

Classes dragged on. Lena could see the outside world in everything. A forest of sand was always beneath her feet; a sky of embers was always above her. Most days she would just take her shoes off and let the classroom floor lick her toes. She allowed Ms. Pluck to serenade her as her words blended into a symphony of stretched consonants. She drifted on the rays of sun that were hidden behind every wall of her cage.

But even in her thicket of imagination, her eyes craved to touch reality. The expanse of her mind felt small compared to what existed outside these walls, whose color's profound sweetness feigned to mask a bitter grey.

To think that manipulating the breaths of her class had lost its music. And that the food forged to satisfy each individual taste bud now only resembled the plastic coating of encapsulated medicine. She went home wishing she could forget it all.

Tulu wheeled over her foot as she walked into her room that afternoon, his purr brimming with excitement, a ball balancing on his head.

"No, Tulu, I don't want to play today." She collapsed onto her mattress, her face buried in a forgetful foam. A soft thud at her legs let her know that Tulu had disregarded her defeat. His whine confirmed it. She peeked out through the ruffles to see her tap-pad now balanced atop his mop.

"Ugh, fine, Tulu, you want a story? Here's a story." She grabbed the tap-pad from between his tangled dreads. "Once there was this absolutely, positively, spectacular and brilliant bat that shot lasers and sound waves from her mouth and everything. And all she wanted to do was help this colony of sea porcupines to be free, because that's what they claimed they wanted. But instead they just sat around being urchins, stinging everybody with their needles, and then they stung the really splendid, completely magnificent bat, and she died, and was Recycled into a girl. The end. The end. The end!" Lena shoved her face deeper into the mattress and let out a muffled squeak.

If Tulu noticed her anguish, he didn't show it. Instead, on cue, he licked her calves until her sobs became laughter, and she was on her feet running, quite poorly evading his efforts. She threatened to go down the steps, but her ruse was fruitless; long ago Tulu had conquered his fear of tumbling down the stairs. That or his circuits were rattled so much from somersaulting that it had made him forget. Either way, he cornered her until a semblance of her old smile appeared.

Lena curled up with Tulu as the city lights dimmed. When his rumblings were that of a robot's slumber, she tucked him in, and like each night for the last five months, she packed her bag and made her way to the hidden tunnels.

Ever since she had found her fire-sword several months ago, she had been marking the paths of Old Brin with hidden signs as she sought any hint of the Outcry. The walls were an invisible mess, tracing the city in circles to no avail. She still had hundreds of tubes and containers left to search, and each one she checked off gave her hope that the next one would lead to her treasure. What she would say when she found them she hadn't quite figured out.

"AHA" may work, she considered. *Or "POW!" Or I could give them a long monologue about how I've got so many ideas that are going to help, but I won't tell them because they're mean and should have listened. But then I'll get all dramatic and say "BUT! I WILL FORGIVE YOU! BECAUSE THAT IS WHAT THE WORLD DOES!"* She glanced up and realized she was on one knee, her hands flailing dramatically in the air. Her face had contorted in a silent shout. She giggled. Then she stopped herself with a somber realization.

All this time she'd been searching for them, all this time she'd been imagining what she would say, she'd never tried to think of how she could actually help them. How she could be more than a burden. The hero in her mind deflated into a small bunny, not an inch tall.

Lena walked along, her feet dragging behind her, in a cold silence. She'd spent so much time trying to imagine these last few months that she'd forgotten to just live her imagination. She shuddered. *Ughh, I've been just like everyone else. There are so many details I must have missed.* She took a deep breath through her oversized mask, like an overweight starfish suctioned to her face. Her mouth wrinkled in a grin as she breathed in a faint scent of her dad. Five months of wearing her dad's mask, and this was the first that she'd noticed it. Her shoulders slumped.

The violet glow of the fire-sword flickered twice and went out. She sighed, shook it, hit it, and spun in a circle for good measure. The soft hue hit the tube's wall again. She watched as it lit a familiar arrow. "Noooooooo! I've already been here!"

She flopped against the wall and slid to sitting. Beneath her weight the paint flaked. In her mind the floor now appeared to be a spackled ceiling. She stood her hair on end and took a moment to be surprised at how much it had grown and how little she had noticed it. *I can worry about that later. I've learned the secrets of gravity, and now I'm sitting on the ceiling, hanging from the rafters, seeing with my ears, and eating mice. There's one now!* She looked across the tube at a splotch of vibrant white. *I've just got to be very quiet.* She stood, balancing on the tips of her toes. *I'll just sneak and...* She paused for suspense. "Pounce!" Her voice echoed in her mask and through the tunnels. Her feet left the ground and her hands collided with the adjacent wall, closing on the spot of light, her "mouse." It mocked her by resting on the tops of her closed hands. Her arms flailed again in an attempt to cage it, but again it stood on her hands, radiating its warmth.

Lena looked back to where she'd just been sitting. A soft eggshell blush illuminated a few splinters of paint that littered the floor. From a tiny hole pierced a strand of light, now balancing on her knuckles. She rolled it delicately through her fingers. Through the air, across the tube, she traced the thread until she felt the cracked surface from which it grew. The tunnel came into and out of existence as her thumb danced along the source of light. For a moment her world was a dying coal. She scratched at the surface and flakes of dried paint embedded themselves beneath her nails.

Across the passage the mouse became a rabbit became a fox became a house and Lena wrapped herself in blankets of torn paint while pastel rays saturated the parched tube. Her mind cried in joy as her eyes laughed in pain. What her world believed to be night, the earth knew to be day. *Oh, what Tulu would say! What everyone else would say! They think they know the time, live the time, and breathe the time. Little do they know.* She giggled as she lay in her canvas. *Little do they know!*

"Madame Sun!" she called out. "Tell me," she paused, for she didn't know her first name. She ran through the list of names in her head and finally settled, quite excitedly, on one. "Tell me, Clara. Tell me, what time is it? And why have you been hiding behind your own portrait?"

The sun patted Lena on the head, her fingers light and warm on Lena's auburn hair. From behind a cloud, she flickered and chuckled at her new name, and at this new stranger.

Lena exhaled with a heavy breath. "You're right, Clara. I guess we all hide behind our own pictures sometimes." Her eyes lifted. "Thank you for saying hello!" She unraveled herself. "I've got to go though! You've just given me an idea!"

She began to run down the tunnel, and then turned back with a second thought. A fresh drizzle now ran along the siding of the tube. "Oh, don't be a baby, you stop those tears! I'm going to show you to the whole world, so you'd better be presentable!" She ran down the tunnel again, into the dark, flicking on her fire-sword. *Goodness gracious! You'd think after a bajillion years, she'd learn to be on her own for a second.*

She followed her stream of arrows and notes, pointing this way and that, warning of stairs, listing treasures found. When she hit a yellow squiggle, she made an abrupt right and ventured down a path riddled with glowing question marks. It was her best guess at the path she'd taken when they'd rescued her. She'd been down the path a hundred times since and had never found anything. *But maybe*, she thought, *that's the problem.* She removed her mask. *All this time, I've been trying to find them, but maybe it would be faster if they just found me. Maybe the only way to find them is if they rescue me again. Rescue me,* she thought, *from danger.*

Sometimes, Lena, girl, you're just too clever. She smiled to herself as she twisted and released the tank's valve, sending the last of her oxygen spindling down the tunnel in a symphony of clinks and clanks.

XVI.

"This has to stop." Talia's lips boiled a bold red, in stark contrast to the green of the room's forest. Her rant had been unimpeded for nearly an hour. "We can't keep wasting time and resources looking after this girl. Every time she enters the tunnels, we've been forced to go on alert, and for five months she hasn't missed a cycle. How the Council hasn't managed to track her to the entrance so far is a mystery, but it's only a matter of time."

Her audience took in her words, but their focus glided along with Lena as she weaved amongst a patch of tomatoes in the background.

"She is persistent." Lin smiled as Lena mimicked the arch of the stalk, a plump fruit balancing on her head.

"People," Talia snapped. "Do you know how much energy we've spent repainting her markings throughout the tunnels to lead her in circles? And not to mention how many sweepers we've had to waste to make sure she didn't manage to hide from us? All of this just so that we could rescue her again and bring her back into the only sanctuary we have left."

She paused as Lena's giggling echoed from the garden. Around her, hundreds of scattered cots lay next to beds of fertile jade, their inhabitants sharing in on the contagious childish laughter that the last several months had robbed them of.

"Tal," Lin said, "we've been cooped up in this place for months. She's the only distraction we've had." She scratched the back of her neck. "She's what they need."

Talia sighed as Lin turned her attention back to Lena. They'd spent all this time regaining momentum, replanting people in society to prepare for their next move. To have their plans undermined by this tiny child would destroy them. It would destroy her.

It had taken Sado's word to save Talia from the wrath the Outcry felt after Esta's death. Only recently had they begun to trust her again, but they were still a long way away from truly listening to her. This child was a liability.

"I motion that we Restore her." She knew the mention of Recycling would only hurt her case. "It's what Esta had suggested."

No one seemed to hear. Their minds drifted free. The air Lena exhaled flowed with a semblance of serotonin.

"You know," Circ said, "if it wasn't for her dad, we wouldn't have Old Brin. He's the reason we're all hidden right now, in what's supposed to be a Recycled city. We owe it to him to look after her." Lin nodded in agreement.

"She reminds me of Isabel." Those sitting in the circle with Talia all turned to look at Joseph. He had never talked about his wife publicly. Everyone knew she had been Recycled for protesting, but he had only ever confided in Esta.

Those five words told Talia that brushing Lena off was no longer an option.

"So what are we going to do with her?" A voice asked from behind them.

Talia and the others looked down to see Lena, a stern expression planted on her face and a half-eaten tomato in her hand. *Just great,* Talia thought. *And now she's consuming our resources, too.*

Lena motioned to the tomato. "I traded my gummy vitamins and mask to Balmy and Judy Hannigan for this. Judy insisted I gave them too much, but I told them that I had more gummy snacks back home, and that I didn't need the mask since I'd be staying here for a while. Honestly though," Lena leaned forward and spoke in a whisper, "Those were my last animal-shaped ones."

She took another bite. "This is my first ever tomato. I've had potato-tomato-pumpkins before, but they're not the same. There's so much life in every bite. If you listen, it goes pop, squish, swish, and the juices jump about with a strange tingling that surprises your tongue." Her eyes traced over Talia with a grin. "Do you want the rest? You look like you need it more than I do." She proffered the half-eaten vegetable.

Shivers ran fresh down Talia's spine. Something about this girl, this child, made her nervous. Talia had managed to nurture the Outcry into an aligned collective, a well-oiled machine prepared to take on the system, and then there was Lena, whose existence seemed to reject any sense of purpose. She'd been holding onto the tomato like it was a commodity she'd been entitled to. She didn't understand the effort that went into cultivating it, and how her frivolity could lead to the starvation of others. Talia snatched the tomato from her.

"This isn't meant for you," she scorned. "This is meant for my people. Do you understand the trouble that you've caused us? Your carelessness has led us to risk our lives twice, like this is all some sort of game. You need to start paying attention to the big picture and realize you're not important; you're just getting in the way. If we find you in the tunnels again, don't expect to be so lucky when you have another accident."

Lena's face tensed. "It wasn't an accident."

"*Excuse* me?" The chatter of the dome faded, replaced by a thousand listening ears.

"I knew the only way I'd find you was for you to rescue me, so I threw away my tank. I've got something important to say to your leader, and I'm not leaving until I say it." She eyed Circ. "So no needles this time."

A hint of a smile touched Circ's lips, if but for an instant. She was clever; he would give her that. There seemed to be a silent consensus of awe at her tenacity.

Talia cringed, ignoring Lena's demand. "And what if you'd died? What if we hadn't come to rescue you?" She watched Lena wince. "You didn't think of that, did you? You just assumed. You're not smart, you're just lucky."

She paused as Lena sunk into herself, her eyes wide and flickering in what Talia hoped was realization. *Sometimes you need to be straight with children,* Talia tried to console herself. *If you're not direct, they'll never learn.* Still, Talia's stomach felt empty. Lena was just a little girl after all. "Look," she began a bit softer, "go ahead and say your idea. You've made it here, so you might as well speak."

Lena's head bobbed left and right, in search of something. Her mouth remained closed.

The room waited patiently. They had grown quite good at that. Talia tapped her nails against the skin on her arm. "Well?" She watched the girl stumble and twist, a look of confusion wobbling on her face.

"Well, what?"

"What are you waiting for? Say your idea."

"Oh!" Lena smirked. "I'm waiting for the leader."

The innocence of her voice sizzled and evaporated off Talia's forehead, like hot steam. She bit out the words "I am the leader." For what it mattered, she was. It had been agreed that she was to be the filter. The face of the Outcry. But if this little girl was going to question it, Talia would just have to educate her. "These are my—"

"No." She interrupted, altogether pleasantly.

Don't hit this child, Talia. Don't let her make you lose your temper. "No?"

"The leader is a man. He has a voice like burnt coals. It's like every word he says is both a test and a lesson, and even as it sounds like it's crumbling away, it's sprinkling the ground with new dirt for things to grow. No, you were there though. Talking to him. And you don't look like someone who talks to herself." She looked around the room. "Who is Caldon, anyways?"

The room full of cots filled itself with talk as it soared above a tittering ocean, whose surface was stuccoed from a blanket of raindrops. Talia walked to Lin and took Lume from her. He squiggled awfully in her arms. It was the first time she'd held him. She held him out like a wet sack of flour and delivered him to Lena, a stickiness lingering in her hands. "Go take care of him. The grownups need to talk."

Lume squealed and bubbled as he was carried off into a forest of commotion. His body bounced up and down in unison with the skip in Lena's step.

Those at the center of the room stood in silence, aware of the speculation that was rushing around them. Circ's gristle interrupted their void. "She's got spunk!"

Lin's laugh turned into a sigh, wishing she'd had her tap-pad out for the exchange. Her fingers itched to document every encounter, and the last few months had made them burn. They'd been told that they had to conserve power, which meant that there was nothing to fuel her writing. "How could she have remembered? About Sado? About Caldon?"

"I..." Talia's mind flickered. If this girl still knew about Sado, and if the Council had taken her, then the Outcry was in danger. The Council could know everything. Every moment she'd worked for, every moment that this group had struggled, could be toppled by the words of a young girl. "I don't know if it matters how. It only matters what we do about it."

"Well I think she's charming." The others turned to see Joseph gazing out towards a group of cots. A family in rags clapped and cheered as Lena led Lume through their camp. His tiny fingers wrapped doughy around her pointers, his toes squished through the dirt, as his knees wobbled forwards. Had there been worms beneath the surface, they would have parted as he crossed their sea.

"Have you seen him smile like that? Have you seen any of us smile like that in our time here?" Joseph turned back around, his hand covering his mouth, stroking the bristles of his face. "Most importantly, have you ever seen Circ smile before?"

They turned towards Circ, whose grin jumped immediately to a stern growl, which slowly bloomed into a difficult-to-suppress smirk. "I don't want to," he rumbled low. "It's contagious. I think she broke my face."

"I'm just saying. Maybe we should tell Sado," Joseph continued. "Maybe he should talk with her."

"That's out of the question. We can't just allow anyone to traipse in here assuming they can do what they want. There is a reason that I'm Sado's filter. I'm to deal with trivialities."

Talia listened as her words were drowned out by Lin's laughter. She pointed. Talia let out a deep, unsettling, sigh. Whatever Lin was pointing at, she knew it would just make her cringe more. Some antic, some little distraction that meant the Outcry was losing focus. No focus meant no progress. There wasn't time for stagnation. She turned.

There, sticking ten inches out of the ground, planted in freshly dug soil, was Lume. Talia took off running on legs that barely knew how to jog. She pushed through the forming crowd and picked Lume from the artificial earth like an autumn tulip. He squirmed in her arms as she held him close. The crowd was silent.

"What did you think you were doing?" Her voice shook.

Lena continued to smile. She pushed back the loose hair from her face, leaving a smudge of dirt on her forehead. "I was planting him. So he could grow."

Talia held out Lume, looking at him for the first time. He flapped his arms in excitement, his lower half covered in dirt, a flower in his hand. She brought him into an embrace and turned, leaving the group.

"You know," Lena called out. "You're not his mother."

Talia's heart sank and her teeth clenched. She continued to walk.

When she got to Lin, she returned Lume to her. "She's not to hold him again."

Lin blinked back. "But she didn't do—"

"Not again." Talia ended her sentence and the conversation.

The room grew cold and quiet. They watched as most of the Outcry huddled around Lena, whether for consolation or warmth. Gurgling broke the silence.

Those near him looked towards Lume, but his eyes lay behind heavy eyelids in a sunlit dream.

The room suddenly stirred with static.

"Talia?"

She turned. In the center of the table, the radio whispered. She hurried over and turned up the volume. "Sado, we're here."

The radio awaited his cue. "Bring her to me. I'll meet her in person."

"But...Sado..."

"Talia. It's okay. Bring her to me."

The greenhouse began to whisper.

"The cabin?"

The radio paused. "No. To her container. Have her there in three hours." More fizzling and then quiet. His voice was gone.

Talia turned to see Lena waiting in silence. They stayed that way as they packed up and left the dome. The room remained still and quiet. In awe. In fear. Lena would be the third person to see Sado's true face. Whether she lived or died, she would be remembered.

Lin watched as the door closed. She turned away, lost without a tap-pad. Her eyes glistened wide. Atop the table lay something so precious and rare she'd only ever read about it. In blue leather, bound in string, lay a book of blank pages. On the book sat a pen.

This night would be remembered.

XVII.

"All the paint!"

"All the paint?"

Lena waved her hands in wild circles, gesturing and running back and forth between each of her walls. She tossed piles of her clothes into the air and tore down the decorations she'd collected through the years of exploring Old Brin. Her room had become ground zero for her animated explanation.

"Every mural," she flung her pillow into a fury of feathers, "every portrait," she ripped a poster into ribbons, "every itty-bitty speck and splotch covering anything that shades our view from the real world. In every city!"

It was the third time that she'd gone through her story. How she'd discovered the Outcry, how she'd made her way through the tunnels, how she'd come up with the idea to tear down the paint from all the cities so that people could see the outside again. No one had seemed to know that some of the walls were translucent behind their century-old lacquer.

After each retelling of her thoughts, Sado had nodded, asked a question or two, and then told her to say it all again. The second time around he'd set on a digital recorder, but she realized that he wasn't really listening. She'd slipped in a few extra details seeing if he'd notice, but he just continued to nod. Those would be a treat for him when he listened to the recording. She knew that somewhere behind his eyes, his mind was churning away at the first iteration. He was planning. Deciding.

She hadn't made up her mind whether he was more or less than the person that she'd expected. In her mind, he had been a goliath. Twenty feet tall with a beard stretching to the earth. Wisdom and lasers shooting from his eyes.

But here he was in reality, in her home. When he stood, it was with a straight back, but he carried a stiff cane of onyx black, with veins of crimson dancing stochastically upwards to a wooden handle. Its roots grew in a soft glaze. *Or perhaps*, she thought, *the cane carries him.* His hair was greyed and loose, remnants of what may have been curls in his earlier years, and his face showed signs that there had indeed been countless earlier years.

Had Lena paid attention to his smell, she would have noticed a fragrance of fresh pine, sewn in with his rolled-up plaid sleeves and charcoal suspenders. *I want to hear you speak, but all you want to do is listen.* She could find a reason to smile in all but his eyes, wherein defined exhaustion.

She tapped her toes to the floor, waiting to be told to start her story again. *Perhaps this time I'll do it in rhyme.* She grinned and wondered why the room didn't laugh at the touch of her ten little toes. *That's Bernie for ya, always so serious.*

Across from her, untouched by her cascade of clothing, an unfamiliar black bag grabbed her attention. It didn't quite call out, but the way it held itself, all rigid and haughty, begged her to notice it. How it hadn't caught her eye before, she blamed fully on its master. But now, as he drifted in thought behind closed blinds, her mind attempted to open the bag.

Its structure told her it was something with a defined shape. Its leather trim and lock told her it was something of value. *A fishbowl? No, fish are only in the movies. A hat? No, that would go on his head.* Lena squinted at the bag, expecting it to betray its contents. It didn't budge.

"What's in the bag?"

Sado looked up to find the eyes of a child pleading towards him. "A precaution. In case I need to erase your memory."

Lena's eyes opened wider, now grappling at the bag. *What does it look like? How does it work?* If only her eyelashes were claws. *Maybe it* is *a hat!* Her mind hesitated. Slowly, it dawned on her that her stomach was churning. *People can erase memories?* The image of a fluffy creature nibbling on a carrot flickered in her mind. Had someone erased her mind before?

She felt the room spin, thankful that she was already on the floor. Her eyes clenched, waiting for the dizziness to subside. She remembered finding the snow globe, a pile of papers, hearing the distant voice of Esta, and then nothing. How had she gotten home that night? Was it so unremarkable, so easy to forget? She felt her jaw hurting and noticed that her teeth were clenched. Her eyes opened and she took in Sado, patiently waiting for her to respond. How hard it was to remember the minor details of a day ago, let alone six months ago. But then again, that's why it frustrated her. Because the minor details were all she ever remembered.

"Does it hurt?" she whispered.

Something about the question amused Sado and he gave a faint smile, still with fatigued eyes. "If it did, you wouldn't remember it." He paused, maybe hoping for Lena to react, but she only nodded distractedly, and waited for more. "But you needn't worry about that just yet. There may be no need to use it if you don't know too much."

Lena exhaled slowly. "But I do know too much," she realized. "I know what your real voice sounds like."

There was silence, and Lena wondered if he was trying to take back everything he had said. "My real voice?" he said with what sounded like approval.

"Uhm, yeah, I heard the voice that was on the radio. That wasn't your voice. So I figured you're hiding your voice." She bit the inside of her cheek. "I...I won't tell anyone."

He grinned. "Yes, it will be our secret."

With his words she inhaled a memory.

Her dad sat across from her, his eyes closed. He was wearing that red scarf and bomber jacket he always wore when he was wishing he could be a pilot. He had always been a dreamer like that. Maybe that's where she got it. Lena hid a nostalgic grin. *That cycle had been an exhausting one. He'd been called in to Racine to work some special disassembly within the capitol, and when he'd gotten home she could tell he wanted to sleep.*

But for whatever reason he'd insisted, or maybe she'd insisted, that they stay up and play Asterisks. She looked across at him, having just answered with her riddle. She waited, and waited, and when she couldn't wait any longer, she yelled out "Dad!" Lena laughed at the thought. *All the time that she thought he had been concentrating, he had really been sleeping. She swore he could fall asleep standing up if the occasion called for it.*

"What's so funny?" Sado interrupted in soft tones.

"I was thinking of a game that my dad and I used to play."

He sat back, more relaxed. Everything about his posture said that he had all the time in the world. "Tell me about it."

Lena sat up, her forehead lifting. She'd been hoping for those exact words. *Words*, she thought. How long ago had it been since she'd heard someone else's words in this container? Nine months? An eternity? She cleared her throat.

"It's called Asterisks and it's a game of secrets. You ask a question, and I answer in a riddle. If you guess the meaning of my answer in one try, then you get to ask another question. If not, then I go."

"And how do you win?"

Lena shrugged. "Not everything is about winning. Here, I'll ask first, and I'll make it easy. What's your position?"

She watched as cogs twisted and turned in his mind. Though his composure stayed solid, she could sense his presence dissolving until she felt alone in the room. Several minutes passed. *Maybe* he *should have asked the first question.* Lena glanced again towards the bag. It didn't glance back.

Sado rolled his cane in his hand. "A girl sits beside me. Her noble steed too. You can't win without me, and it only *seems* that there are two."

Lena sighed. She should have done the riddle first. How was that supposed to mean the leader of the Outcry? He must have taken "position" literally. And no one had said he had to rhyme. What a mess! She spoke slowly, so as not to upset him. "Well, that was a nice try, but how about instead you ask a question, and I'll do the riddle first?"

He looked at her with patience, but still there was a bit of disheartenment in his posture. "All right. Why do you want to go outside?"

His words hit her like a door to the face. Even his questions were difficult. She wasn't used to playing this game with such open-ended possibilities.

Okay, I want to go outside to be with the trees. She paused. *No, that's stupid. I want to go outside so I can be a bat.* She hesitated. *Good, but I can do better.* Her mind rumbled on for a few moments longer, until she looked up, a proud grin on her face. *I've got it!* "I lick the air. I dance on the ground. And you could jump right through me, were I round." She smirked. Maybe there was something to this rhyming thing.

She watched him think for a moment before she became bored. *I bet Lin would be good at this game. I hope she liked the journal I left her.* Sado cleared his throat and she looked up.

"You want to see fire." He rested his hands on his knees. "You forget that I've been outside."

She crossed her arms and huffed. "I want to *feel* fire," she mumbled. Clearly she had to step up her game. "Fine, you get to go again."

"What did you think of the capital?" He sat back.

Lena threw her hands up in the air. If he was going to ask questions without one-word answers, then she was going to give riddles without one-word solutions. She stood up and paced, pausing at each turn. "Gold made of copper, with water made of mud, zealots made of parrots in bright green suits, a credit in the movies is one less credit on the streets, yet a path paved with bodies still reaps a noble feast." She ended her rant breathless.

Without a microscope, it was difficult to tell if Sado reacted. He sat silently, letting Lena's breath become steady again, and then gestured defeat.

"You're not even going to guess?" Lena frowned.

"You clearly have some questions on your mind. How about you ask them?"

She could feel her thoughts pushing up from her pores, and she wondered if they were visible. The words poured from her mouth. "What happened to Esta?"

The way he exhaled told her everything she needed to know and exactly what she didn't want to hear. Numbness filled her body like a glass, and she could feel it slosh around on her insides, a cold metaphorical substrate that made her mouth taste of hot salt and her ears sound of distance. Somewhere Sado was talking, mumbling in a muffled continuum, but it only trotted on the horizon. A faint echo of a throat.

When she thought about it, she had barely known Esta. So she didn't think about it. She just felt it. And the cries of Joseph and Lume and all the lives that Esta brought into this world bled beneath her temple. It was hot. Beside her vision, a vein pushed and pulled with the heaviness of her heart's beat.

How long had it been since she'd lost her dad? She could remember him clearly now, but what about in five years? In ten? Lume had known his mother for a month. What would he have of her but the echoes of her voice in forgotten dreams? She thought she felt a hand touch her shoulder and she looked up. Sado still sat across the room. Lena turned her head, but there was no one else there. She sighed.

"Was it the Council?"

Sado nodded.

She bit her tongue, the feeling of her teeth imprinting on her taste buds.

"There's something you should see." Sado stood and went to his bag. He opened it, and from it he pulled two oxygen masks and a tap-pad. After a few quick motions he set the tap-pad back in the bag and looked at his watch. "Let's go for a walk."

"But what about..."

"It'll be okay. It's not that far, and I know this city better than any Council patrol." He strode out her door and down the steps, leaving her in disbelief. She shrugged. *It's not like I haven't gotten in trouble before.*

Still, she hesitated. She didn't know what to think of Sado. She had built him up as some piece of history, had hoped that he was a library containing vast knowledge, but now she saw him as just a man, with a face and voice. Would he truly be able to lead them to the outside?

Her footsteps reverberated, and when she got to the bottom of the stairs, Sado stood with the door open, mask on and waiting. She slipped on her own mask, and a shiver feathered her back. How he had managed to get the door open without it being the change of a cycle made her mind itch.

They flowed like a current through the city, down alleys and under bridges that she hadn't known existed. Having thought she was the master of these grids, she now felt dwarfed by Sado's expertise. The way he moved, he could have designed the city. For all she knew, he could be redesigning it as they walked.

He glanced at his watch again and his pace quickened. Most would have failed to keep up, living in a world where running was a felony and moving quickly was a job left to the automated sidewalks. Had she not broken that law long ago and dared to scurry, she would have been left in the dark. She gave silent thanks to her dad for the spare oxygen she'd needed to satiate her lungs. Still, she'd have given all that up just to have him around.

They turned a familiar corner, and where Lena could have sworn should have been a wall was another alley. The darkness hid their movements, but it was unnecessary, as they didn't cross another soul. Before they turned past another building, Lena glanced back down the alley to see a dead end from which they'd emerged. Or perhaps the darkness was just playing tricks on her. Still there was silence.

Just as Sado's pace became near unbearable to imitate, he stopped at the side of a building and ascended vertically. When Lena got closer, she found that a maintenance ladder had been built into the side of the container complex. She wondered if all containers had them. One barely ever had time to take notice. And so, she climbed.

When she reached the top, she found Sado crouched and peering over the side. She crept next to him. Below, a group of white-uniformed officers lingered outside a small windowless container. Their lights bled out onto the streets in broken strands as they surrounded the door. Sado gestured to be quiet.

One of the officers motioned to the others, checked his watch, and then pounded on the door. In their hands glowed batons of dancing white static. A bell signaled the changing of phases, and a moment later the container opened. From it, a woman with a worn complexion and the body of a steam engine stepped out.

Lena strained her ears to hear her speak. "Offishers, how may I help you at thish late hour?" Diffidence blanketed her tones.

"Ruebid Pluck?" The uniform inquired.

"Yesh."

"You've been accused of aiding the terrorist group known as the Outcry. How do you plead?"

There was a moment's hesitation. The doorway slouched around Ms. Pluck as if to hug her goodbye. The inside of her container whispered in a silent agony, pleading at her not to go. Nothing but darkness on the streets surrounded them, yet its wordlessness throbbed at Lena's ears.

"Guilty," Ms. Pluck sighed. She straightened her spine and pushed back her shoulders. "Guilty and prou—"

Before the last consonant left her lips, the end of the officer's flickering baton touched her side and she fell limp to the ground, a teacher no longer.

Lena's mouth opened to scream and her body desired to leap, but she found herself restrained in Sado's grasp, her mask covered by his hands. She writhed and pushed, but his grip held her firmly, and she collapsed, defeated. All she wanted to do was cry, but her eyes fought back, holding onto the bits of sanity she knew would be lost if they became flooded. The pack below picked up the fallen teacher and compressed her body into a small case. Four of them lifted it and they processed back into the darkness that had birthed them. Their lights faded behind another building, and the streets were again unlit.

Lena sat, staring into the ether. Only when Sado broke the silence did she remember to take a breath. "This is what we do."

"We?" She bit back the threat of tears.

"We, as a society. You're just as guilty for letting this happen."

She swallowed dryness. "But I didn't know it was happening."

"Ignorance is not an excuse, it's an offense. Those who sit idly by, those who close their eyes, and those who instigate are all the same. Three names with one face."

Lena didn't speak. They made their way back to her container in silence, and even as she crawled in bed, her mind was as empty as the night. She felt numb.

Sado pulled up the covers over her as Tulu dreamed in the corner. He glanced towards his bag and back to Lena. His voice was solemn. "I can make you forget. I can make it like it never happened, and no one would look at you differently for doing so."

She stared up at him. Beneath the tiredness in his eyes, she saw the wilting of hope. "Do you think that we'll ever be able to live together with nature? On the outside?"

"We already can," he whispered. "Our cities are a testament to this. We just need to be willing to try."

Her mind sank back. "Then I should remember this." She quivered. At her words she thought she saw his face twitch a smile, but in an instant it was gone, and she was too tired to wonder if it ever existed at all.

"If you'll listen," he began, with an intonation more awake that she'd heard from him. "I have one more thing to tell you." He moved to the side of the room.

She looked at the time displayed on her ceiling. Only seven more hours remained until she had to go to her now-teacher-less school.

Sado sat down next to her. "Your father was one of the first members of the Outcry. Back before we even had a name."

Lena's heart raced for a moment and then settled back into her body. She had had her suspicions about her dad, but he'd never mentioned the Outcry. She knew why, though. Back then she wouldn't have understood it. Couldn't have. Still, she wished they could have shared the secret. "You knew him?"

He nodded. "He would have been very proud of who you've become."

She felt a warm froth wash over her. Sadness, happiness, fatigue all blended in a ripple of her senses. Her eyes felt hazed.

When she blinked again, the time displayed that two hours had passed. She looked over at Sado, confused. Before she could ask anything, he cut her off.

"We can't carry out your idea to tear down the paint. It's too risky." He said this with a puzzling smirk on his face, and his speaking was rushed. He gathered his bag, placing items that Lena couldn't identify into it. Without another word he disappeared from her room and he was gone.

Sleep crept over her before she had time to question his mysterious behavior. Only a few hours till morning.

XVIII.

The alarm's clamor perforated through down and fabric. The muffled sound pulled Lena away from the momentary sleep that last night had permitted. Her head felt stuffed full of the feathers that frosted her bedroom floor. There was a throbbing in her sinuses that threatened to cross the border into a headache. Her body felt uncharacteristically cold, but it wasn't clear whether the chill was a result of her overly warm forehead or something entirely different.

She kept her eyes closed until the snooze button stopped acknowledging her requests. Tulu sputtered for her to arise.

"Not now, Tootles." She groaned, slipping out of bed one toe at a time. When she managed to stand, her feet rested on the soft cotton twill of a dress. She pulled it up over her head and felt the blue denim tumble down her like woven petals. She shook her hands through her hair, ruffling it to match how she felt. Her mirror smiled back at her, then faded to an exhausted scowl.

Why did Sado leave so abruptly? She felt a wheel on her foot and looked down. Tulu purred, a ball balancing on his head.

"Tulu. No!" Her foot pulled away from him.

She gathered her bag and went to the door, looking back to check if there was anything she'd forgotten. Tulu whimpered, pushing at her heels.

"Agh!" Her breathing rose and fell hard. She growled and went into the hall, slamming the door. Behind her, she heard a thump. And then another. Tulu's sobs were stifled by the sounds of him running into the divider between them. The pounding matched the throb of Lena's heartbeat pulsing in her temple. She clenched her teeth as she left the house.

Her eyes stayed trained on her feet as she let her body coast on autopilot to school. She glimpsed a knot of people whispering and pointing at something in the distance, but her mind stepped through the previous night, oblivious to the world.

She sat down in the tube, thankful for the small container's warmth on her bare shoulders. Warmth that the city seemed to lack today. She wondered if it was caused by her lack of sleep, or perhaps because she was wearing a dress. But she had never remembered the air being anything other than temperate.

She refocused on tracing through what Sado had said, hoping there was some hint at his departure, but after they had returned to her home she mainly remembered sleep. Or rather, didn't remember being awake. She avoided the thought of Ms. Pluck, knowing that when she got to class that would be all she would think about. Her feet carried her to the front of her school, and it wasn't until she bumped into Molly that she looked up.

Around her, where most days a blur made up the steady current of a human river, hundreds of people were as rooted and as immobile as a forest. They all stared at the city's ceiling. Their mouths moved like guppies, their words babbled like brooks, and yet in the liquid commotion of their noise, a single thought permeated their minds. Lena looked up.

Not to murals. Not to portraits. Not to itty-bitty specks and splotches shading her view. Instead, she saw the sky. Behind the thick translucent panels of the city's exterior, clouds shifted and stirred. The sun scattered its array of spindles down over the landscape of an emerging spring.

Lena collapsed to her knees. Many others, she noticed, had done the same. She watched as some parents blocked their children's views, directing them into the school. She saw bulging eyes, frightened eyes, teary eyes, some crying over the beauties of the forgotten world, some crying for the lost works of art, torn down by terrorists – or revolutionaries.

The signal for the changing of phases sounded, but the river remained frozen. It wasn't until a group of white-clad uniforms appeared that movement rekindled. Lena and her classmates were herded into their classroom, the lack of their teacher not registering in the distraction.

Lena found her way to her desk, again blinded by the rush of thoughts igniting already fatigued neurons. *They did it. They really did it. They carried out my plan. How? In so little time. With such short notice. They would have needed hundreds, maybe thousands to do it. All coordinating together, all acting at once. How is that possible?*

Why hadn't Sado told her? She could have helped. She should have helped; it was her idea after all. She sighed. *He knew I would have insisted on helping. It's why he said no. It's why he rushed away.* She wanted to hate him, to be angry with him, but it was hard to do so when she understood him. Now all she wanted to do was to express her excitement to Tulu. She just hoped he'd forgive her for being so harsh that morning.

"Class, I understand that there has been quite a bit of excitement." Lena heard the familiar raspy voice, but it seemed out of place. "But you'll notice that your teacher, Ms. Pluck, is not here." Lena looked up. Her heart became caught in a flickering of short, quick breaths. Her eyes flared. "Until a replacement is found, I will be substituting for her. You may call me Paxton."

Molly raised her hand. "What happened to Ms. Pluck?"

Paxton gave her a warm smile. "She has been recognized for her accomplishments as an educator. Though she wanted to stay here and continue to teach, she realized that her talents were needed urgently elsewhere. She promised to write letters to you all once a month, so if you'd like to write back, I will make sure you're able to do so." He looked back at Lena and nodded. She blinked wide-eyed in response.

He was just like she remembered. His voice was aged and sincere, crafted with subtle notes of pride and sympathy. His tone made her want to trust him, even though she knew who he really was: a liar. That was his job, after all. And he'd considered himself an artist. Her mind didn't want to deal with him right now.

Just as he began to speak again, his tap-pad lit up and he walked to the desk. Someone behind its screen talked to him in a rushed voice. Lena couldn't make out the words, but the tone was anxious. She realized then what was happening. The balance had tipped overnight, leaving the Council scrambling to assert their authority in the Outcry's anarchic wake.

Paxton's composure remained firm, despite the news he was hearing. He looked out over the class. "Students, I've just received word that I'm to send everyone directly home. You'll receive further information on the C-Phase news." The classroom door slid open.

One by one they stood and walked away, wary and concerned. As Lena stepped through the door, she glanced back. Paxton's calm had fractured; there was worry in his face that hadn't existed moments before. He caught Lena's eye and something about his look told her she wouldn't see him again. Or that he wouldn't see her again. The door slid closed between them, and Lena was left being herded with the flock of people told to return to their homes.

No one around her spoke. Throughout the masses of people, scattered white uniforms reflected unfamiliar sunlight. The buzz of the now-unnecessary overhead lights washed over them. The crowd looked at the ground, avoiding eye contact with the outside world. Their submission was brought on not by force, but by the patrol's mere existence.

Lena ran her hand along the glass, feeling the liquefied breath coat her fingers. She spelled her name in the window's impermanence. The autograph of its artist. Layer by layer a thicket of wet nothing painted over it, and when she finally turned, it was again a wall without a name. She stepped forward bumping into a white pillar.

It turned and spoke to her. "Are you all right?"

Lena blinked the mist from her eyes and realized that the pillar was really a man, and the man was in uniform. "What's going on? Why are we being shepherded?"

The pillar gave her a soft grin. To her, man or not, he still resembled a pillar. "I imagine you know as much as any of us. We're asked to lead people home, and so we lead people home. We're just sheep leading sheep." He patted her on the head. "Now go on ahead, little lamb. Lest you be a black sheep."

Lena smiled and walked on. From behind her, she thought she heard a feigned *baa,* but she didn't turn to see, for in her mind, a ram was its maker.

The flock grew smaller until there were just a few stragglers left, and when she glided around the final corner to her home, she was alone.

Now, without the scrutiny of the pillars' gazes, she grinned with pride. She didn't know what would happen tomorrow, but she'd played an important part in today. She had a story. *Tulu will be so proud!* She hoped her dad would have been, too.

Lena looked up at her container. Bernie stared off into the distance, inert. His paneling looked warped with lethargy, causing her ecstasy to flicker. She'd never seen him look so hollow. Lena touched her hand to the door's panel. Nothing. It remained closed. Something wasn't right.

She crawled through the flap, ready to push the mound of pillows from her path, but there was no need. The feather-filled sacks lay scattered about the hall, naked geese lying mangled in a sea of their own quills. It was eerily quiet.

Lena stood. Her bare hands touched the wall and felt the chill brought on by the unpainted world. She shivered.

"Tulu," she called out. "Tootles, I'm home!" She waited for a response, her feet pausing at the base of the steps. She exhaled and her breath emerged as a white fog. The top of the steps blinked from yellow to black, giving a motion to the motionless. As hollow as her home felt, there was a stale aftertaste lingering in the air, as if another body had recently occupied the space. Had someone been in her container? Were they there now?

Lena removed her shoes. *You're just being silly,* she forced herself to think. She began ascending the stairs on the tips of her toes. She lifted herself over the distorted sheen of the creaky third step. *I assemble monsters with my mind. I build them of broken glass, and forgotten words, and knotted yarn, I forget as they gobble up my memories, and I crawl as they pull upon my strings, but even when I write that they've trapped me in a tiny box wrapped with twisted burgundy bows addressed to return-to-sender, and I dream of wanting to dream...* She stopped at her door. *Even then, I know it's all just swimming in the fabric of my mind.* Her hand touched the brass knob. *It's just my imagination.* She pushed open the wooden barrier to her room. It swung, a sorrowful creak played its melody for a moment, and the door came to a stop with a soft thud, only halfway ajar.

"Tulu," she whispered. She looked down; a thick thread lay disheveled in the entranceway. She knelt down and touched the braided lock. She pushed the door again, and again it stopped with a hollow thud. Her fingers clenched into tiny fists, the ridges of her nails throbbing against warmed skin. She slid around the door into the black...the red...the black...the red.

She held her breath, her teeth on her tongue. Against the back of the door lay a pile of lifeless yarn. From it ran a rat's nest of wires, insulated conductors vacant of music. The wires stopped two feet away in a body of shattered circuits. Circuits and twisted metal. Metal and wheels. Tulu's remains.

Lena fell into the pieces of her friend.

Wordless.

Just.

Broken.

...Fragments.

Water fell from her eyes.

Metal

Yarn

Cut Her.

Skin.

Water fell from her skin.

Red in the red.

Red in   the black.

She needed a friend...to pick up

her pieces.

Behind her, masked voices behind muffled faces blinked white in the black. She heard them speak at her. "What's she doing rolling in that broken junk?"

She wasn't sure what they were speaking about, so she listened more, pressing her face into Tulu's hair.

"Grab her, she's going to hurt herself." Lena felt a tug at her arm. She bit and flailed, but it remained attached. She wasn't sure if it was her tongue, or the creature's hand, that her teeth embraced. She felt no pain. Her pain had already fallen to the floor in puddles.

"She bit me!"

"Just pick her up!"

"She's bleeding."

"Our orders are to bring her in if she's cogent."

Lena screamed. "He's bleeding. Tulu's bleeding. We need to get him help!"

"And if she's not?"

The walls cried.

"We burn her."

XIX.

She had never truly known sunshine. Never really noticed how she could squint and swirl her head with a quick glance of its palette and paint the landscape red. "Paintbrushes made of eyelashes," her dad used to say. Today she painted the world red, not in anger, not in love, but in order to see everything through a rose-colored filter. She needed to forget the life that now floated above her. Away from her. The life that was no longer hers.

***

Circ hesitantly flicked the screen of an unlit digital dial in front of him. The hardened plastic returned the sharp impulse, and he stuck his sore finger in his mouth.

Behind him in the passenger cabin, Lin stared curiously at the nylon belt and metal buckle attached to her seat. "How do you think people worked these things?"

She clapped them together with a loud clink, but they remained disconnected. "There must have been video instructions or something." She pushed a button above her and a small light blinked on. Beside it, the approximate silhouette of a woman stared back at her with a round head. "Circ, have you ever flown one of these before?"

A chuckle resonated from the cockpit. "Sure, it's just like piloting a tube."

"Oh." Lin relaxed, then ruffled her forehead. "Wait, aren't those on tracks?"

"Isn't this?" He smiled as the engine purred to a start. "I knew it was one of these buttons." The dial now flurried numbers.

Next to Circ, Joseph clutched a little black gurgling box with blood-drained fingers. His seatbelt was tied in a knot about his waist. His eyes stared down, locked on the radio, avoiding the window and the world outside of it that threatened to get closer.

"Joe, you're awfully quiet. How about you tell us the story of when you and Circ worked the tubes, and how you fought over that one-legged tube woman?" Lin grinned, triumphant as her belt and buckle clicked together. She pulled out the notebook and pen from her duffle bag. Her hands weren't accustomed to writing words, and each letter felt like it was its own separate drawing, but it was better than nothing.

Joseph sighed, something he'd only recently grown accustomed to. It was fascinating how quickly the body adapted to not breathing on cue.

"I..." He began but stopped as the aircraft lurched forwards, giving his stomach an out-of-body experience. The three of them accelerated down the ancient runway that sat atop Old Brin. The runway was truly a signifier of the city's age; newer cities only had hopper pads atop their roofs. Joseph clamped his eyes closed and clawed at his armrest. "Limit to fuel; fuel to create; create to limit," he whispered in repetition.

***

Still, to wake up in the grass, to feel her bed living beneath her, the earth growing about her, welcoming her, she couldn't be more alive. For who can be more alive than the earth, and as she knew it, she, today, was the earth. Each moment she got up was a moment she spun around and tumbled back to the lively bed, her mattress of green. Dizzier and dizzier, the world spun, and she spun, about her axis, about the world's axis. The sky stayed blue and still, or was it red and flowing, she couldn't tell, for each attempt to rise was just another twist to fall.

***

For a brief moment the plane lingered on the edge of their world, and they questioned if they could truly leave its surface. There was half an expectation for the wheels to stay attached to the ground and for the craft to wrap around underneath the city. Their minds liberated those thoughts as they plummeted over the edge, weightless and free.

Lin yelled in delight, her arms flailing above her, gripping tightly to her notebook, red and yellow lights flashing throughout the cabin.

Circ pulled back hard on the yoke and their stomachs hit their seats with an audible *thump*. Beads of sweat freckled Circ's brow, but his face glowed with accomplishment. He wanted to say he felt young again, but the expression had grown meaningless. This felt far more exciting than youth.

***

She welcomed the silence that resounded each time she settled back into the earth. A smile at the knowledge of her own silliness was planted and growing on her face. How funny to be unable to move and yet to always be moving. How silly to be the earth. Even the grass was red now, having looked at and praised the sun for far too long; was it an eternity, or was it just long enough, for maybe it was okay to see light like it truly was, as blinding. Maybe the earth sees the grass as red, or, she thought, maybe I do.

The rustle, or rather the inhale, of the grass as she stood, was intoxicating. Maybe someday she would be as intoxicating as the brush of grass, as the music sewn by the wind, but not today. Today she would stand, hear the call of the grass, and tumble to its beckoning. And then silence. A chorus of nothing. And at once, a pounding. Was it the molten core inside her? She could taste the iron, shifting, rotating, revolving, whatever iron does in its natural state of hot chaos. She felt the pull, the attraction, to the magnetic satellites about her, she could feel her entire mass shifting and stabilizing, and saying, "I am stronger than you, tiny pebbles of dust." Slowly, and then quickly they would fall to her, she knew, maybe not today, maybe not while she was the earth, but as long as someone was the earth, someone with a furnace inside them, the dust would come. That's what things do. In an open fire, things flee, but once it's controlled, they flock. As long as the iron moves, and shifts, even if it broke her apart, until it broke her apart, they would come. Or at least she hoped.

***

Circ tapped on the autopilot and the craft took over. He hesitated and decided against telling the others that he could have done that from the start.

"Young'n like him never had a chance with Gladice. She was a fine lady. Now, where are we headed?" He tapped Joseph on the shoulder.

Joseph looked up, still rearranging his shaken-up pieces. "I...we...are to continue heading North-Northwest. That was the last direction they were seen taking her."

"That's hardly specific enough to find her. There's a whole world that's North-Northwest of us."

"Well," Joseph began to regain his composure. "Keep an eye out for smoke, or a fire. Sado had said that they'd likely drop her somewhere in the middle of one. And they won't have gone far. Their hoppers aren't meant for long distances."

Lin's seatbelt unclicked and she walked to the front of the craft. "I'm really starting to get the hang of those things." The smile she wore dissolved as she looked out on the grey expanse flickering in the distance. "What if we can't find Lena? There's so much world. And she's so small." She picked at her thumbnail. "Besides, how do we know she's really out here? Why wouldn't they have just recycled her?" The question had been ruminating in her mind since the call.

They grew silent. Lin looked down at the radio in Joseph's lap. Its quiet unsettled them. Three hours before, Sado had alerted them that Lena had been taken. His voice had come over the radio, frantic and full of distress. His lack of composure came unanticipated on the day they should have been celebrating the Outcry's victory.

They'd taken the plane and flew off on his orders, but his orders were few and far between. A general direction, the expectation of a fire, and a required haste. It wasn't much to go on, but it was worth the risk if it meant saving Lena. As the entirety of the Outcry had tried to volunteer to participate in her rescue, the decision to send a rescue mission was unanimous. One of the few things that they'd ever all agreed on. Still, Lin couldn't help but feel that there was something odd about this, about the effort of taking Lena so far away to dispose of her. There was something they hadn't been told. Lin may have trusted Sado, but that didn't mean he was without secrets.

Circ turned to her, taking his eyes away from the wild expanse before them. The sadness in his voice extracted Lin from her thoughts. "When my son was born, they said that he didn't have much of a chance to survive." He stared off into the back of the plane, and when he spoke it was barely audible.

"They refused to try to save him, saying that even if he got through his infancy, he wouldn't live a full life. He was deemed as non-optimal. Said he'd just be a burden." He took a breath. "A waste of air." His eyes shook. "He lived for thirteen years before they took him. Thirteen beautiful years that he fought for and defied their sentence. He'd learned to breathe just like everyone else. Learned to walk in step. And he was so happy about life. About his struggle. He had to fight for something, and that gave him meaning. More meaning than most." He stopped, mouth slightly open, choking back the next few words.

Lin glanced at Joseph with concern. He shook his head, signaling her to wait.

When the words finally emerged, the blood from Circ's face had drained, leaving him pale. "One day, they just took him. Said he was discouraging to the other kids. Said that because he'd had to try so hard to live, to just be normal, it made the others see a way of life that wasn't productive. Wasn't realistic. Non-optimal.

"So in the end. Even when he had fought so hard. It didn't matter. But then again, sometimes death is more important than life. He brought me here." He paused. "Will we find Lena?" His eyes connected with Lin's. "Maybe. Either way, she's already united us. Her life has had more meaning than most." He turned away, looking back onto the rolling clouds. The plane began to shake.

Circ's eyes lowered. "You'd better take your seat, Lin. We're passing over a storm."

***

Lena stopped, if only for a moment. From her scarred surface pulsed a molten red. Layer upon layer it grew and solidified in her eternal breath. Liquid islands flowed from her veins. She no longer needed to spin for her dizziness spun for her.

And in her momentary calm her mind reeled sun-bleached frames of a girl's dead father. And a girl's dead teacher. And a girl's dead friend. And as desperately as she wanted to, she couldn't cry. For the air stole her tears.

***

The plane pivoted and twisted as they jolted over a pocket of hot air, and the computer calmly told them to "please fasten your seatbelts." Outside, the world was dry. Grey clouds rumbled together, spindling dust and dirt with their palpable thunder. For an instant, the sky bleached their vision. And then it passed.

Beyond the ruffled grey, the sun balanced on the horizon. The air became smoother again, just as the little black box in Joseph's arms began to crackle.

"Joes... kshhhh shhhhhh... aken off yet? Kshh shhh shhh."

"Sado!" He held the radio close to his mouth. "We're heading North-Northwest, over the Great Plains."

"Kshhhhhhh sign of a fi kshhhh shhhhh?"

"We just flew over some thunder clouds. Air reads to be pretty dry here. We haven't seen a fire yet, but we're bound to be close."

"Kshhhhhhh ehh kshhhh ehh kshhhh."

Joseph looked at the others, but they both shrugged. "Sado, we didn't get that. Could you repeat?"

The radio continued to fizzle. Beneath the aircraft, the air burned a brilliant red. The layers of grey cloud became ribbons of thick black smoke, wrapping and folding themselves onto the sky.

"Kshhhhh ook for a kshhhhh hey could land kshhh shhhh oppers shhhhhh."

Circ turned off the autopilot and brought the plane down below their cover of black cloud. The craft maneuvered smoothly, and Circ silently thanked all the hours of flight simulations he'd had to endure.

It concerned them that they hadn't noticed the expanse of flames. From above, it had only appeared that the ground was in mid-autumn. A dusting of red among the leaves blowing in a faint wind. From their current altitude, it was clear. Invasive undergrowth burned beneath thousands of acres of pines.

***

Warmth, she could hear. The sound of her infinite sea of grass metamorphosing to an ocean of entropy. An orchestra of static, crackles, and pops, to which her winds dared to dance. She was an updraft reaching for a bird in the sky, and then again falling back into the earth.

***

"Sado?" Joseph spoke into the box. "We're on the fire. But it goes so far; I've never seen anything like it. I don't even know where we can begin looking."

They waited while the radio seemed to consider the statement. A quarter of the sun now hid behind the edge of the world.

"Circ," Lin started. "We're losing light. We've got to cover more ground."

"The only thing we've got is our eyes, and if we fly any higher, they'll be useless too."

"Look kshhhhh an opening. They would have ksshhh and in an open field."

At that the radio fell silent. Static ceased and they were on their own. They glided in silence while the sun took its time sinking. Twilight lit the landscape below, casting its orange hue on the fiery tides. Lin scraped the forest floor with relentless eyes. She rubbed away the dry and sleep, and she pulled at her hair to keep her senses. Her peripheral vision ignited as herds of deer and flocks of birds abandoned their homes, leaving the dwellings they once knew as safe for a world that made no promises.

"Any fields that used to be here could have been consumed hours ago," Joseph choked. "We're looking for salt on the beach."

"Or a dancer in a meadow!" Lin tried to jump up from her seat but her buckle pulled back on her waist, causing her body to flail.

Joseph and Circ looked back at the knotted mess that was Lin pressed face-first against the window, her leg anchored to her seat by her seatbelt, her arms bound behind her in her green sweater.

Joseph shook his head. "I can't say I've heard that expression."

"Turn around!" She shouted as she pulled her leg free from her seat. She rushed to the front of the cabin. "I saw her. She was dancing like a little ballerina in a clearing."

"Lin, I know you want to find her. But, the likelihood of—"

"Circ!" She ignored Joseph. "You turn this plane around, or so help me, I'll—"

Before she could finish, the plane made a sharp U-turn. Circ howled in delight. Joseph retreated into his stomach and Lin was tossed sideways, her sweater twisting back into place.

"There!" she said, clawing her way back up to the window.

The three watched in disbelief as a small girl twirled and spun and fell in a narrow glen encircled by a burning forest. As they flew over her, she stood again, spun, and once more fell. Joy and sadness plastered on her face.

"Well," Circ breathed. "I guess I'd better learn how to land this thing. And quick."

Lin crossed her arms over her chest. She turned back with an I-told-you-so smirk but Joseph was no longer sitting. She twisted her head further to see him towards the back of the craft, pulling on an exosuit. The harshness in his brow had all but vanished. She smiled and turned back to see Circ directing the plane where to land.

The fire grew steadily closer to Lena as she continued to dance and fall.

As the wheels touched the ground, Joseph flung open the door and leapt out in a run. When he reached her, she appeared to have finally settled into the patch of grass on which she lay. Peaceful.

He smiled down at her, but she looked through him. Her glassy eyes told him that she was far away. Or perhaps too large to see the small things. He placed her gently over his shoulder and walked back towards the craft. *I won't lose you, too.*

***

In an instant, the short type of instant, not the eternal instant some may experience in moments of clarity, her world, or perhaps just her, was tossed upside and left, right and towards the middle, and perhaps a slight bit counterclockwise. A man, no, it must have been the moon, she thought, was beneath her, or was he just adjacent in space, nevertheless, his gravity was pulling her. She was dizzy, perhaps from her natural rotation, for what does the earth look at so that it doesn't get dizzy when it spins. Obviously the sun, but that's why the world could only see red. The red, of course, being the sky, for her skin was a pale orange, or was it green, she no longer knew where her grass grew.

The moon shook and shook, or perhaps it bounced; all she knew was that her waves shifted and stirred like a nervous cup of coffee. The thought made her giggle, and the moon stopped for just a moment to smile back. How nice it was that a moon was out tonight, maybe he was intoxicated, or intoxicating, she didn't know the difference, but someone was toxic, or something. Could a person be toxic? She wondered what people thought about all day, as they drifted above her ferns, or skirted around her roots, in their little bubbles that they seemed to exist in, to persist in. She wondered if people knew the warmth of fire upon their skin.

For to float through the absence of space, even with a fire in your heart, is still cold on your skin.

***

In the distance Joseph could see Lin and Circ as they stood outside setting up a tan stretcher. On his shoulder, Lena giggled and he paused and smiled at her. What a peculiar child, to find time to laugh this day.

***

Another bump from the moon, and a brief flash of the red earth. Why was it below her now? Or was it above? Can the earth see itself? Oh to see! She had forgotten about her eyes, about light being more than just the resultant from excited matter. Light and air and sound, they all seemed like the same notion to her now, but if she could remember to see, why couldn't she remember to breathe? Was she breathing with her eyes? But of course, she thought, the earth breathes with its grass, with its trees, and so must I, for my lungs are alive.

She called upon her trees, and her grass, and her ferns, and all parts of her to breathe. At first her body didn't react, for who can tell the earth to do something, even itself. Slowly, though, she listened, and pulled upon the sky's breath. It flowed across the buds of her tongue, each blooming in delight; it flowed down the valleys of her chest, into her aquifers until finally she exhaled.

At first her breath was dictated by tremors threatening to rattle her structure, each push requiring a pull, no matter how shallow she managed, but soon she, or her surface, settled. *Was she a she? It had been so long since the days when she was a girl and not the earth.*

An entire instant had passed. She noticed that her eyes had clamped shut, and what once was grass below her skin now felt like a canvas. Was she a painting? Her body, or her earth, no, this was her body that felt clammy. Not fresh or salty, but damp and hot, and yet still craving moisture. Her lips, as cracked as the ocean floor, and as dry as small talk. She almost giggled again but filtered the noise into a grin. She was afraid to open her eyes but didn't know why. Most days she was afraid of something, more some cycles than others, but today it frightened her. To be scared of fear was her one real fear.

***

When he got to Lin, he laid Lena down. He touched her shoulders. "I'll be right back. Just stay still."

***

Her ears perked, as much as a bird's ears can perk, as new sounds emerged. Was she a bird? She couldn't remember. The sounds, a symphonic compound, broke down into the instruments of her surroundings. She thought she heard a man speaking, yes, it was a man, but was it speaking? She knew words, she had to know words since she was thinking, or, at least that was what she reasoned. Something about sitting still, or standing still, something about being still, for certain. She thought he was addressing her, but how can one command the earth? Or a painting?

204

Either way, it couldn't be her. She was spinning in a field somewhere outside. Outside? Too much was unclear for her to sit, or to stand, or to be still. Slowly, she pulled apart her eyelids with the tiny muscles in her head. She had been using them all her life, but now everything felt new. She felt like she was teaching her muscles for the first time. She must have been a baby when she did this last because she didn't remember. All she could remember was how it felt to blink. And it didn't feel like this.

***

The three of them stepped away. "How is she?" Lin whispered.

"She seems dazed." He looked back at her still figure. "I'm not sure if it's just the smoke that got to her, or if they did something, but she's not all there right now. Her hands are a bit cut up too, so she'll need to be cleaned up. We'd better get her on support, and make sure we keep her awake so we can find out if they dosed her with anything."

"Okay, I'll—"

"Man!" Lena called out.

They turned and hurried to her. Her eyes were now open, with a milky glaze.

"Lena," Joseph spoke slowly. "I need you to stay still and stay awake for me. Can you do that? Just keep those eyes open. We'll do this together."

***

At first, the air seemed glazed, almost frosty, minus the sweet or cool. She was outside, that was certain, but the sky

205

flickered in the darkness like the light in the crawlspace below her front stairs. She couldn't tell if it was the stars or the sky that was blinking; was it white on black, or black on white?

Her first real clue among the plethora of false positives was the smell of ash. Or black snow. But black snow didn't smell, and it wasn't quite winter, so she doubted that that was what was accumulating on the tip of her nose. She had thought about calling the man who talked of stillness, but she didn't know what to call him, so she had shouted "Man!"

To her, her shout only seemed to radiate from her eyes. Perhaps it was her mouth, but who can say what it's like to shout from one's eyes. She could, or so she thought. Nevertheless, someone came, and when one came, many came, for they were all still magnetic dust trying to steal her molten core. They all talked at once, but luckily for her she had multiple ears, and so she heard her parade tell her again to stay still, to just stay awake.

***

Joseph and Lena stared at each other for a long moment. Their eyes locked together, his pleading for her to stay focused, hers teetering on a questionable reality. The instant she blinked was the moment he knew he'd lost that battle. Her eyes didn't reopen.

***

Who were they to tell the earth to do this or that? Without a thought, or perhaps with just a single thought of opposition, though she would never admit it, she promptly fell asleep. A sleep without dream, or rather, who can say what is dream and what is not when one is asleep? Certainly not the earth.

***

Joseph exhaled deeply. He touched her head. There was clamminess to it, but it wasn't overly warm. "Let's get her inside," he said. "Lin, get her hooked up to an IV and an oxygen mask. Circ, we're to take her to the cabin."

Circ looked nervous. "Are...are we going to meet Sado?"

"Our orders are to leave her there."

"Oh," his face ruffled back to what he'd grown accustomed to over the years. Some things never changed. "Maybe we'll meet him another day," he said half-heartedly.

As dusk turned to dark, they carried the stretcher into the plane, silhouetted by an ember forest. Joseph gazed down at the slumbering child. He didn't want to care for her. He'd even tried not to. It seemed like everything he'd cared for had been taken from him. She was a symbol of his memories. She was the spirit of his wife, Isabel; the wisdom of his mentor, Arthur; and the hope of his friend, Esta. He touched her cheek. The aircraft doors closed behind him as they took off away from the fire.

"Don't let him change you," he whispered. And he sat back, a little less afraid of flying.

XX.

A wood cabin sat cradled in a gulley of trees, shadowed behind the body of a mountain, just a little ways away from a snow-fed lake. Overgrown with threads of ivy and blankets of moss, its exterior blended into its evergreen neighbors. The structure itself lay untouched, preserved in the cool mountain air. Several of its wooden supports showed signs of having been replaced within the last decade. Inside slept Lena, her body and her mind drifting worlds apart, one in dream, one in reality, though, which was which she couldn't say.

Next to her crackled a small fireplace. The embers tittered, making the sound she imagined autumn leaves might make while scampering across a tap-pad. Her taste buds alighted with a hint of burnt pine. She awoke with a mental start.

She shifted to yawn, but as she moved she became aware of a cold steel needle protruding from her arm. It countered her motion and wiggled in her veins, sending shivers down her spine. With more force than intended, she yanked it from her arm and tossed it away from her. It reached the apex of its toss and stopped, held momentarily taut by the tube leading to the medical stand adjacent to her, and then fell. Next to her it swung back and forth like the pendulum of a sad grandfather clock. All in all, the gesture was substantially less dramatic than Lena had imagined.

Her thoughts drifted momentarily over the last few cycles, but as soon as the image of her sweet Tulu surfaced, she shoved it into the back corner of her mind. The corner she reserved for the pieces of the world that she couldn't handle. This was the corner where her dad, Ms. Pluck, and Esta sat with their new corner-mate Tulu. She found the indent in her tongue that she'd so often bitten down on and refocused her eyes to the strange new environment in which she existed.

The bed was hard and lumpy, stuffed with foam and straw and coils and maybe the occasional rock, patched together with grey strips of tattered adhesive, charred and browned from two centuries of neglect, and topped with an eggshell-white duvet. Lena loved it immediately. It didn't mold to her form, or heat her bottom, or even wish her to have a good day at school. It was just a mattress. Just as it seemed. It didn't try to be anything else. For a girl with an imagination, it was perfect.

Her mind jumped from her bed and explored while her body only slowly, shakily stood. Around each palm, cotton fabric was wrapped. She wiggled her fingers and instantly regretted it as pain flared across her hands. By the time her eyes had made it to the door, her knees were wobbling, pleading for her to slow down. With a deep sigh, she re-centered herself and noticed that her body was having trouble supporting itself. *Hey you! Come on, pick up the pace,* she thought-yelled. Her knees went "wah-

wah-wah" in reply and she collapsed to the ground. The wood embraced her hard, and immediately she had knots in her stomach. Around her, the cabin seemed to chuckle.

A cane leaned against a table of streaked koa wood. Its posture was familiar, but she couldn't quite place it. It looked down at her with its mahogany handle and white-veined black body, a bit too uppity for her taste and a bit too off-balance for its own. If it had arms, it would have waved them in circles as it pivoted about its one good leg and tumbled to the floor with an "oof". Lena grinned and wrapped her hand carefully around the fallen snob. It cringed at her touch, and she winced at its. With a push and a shake, she stood. Her third leg stabilized her, reluctantly.

This time she slowly let her eyes stroll about the room, taking in her mattress, the fire, and her neatly folded denim dress atop the table. Her eyes bulged and she looked down. At the sight of herself in baggy flannel, she exhaled in relief. No wonder only her face had felt the cold. She noted to ask how she'd arrived in these clothes later, once she'd figured exactly where it was that she'd arrived.

Next to her denim dress stood tall a soot-stained radio, proud and industrious. It avoided making eye contact with her, but, from the corner of her vision, she could see it glancing over at her in curiosity. She smiled. Behind the radio, a window looked out into a leaf-covered world, its lens distorted with both age and moss.

Though her brain toyed with the idea of jumping through the glass portal, only two of her legs consented to bend, while the third remained rigid and refused to heed to her instinctual desire. She crept closer to the window, but as she did something inside of her growled. A lion maybe, or perhaps a Snarglops, she wasn't sure. Whatever strange feeling it was made her feel weak.

"Growlllll," her body said again.

She clutched her stomach. Whatever it was, it floated about her belly, angry and on the prowl. "What do you want?" She tried to comfort it.

"Grummmble gurrrgle rumble gurrrrrgle urrgle gurgle urrlge," it complained.

Her mouth salivated and her mind flashed images of green-golden-maroon wafers. Whatever strange magic her stomach was making, it seemed to want something. "Food?" She inquired.

"Gurrrgly gooo!" It purred.

How strange, she thought. She'd never really wanted food before. She'd always just had it. She scanned the room for a tap-pad to take her order, but there was only the chattering fire that seemed to speak a language similar to that of her stomach. *It must want food, too.*

Past her bed, on the other side of the room, a door stood crowded in its frame. It beckoned her and she beckoned it, but alas, it remained firm, and she was forced to go to it. One step at a time. "Flip-flop-clunk. Flip-flop-clunk. Flip-flop-clunk," went her three feet. The touch of the frigid brass handle let her know that the outside would bite, even though sun lit the room's interior. She turned it. It creaked. She squeaked. And it opened.

Wind rushed past her and nibbled at her ears as she wriggled in delight. The world was full of air. Stretched out in front of her, tall towering timbers punctured up through the earth's surface like verdant stalagmites. At the sound of the door, birds by the bushel leapt into the sky. A small voice ingrained in Lena told her to flinch and to run for her life, for the beasts of the air would soon attack. But nothing happened. Nothing but a wispy breeze that spoke of the birds having relaxed in the higher branches of nearby trees. Her world had been so wrong.

Her stomach moaned again. Lena flip-flop-clunked across the forest floor, towards her closest tree neighbor, as blades of grass licked between her toes. Scattered about the tree's base, in a fresh coating of leaves, were what appeared to be hand-sized spiky, brown eggs. She watched as a petite quadruped scampered across the grass and picked one of them up. The critter had a tail like a duster and it moved in a fidgety, squirrelly manner. For lack of a better name, she called him Squirrelly.

"Whatcha got there, Squirrelly?"

He poked his head up, keeping tight hold on the tree egg, which was as large as its body. "Chhhht-chippety chhht chht eirppp teet teet?"

She squealed. It was so infrequent for her ears to behold a foreign tongue. Its squeakiness was unlike Stubby's wisps, or Tulu's language of sputters and vrooms. The tittering reminded her more of the girls in her class back when her world was simpler. Her brow furrowed at the thought. She cleared her throat. "Chyip chyip chippety teet terp choodle."

Squirrelly pondered her statement for a moment, then, without another word, lowered his head back to the task at hand. He chewed and pulled at the scales of his conic foe, slowly wearing away at its husk, tasting, constantly tasting. Lena's stomach growled again.

She flopped her body down to the nearest unoccupied cone and cupped the woodened flower in her hand. Its scales, sticky with sap, glistened in splotches of scattered sun. With her molars she pressed slowly down on the cone's point. At first it only creaked, then one tendril at a time it splintered and crunched, a cycle's worth of fiber in every bite. It didn't taste bad. She chewed. It was mildly sweet. She chewed. It resembled a petrified wafer. She chewed and chewed and chewed.

After a phase, she licked the residual sap from her fingers and got up. Her stomach no longer groaned for nutrients, though she thought she could feel it whimper.

Now sated, she took a breath of her crisp reality. *I'm,* she combed across the forest ceiling. Fractals swayed in melodic procession, like fingers dancing atop ivory. *Outside.* She could feel her body trembling.

Her feet brought her to standing and hobbled her over to the tree. "You're so tall," she said as she wrapped her arms around it. "Your skin is so rough and grooved and you've got so many nooks and knots filled with little bitty spiders, and cobbly webs, and green fuzzies."

Her eyes followed its trunk to its branches to its canopy, and her mind reoriented her ground to be the tree. She considered walking up it, but instead she spun in a circle and what was her ground became her ceiling, and she fell sideways to the dirt in a fit of laughter. Everything her dad had said about the outside had been true. Even in his words he couldn't capture its beauty.

Every splinter of the forest was full of life. For a phase she buzzed along with a straggling honeybee and counted the hairs on its legs. When it led her to a small brook, a frog eyed her cautiously, so she hopped beside it. She smeared mud on her face, and together they hopped alongside the water, telling each other tales of their grand adventures. As the wind picked up, she let it carry her away as fast as her legs would let her fly, and when she couldn't breathe, she let the earth breathe for her.

In the infinitesimal moments when she thought that she'd explored the entire world, a leaf or a mouse or a dear would appear and lead her to an entirely new domain. And when the world seemed too big, she looked down. An ant crawled across her toe, making its way towards a system of tunnels and burrows with thousands of its brethren.

Next to the ant's architected network grew an umbrella. Lena smiled at its gills, and when her eyeball was as close as possible, she noticed its intricate pores and spores, and she finally understood. *There are galaxies in anthills and universes on mushrooms.*

The sun was still high in the sky when her body told her that the cycle was over. Time had been arbitrary in a world kept dark. She made her way back to the cabin. She couldn't tell if the stuffiness behind her eyes came from the oversaturation of her senses, the overabundance of sun, or the overconcentration of oxygen in the air. Whatever it was, she wished it were over. A headache beat her forehead red, and by the time she'd picked up the cane and reached the door, she was rubbing her temple blearily.

A hundred smells hit her as the door opened. Sweet, spicy, hot, zesty, tangy, salty aromas coiled about her. Nothing had prepared her for this. There was nothing she could compare it to, for her world had lacked scents. It wasn't like the foulness of 701 or the fondness of her dad. Instinctually, though, she knew these smells belonged to food. Her stomach knew, and it crawled and tried to leap ahead of her. It was too late when it remembered that it was attached to her, and what leapt forward across the entryway was her morning meal of pinecone in all its fibrous glory.

In front of her she heard Sado sigh. He set down the stirring spoon and brought Lena over to a chair. Its curved basin was full of rocks and creaks.

"You've been gone for quite some time. I was beginning to wonder if the world had managed to consume you." He glanced at the entryway. "It appears to be quite the opposite."

She grinned behind her queasiness. "What's that expression? When in Racine..."

He chuckled. "I guess I should have left a note that I would be out getting lunch. I didn't think you'd be up for a few more hours. Joseph left you here in quite a state. They did what they could, but it was up to your body to push the smoke from your lungs. And I'd imagine the excess oxygen in the atmosphere here has left you in quite an airy state. But you're quite a survivor, aren't you?"

"There's more air here?"

"The concentrations are different than what you're used to. The cities teach our bodies to need less in order to consume less. And what you know as O_2 is actually a mixture of all sorts of compounds. It's designed to make our bodies efficient, to transport the elements we need to where we need them, when we need them. Nothing more, and usually nothing less."

Lena eyed him and he sighed. "Sometimes a free market is not as free as it would like to think."

"Are...are we being poisoned?"

Sado stood and filled a bowl with food. He handed it to Lena, along with an oddly shaped metal instrument, like an oblong comb. "Sometimes." He smiled as she studied the fork.

"It depends on what the capital needs. I've been to rallies where the capital will increase the amount of oxygen in the air to calm crowds, and I've been to concerts where they'll reduce the amount of helium so that basses can hit a note lower."

As he spoke, Lena stuffed her face with the contents of the bowl. Small grains, squishy beans, and a cornucopia of spices assaulted her mouth and the space surrounding it. Some bites were too hot, some were too salty, others included a chaotic mixture of pumpkin and peanuts, but every time she cringed it reminded her that she was alive, that there was room for mistakes and accidents and sorrow in life. She looked up at Sado, rice clinging to her eyebrows. "Why are you telling me all this?"

"Somehow you've managed to unify a group of people that started as a bramble of refugees. What Talia and I have been trying to do for near a decade, you've accomplished without trying in just a few months. Lena, you'd never been part of my plan, because you were just an extra body that we had to worry about, but it seems that that is what the Outcry needed. Something that they could care for and want to protect."

Lena wiped the food from her face, revealing a scowl. "I can take care of myself. And why do you let Talia be in charge when you're not there? She's mean and she doesn't care about anyone but herself."

Sado sighed and patted the top of Lena's head. "In time, you may understand. Her life hasn't been as easy as you may think, and it may not seem like it, but a lot of it is an act. If you got to know her, you would find she is quite amiable."

"Amiable? What are you, a politician? I don't care about the life she's had. I don't trust her. Just because she's broken a nail doesn't mean she can treat people how she does. Like children. Like we're just a bunch of breathers."

The fire crackled hungrily, casting soft shadows about the walls. Sado added new wood to the embers, stirring them in silence. Lena waited. She knew she was right. At least, she thought she was right. If she wasn't right, she at least knew she wasn't wrong. Right?

Sado spoke softly, barely audible over the new logs crackling with flame. His eyes looked fatigued. "You've found your way to us over and over. Why do you want to join the Outcry?"

Lena let her fork clink down onto the plate. It rattled and then resolved to be silent. "I don't." She smirked at his confusion. "The Outcry isn't right. The capital isn't right. But neither are wrong, either. They're just," she scrunched her cheeks, "different."

She looked down at her feet. "When you learn to work together, and not just be a bunch of whiny adults, then I'll want to join. But not the Outcry, and not the capital. I'll join the world that should be."

The cabin filled with Sado's laughter. It rattled the rafters and a thin coating of dust and dirt snowed down from them. "You certainly are a dreamer, aren't you? And what would you have us do? Vote? Can you imagine a member of the Council who desires to reintegrate with the earth just so he can lose any power he holds?"

Lena stood, her legs no longer shaky. She looked up at Sado, her eyes glaring. "No. You need to become

President Durin. A single faceless leader. The Outcry will think they're in control. The Council will think they've won. All while you teach them to work together and lead us back home."

Her eyelids quivered, and her hands were clamped into blood-drained fists. Her heart stomped. It brushed her with a flutter of warmth. This was the sensation she felt any time she was proud of herself. Or maybe any time she deserved to be proud of herself. Whatever it was, she didn't want the feeling to stop. It wasn't often she'd think of an idea that was any bigger than just an idea. It tasted sort of funny. Unusual, at least. She wondered if it meant anything. But wondering that meant she was trying to think of more things bigger than just ideas. And she'd already done that once today, so she felt tired. Her eyes flicked back to Sado, whose eyes were doing that thing they did when he was deep in thought and wasn't really in the room. She waited.

When he entered the room again, Lena was sitting, picking at the last bits of grain from her bowl and off her chin. He cleared his throat. "It'll never work," he said, but he sounded uncertain.

"Why?"

"There's no way I could make it that close to Durin."

Something about his words reminded Lena of a soap opera. As if he was trying to lead her down a path that was already written.

He can't get close, she thought. *Well...what do I do when I need to get close to somewhere?* She crinkled her nose. *I get rescued.* She shook her head. It clicked, and she smiled. "I get captured."

He eyed her. "What's that?"

"You could get captured. They'd take you to the capitol. For questioning. And then... Then you could escape. And find Durin. Bing bada boom. Then you're the king. Easy peasy." She scraped a burnt piece of corn from the table and popped it into her mouth triumphantly.

"I'm too much of a threat. I wouldn't get anywhere near him without a hundred guards barreling down around me."

"Or her," she corrected him.

"Or her?"

"Yeah, you said near *him*. But we don't know if Durin is a girl or a boy. It's just an old face and a voice. Right?"

He grinned. "Or you." His face seemed to be lighting up towards her. Not quite maniacally, but questionably close.

"I'm tired. Can you just spell it out so we don't need to do the 'or this, or that, what is who, why is where' and all that. What are you talking about?"

Sado sat, taking in another moment of calm. "They think you're dead. If they find you alive, they'll bring you in for questioning." A breath. "You wouldn't be deemed a threat." Another. "You could get Durin." He exhaled. "This could work."

Lena's chest was ablaze with fireworks. Was he serious? He looked serious. But she was just a girl! That's what everyone said. Everyone always and anyone forever as long as she remembered.

A task? A mission? What did he mean by "get Durin"? Get him what? So much could go wrong. She could trip! And get locked in a closet. Again! Wasn't that how this whole mess had gotten started? How could he ask her to get locked in a closet again? After all she'd been through. She was ready to retire. To watch her kids grow old. To nap for an eternity. To be ground into soil. To give birth to a plant. She could feel leaves growing on her arms already. Somebody was whispering to her. A plant whisperer? Maybe it was just someone far away? Someone was saying, "Lena." But that was her name in a past life. Before she was a plant. Her name was now Achillea Millefolium.

"Lena," the voice said again. She rubbed her leaves to her petals. Sado was looking back at her.

"Lena. It's all right." He kneeled over her. Her body lay on the patched bed where she'd awoken earlier. "It was just an idea. No one would force you to go through with it. It'd be your decision. And I'd be right behind you all the way."

She took a breath. The room seemed dimmer than she'd remembered it. "Once they captured me, how could I escape? How could I get Durin? And what would I do once I did?"

"I'll teach you. All you need to do is get close. And I'll be waiting for your word." He pulled the cover over her.

"We can work with your strengths. Is there anything you're particularly good at?"

She thought for a moment. "I'm really good at faking accents!"

Sado leaned back, a new wrinkle forming across his brow. "Well," he paused, "I guess it's something."

XXI.

The beat of her heart matched the cadence of her footsteps as she scrambled along the forest floor. She darted behind a tree. The inhale of winter air was sweet. She forced herself to keep moving.

Lucent emerald cascaded down from the canopy, speckling a powdered white. Each footstep imprinted the snow as a fleeting memory. She dared look back. Only quiet. And trees. She turned and continued to run.

There wasn't time to think. Not about how she'd been on the earth for nearly three months, nor about how Spring would soon bring about a valley of birdsong, or even about how the air tickled her hair, now as jagged as the rocks she'd used to cut it. There was only time to run.

She could feel her stomach knotting itself into a cramp. It pinched her right side. Dehydration perhaps? She'd been on the go for nearly two days. What was it that Sado had said? Be careful of bears? She laughed and her cramp flared. Through the wince she refocused. No, it was something else he had said. Right before he set her loose. *If you're not hunting, you're being hunted.* Her body shivered, and she shifted her eyes left and right. *A little further*, she thought.

Just as the trees thinned near the edge of the woods, her stomach pulled her to the ground. *Not now!* She heaved and painted the blank snow with a palette of blistered berries and shredded carrot. So much for the morning's breakfast. *Though when did I have carrots?* She pushed herself up and stumbled forward, holding her side. The sound of mechanized wheels whispered somewhere behind her. The rustling of bushes ignited an angry bird choir, not quite ready for their concert. In front of her, she could see the ridgeline. The forest opened up to what may have been the edge of the world. On its rim stood a lone willow tree, seemingly having contemplated its fate for a hundred years. The end was in sight.

She lined her body up with the tree. Her eyes traced over the path. *Good*, she thought. It looked untouched. She smiled. Her plan could actually work. Her eyes continued down to her feet. All she had to do was make sure she didn't slip. Or trip. Or stumble and fall. Or any number of a variety of actions that would result in her messing up.

She watched as her shoes moved up and down. They seemed faster than she remembered. Snow sunk and fluffed in spurts of mist around them. Her legs were pistons and her soles were stamps, marking the ground with impermanent checks of approval. She was reminded of Ms. Pluck on the day that she first heard the voices of the Outcry. Ms. Pluck had seemed so much like a steam engine chugging towards her. How far she had come since that day. And how far Ms. Pluck would never go again.

Her chest strained in lament. Or fatigue. She wasn't sure. Her mind flickered with images of the tubes. How had Ms. Pluck managed to catch her that day? She'd been planning to blend in, to go unnoticed, but something had gone wrong. *I remember standing there, thinking that if those jerks didn't push and lock me in that utility bin—*

Thwap!

A pellet of frozen paint shattered and bled down the back of Lena's neck. The impact pushed her forward, and she flopped onto the ground, her face filled with powder. The numbness muffled the throbbing that had begun to swell behind her eyes. She lay in defeat, sprawling sunken under a foot of snow. At the sound of metallic squeaking, she rolled over and let out a shriek. Behind her, in rusted sheen, sat a glorified trash can. It revved its motor, reveling in its victory. On its front were two nozzles. The smaller one was covered in burgundy paint, while the larger one emitted a slow cranking sound.

"Now I hardly see that as necessary," Lena sat up.

"Ker-thunk!" A fluorescent orange net shot out of the nozzle. It blanketed Lena, and without another word the silver beast drove back towards the forest, dragging its captive in tow.

By the time they'd reached the cabin, Lena was a large snowball. From her jutted twigs and leaves and all manner of forest paraphernalia. Sado's laughter let her know that they'd arrived.

"I don't know why you have Mortin drag me all the way back here. Once I get hit, the game is over." She pushed and twisted about in the net and the ground became coated in ferns. The light on Mortin's head switched off, and Lena, as a triumphant fish, wiggled free.

"If I'm not mistaken," he cleared his throat, "there was a certain incident where you were tagged, but you claimed otherwise." Tree shadows played on his face as he smirked down at her.

"I still don't think that counted. The paint didn't break." The back of her head flared again.

"So what happened this time?"

She grumbled and didn't answer.

"Got distracted again," he answered for her. He sighed, his jovialness sobering.

"I did a lot better. I was leading him to a trap." She glanced at Mortin and continued in a whisper. "I was leading him to the ravine. I covered up a sheet of ice near the old willow tree. If I had just made it a little further, he would have slipped and slid and tumbled right off the edge!"

"But he didn't. You lost focus."

Her arms crossed. "If I don't stop and let my mind wander, then I'm no better than someone from the cities."

"Yeah, and if you stop at the wrong moment then you may never have time to let your mind wander again." He paused. "You *are* someone from the cities."

"Sure, but I made it outside."

"And once you start thinking like that, you're no better than the Council." He looked away, his face sullen. "I think we're done here." He turned to walk inside.

"No, wait! I'm sorry for being such a Snarglops! I'll try harder. I will, I really will."

Sado looked back at her. His eyebrow rose. "What, pray tell, is a Snarglops?"

Her shoulders sank in relief. "Well, no one really knows. It's like a monster. Some say they crawl out from the corpses of kings." She made gurgling sounds and squished her face as if she were being born from the precipices of death. "Because no matter how hard a king may try, he can't take his power with him when he dies. And it's all gotta go somewhere." Her head shook up and down in affirmation.

"Though some say," she kneeled down and whispered, "Snarglops are lies that grow and grow," she stretched out her arms, "until finally they're so big that they eat their weavers. Nom!" She slapped her hands together. "But I believe," she traced a crescent into the snow, "that it's a beast who in the moonlight looks like a friend."

Sado blinked, unsure if there was more.

She sighed. "But I just meant, I'm sorry for being a jerk."

His lips blinked a calculated grin. "It's important that you realize that you're no better a person than anyone, because as soon as you start thinking otherwise, then you're much worse. Do you understand?"

"But people always thought they were better than me. And they always teased me for it."

"People are afraid of difference. You, Lena," he placed his hand on her shoulder, "upset the balance of things. All about you is an air of change. When they are afraid, people will do what they think they need to do in order to protect themselves. Use your imagination, Lena, and think about what it's like to be someone else. You might be able to see things that were once invisible to you." Sado turned around to walk to the door.

Lena's eyes lit in concern. "But I thought we would continue training. I'm sorry for what I said. I will try. I will."

"We will continue, but you've had a physically arduous day. Let us train your mind now."

"I don't see why I need to learn about history and society and all that boring stuff. If all I need to do is lead you to Durin, then I should be learning to sneak and creep and slip in and out of the shadows."

"The time and chance to learn should never be wasted. While your body rests, your mind can be active."

"But I'm not tired." Leaves fell from her hair. She was autumn on a winter solstice.

Sado stopped and stared at her. She felt his eyes burrow into her. She knew she was breathing heavier than usual, and that her muscles were sore, but she had to push. She couldn't have him taking it easier on her, else they'd never get anywhere. Her shoulders pushed back and her chest puffed out. Whatever it was that was next, she'd be ready. She had to be.

He shook his head and walked inside.

Her chest deflated in defeat and exhaustion. She wasn't weak, though. She couldn't let him think that. She knew how others thought of her: how she was always being taken care of, always being rescued. Just a child. She ground her feet into the earth. If he wouldn't let her train more today, she'd have to take it upon herself.

She twisted towards Mortin. He sat in a fading light, casting his mundane shadow onto the snow, staring out into the forest as if bored. His blasé expression told her that she was just too easy to catch. Not even a challenge. She scowled.

"How dare you! How dare you! Look at me!" She strode towards him and slapped him on the side. The anger in her hand boiled through her, and she stifled a scream. She forced the pain up her sinuses and out her eye in the form of a bubbling droplet of water.

"Time for a rematch. I'm serious. Get ready." She slid open the back of Mortin, exposing a panel of knobs and needles. "Let's see, he usually pushes about here." Her finger stabbed at a faded orange button. "And then he twists," she raised an eyebrow, "maybe this one?" Mortin's light pattered red and yellow. "And then..." She stopped. A shadow spread across Mortin's bare back, hiding his controls in a diffused grey. Her pupils dilated.

"What are you doing?"

She turned to see Sado's outline bracketed in the harsh glow of the doorway. "What are *you* doing?" she said while holding her glare. *Good one, Lena. Turn the tables. Throw him off. If he's not going to train you, it's his loss.*

Sado stepped from the doorway. In one hand he held his cane, in the other was a thin leather case with a warm green handle. He thrust it at her, and she caught it with two shaking arms. She looked at it, and then to Sado. With his left hand he twisted the top of his cane and pulled. A thin blade slid noiselessly from its body. She inhaled.

"It's time for the next phase of your training. It's time we make you less helpless."

She blinked to Sado, to the object in her hands, to Mortin, back to— She whipped her head to Mortin as he beeped and sputtered. Mortin blinked green, chirped three times, and without a word, drove off into the forest. Only his cylindrical silhouette cast of bushes remained. She bit the inside of her cheek as the heat of Sado's scowl radiated down upon her. *Helpless.*

XXII.

Light saturated the tunnels the instant that Joseph opened the door. He squinted and lifted his hand to slow the flood. It had been hours since he'd seen more than a few strands of light and cycles since he'd seen real daylight. They had spent the last week navigating the maintenance tunnels, slowly sneaking back and reintegrating members of the Outcry into the cities. His legs trembled. They threatened to give way, but he recognized their bluff. He'd made it this far, and the radio was in sight. Had Lena spoken that moment, he'd be able to hear her over the static. And that gave him strength.

He felt Lin squeeze his shoulder from behind, and he turned back with a soft grin. As the door slid closed, Lin removed her mask, and he realized that he still had his on. When was the last time they'd had fresh air? He shook his head, removing his own tank. A rich gulp flooded his lungs. As he pulled in deeper, he felt his ribs expand and his back pop in three locations. *To breathe freely,* he thought.

He turned back to the nursery, his eyes now stable with its luminance. Among the forest of potted plants remained a collection of several hundred people. He swallowed hard and directed his words quietly to Lin. "Are we even making progress?" His head felt light.

Lin remained silent and he followed her gaze to the radio.

"Lin," he raised his voice, "we plant ten, maybe fifteen, people a day. How long can this continue before we're caught? Talia can't just keep creating new records, can she? Our luck has got to run out at some point."

Lin turned to him abruptly. Her face was stern and exhausted. She pointed at him and pushed her finger hard into his chest. "Joe, this is bigger than you. You've got to compose yourself, because these people," she lowered her voice until it was barely audible, "these people need to believe we know what we're doing. They need to believe that the Outcry is about to take control. Because if they don't," she glanced from side to side, "if they don't, then their hesitance and uncertainty will boil into panic, and then we've lost everything. If we want to control our future, then they've got to believe that we're in control of the present." She looked him hard in the eyes. "So keep it together."

He blinked, wide-eyed. Silence filled the space between them as she sat at the table and flipped the radio on, constantly making small notes in her journal, as if on the brink of discovery. He eyed her cautiously. She had been on edge since they'd left Lena at the cabin, but she'd refused to discuss it. They were all worried about Lena, but he didn't think that justified Lin's temperament. He sighed. *Youth.*

An hour passed without words. When the radio finally gurgled Lena's long-drawn "hellooo", Lin's attitude turned to excitement.

"Lena! You're late!"

The radio paused and Joseph could feel Lena's scowl through the box. "I'm not late! Your world is the one that's constantly moving. If you'd stop chasing the sun, maybe we could have more than a few minutes of conversation!"

Lin laughed and it forced a smile from Joseph. It felt like an eternity since last they'd all shared a laugh. It was only a few minutes a week that they had an opportunity to talk with Lena, but it made the days worthwhile. It gave them moments to look forward to. A reason to keep going.

Once Lena had learned that her father was Joseph's mentor, she'd insisted on hearing stories about him. How he had led the rewiring of Old Brin to keep it afloat. How he had been instructed to help reconstruct the capitol so that no one person could navigate it. How he had been caught.

After she had learned that his death hadn't been an accident it had taken weeks for her to want to talk about him again. Joseph felt helpless on his side of the box. Even if he could have comforted her, their short window of communication didn't allow it. He remembered one of their conversations stopping when the word "Tulu" slipped from Lena's mouth. The name was a trigger for her detachment.

"I'm starting to learn how to hold a sword!" she squeaked.

Lin and Joseph looked at each other, eyebrows raised. "That's nice. What's a sword?" he asked.

"It's like an electric baton." She paused. "But without the electric. And sharp. Really sharp!"

Lin looked off into the distance with a twinge of apprehension, then refocused and scratched something into her notebook. "Why do you need to learn that?"

Static crackled momentarily and then Sado's voice resonated over the radio. "Because I've decided that it would be advantageous for her to know how to defend herself."

"But she's—"

"I've decided," he cut her off. And that was that.

A few minutes later the conversation ended, not from disagreement but from distance.

"I'm worried," Lin said as she turned off the radio. "If Sado is teaching her violence, then Sado is expecting her to have to deal with violence. And if that's the case, there is something he's not telling us."

Joseph touched her shoulder. "If Sado thinks it's best, then we've got to trust that he knows what he's doing. It's like you said, we need to support the Outcry's decisions."

She pushed his hand away. "Our new foundation should not be laid with blood."

He winced at the words. He knew them all too well. Esta's voice repeated them in his mind as his heart beat faster.

"I know what violence can do to a kid. When you start to get your way because of it," she bit the words, "when it becomes easy, it's hard to see other solutions."

"Lin, if there's something you want to talk abou—"

"I don't," she ended his sentence.

It was seldom that Joseph heard Lin speak about her past. She would relive her happier moments with vivacity, but the rest was a locked door. He knew she'd grown up in an orphanage. He knew that the Council had Recycled one of her best friends. But anytime she spoke of her past, she became distant. Disassociated. There were never any specifics, just vague wisps of a sad story. She was similar to Lena in this way. She'd spent her entire life building up precautious barriers; to tear them down all at once would be detrimental. Thick skin filled with a fragile sense of reality. *Careful,* he cautioned himself. *Little by little.*

XXIII.

"How's she doing?" Talia's voice whispered over the radio.

"She's making progress, but she needs more time." He glanced over his shoulder to a narrow hallway. It was empty.

"I'm not sure how much longer we can hold out. The Council has started screening everyone. They're tagging names to breaths. We're not just numbers anymore." The radio fizzled in a forced laugh. "I guess we got what we wanted."

"You know that I can't rush her training."

There was a pause. "I just hope you're right about her."

"Me too, Tal." Sado glanced to the hallway again. "I think she's awake. I'd better go. Be safe."

"I mi—" He clicked off the box as Lena walked into the room. She rubbed her eyes. Her hair, in typical fashion, stuck up in five different directions.

"Morning," she yawned, stretching. "Were you talking to yourself again?"

He chuckled. He'd forgotten what it was like to have such good hearing. "I tried the radio."

Her eyelids leapt open. "Did you hear from Lin? It's been almost three weeks! Did you know she used to write speeches for the Councilman from Deloy? She said that politicians have a certain way of speaking and if you listen, you—"

Sado held up his hand. "Just static. They should pass over again tonight, so let's try then, and we'll see if we can hear from Joe and the crew."

She smiled at that, and he exhaled in relaxation in a way that he hoped was unnoticeable. He wasn't used to children, had never really spent much time with them. Until he'd met this one, he'd assumed them to just be placeholders for people. Just breathers. But he saw something in Lena, undoubtedly the same potential that others had seen. He only needed to direct it.

Lena stepped softly to the left and he refocused on her, though he let it appear that his eyes were wandering. He'd noticed when she'd walked in that her hand was fidgeting behind her. Her back was straightened in a minutely more uniform way. Most likely she had the sword tucked up her shirt, in hopes to surprise him. He thumbed the knife concealed beneath the table and slipped the blade up his sleeve.

She'd been edging her way between him and his cane, which lay propped against the stack of logs. *Smart girl, trying to cut off my resources*. He resisted a smile. He knew that she believed he was drifting in thought, upon some alternate edge of reality. Similar to how she daydreamed. The problem, he had ascertained, was that she still assumed that other's minds worked in the same way as hers. Sure, he was aware that she believed herself unique, but until she studied how memories and thoughts moved through the brain, she wouldn't realize how unique of a mind she had.

He turned his head away from her, just enough to give her a sense of the upper hand. The fire cast a soft glow in the pre-dawn and Lena's shadow launched into the air towards him. Her blade slid out from behind her, and he listened as it plucked a group of threads at the base of her shirt.

Sloppy, he thought. He pushed the knife outward, against the inner edge of his cuff, and twisted his body to standing. The sword met his sleeve met his knife, and in the moment of their collision, he threw his weight into his arm.

Lena's eyes flared as in one instant his arm stopped her and in another his leg swept behind her and slammed her to the ground. He pushed down the sword's edge until it kissed her throat. He grinned.

"You must not assume that you have the upper hand. For only when your opponent is buried in the earth will your hand be above his." He stood, leaving her wide-eyed on the floor. "Now, it's time for breakfast. No weapons at the table." He pulled the knife from his shirt, displayed it to her, and slid it back under the radio's mantle.

***

The day passed by in an instant. They ate, he taught, and she failed to learn. He bit back his frustration.

"Point to the pommel."

She touched the base of the sword.

"Good. Now, where is the fuller?"

She ran her finger along the blade's indentation.

"Very good! And find the center of percussion."

Lena held the hilt straight and tapped the pommel. Her eyes tread lightly up the steel and stopped at the point where resonation was nonexistent. She nodded towards it.

"Exactly! Now tell me the purpose of those three things."

He glared down at her. As he expected, her mouth contorted and she shrugged in uncertainty. "To better slay the beast?"

He exhaled audibly with the intention to make her shrink lower. She did.

"Every piece of the puzzle plays its part. You must understand how each component affects the whole. Now what did I tell you are the three most important characteristics of a sword?"

Her ears perked. "Oh! Its balance, its weight, and its deadliest point."

"Good. Now, what is the purpose of the pommel?"

She blinked, scrunched her nose, and crinkled her forehead. *Please, Lena, just say it. Balance, the pommel gives the sword balance!* His eyes opened wider as her lips took form.

"Baaahh..."

Yes, just say it.

"Ahhh, I don't know." Her body slunk to the ground, and she covered her face.

Sado raised his cane from its sheath and tapped her on the shoulder. "Dead. Never let your guard down. Never look away."

Lena looked up. He could see weariness and worry in her eyes. Maybe he was working her too hard. But if she couldn't handle this, then she wasn't worth his time. He didn't want to send her to be slaughtered, but if she wasn't going to be a leader, she was useless. He didn't need another follower.

He sat down next to her on the floor and they breathed in silence, slumped in defeat. From the corner of his eye he could see her staring at him, pleading at him to make eye contact. He looked away.

He wouldn't be able to just drop her back at home and pretend like nothing had happened. They both knew that she was in too deep for that. He wasn't worried about what she could say to the Council. He was worried about what she could say to the people. The Outcry's protectiveness towards her could ignite a revolt, and he'd already seen that that wasn't the answer.

To bring the earth to the people, he needed to bring the people to the earth. All the people. Otherwise, they'd be back where they started: stealing from the world, crippling it, and looking for an escape. No, he couldn't let her go back home. *Kill her now, or feed her to the Council?* He sighed. Which would be more merciful?

Lena cleared her throat. He finally met her eyes. "Let me try." Her voice didn't whine or plead. It only stated. Maturity he didn't expect.

He gave her a soft smile. "There won't be anyone to catch you if you fall."

She nodded.

"When you get into the capitol—"

"I know," she interrupted. "Just get caught." She picked herself off the ground and walked to the radio. She was quieter than usual, Sado noted. Even her thoughts seemed to permeate the air less. "Can I talk to them before I go?"

It hadn't occurred to him until now that she might consider Joseph, Lin, and Circ her friends. To him, they were just followers that stood slightly taller than the rest of the crowd. Noticeable, but not noteworthy. For her, they were probably the closest thing to a family that she had left.

"We can hope they'll answer, but there's no guarantee." He pushed himself to stand. A sharp pain prickled across his knee and he winced. Age asked him to stay on the floor, but he ignored its request. "Twist that copper knob until the dial is on thirteen. That should be tonight's channel."

She eyed it steadily. "This microphone is for talking into?" He nodded. "What's this other mic for?" She pointed to the heavyset box in the back corner of the table.

"That's for voice manipulation. It's used if you think unwelcome ears are listening. We should be all right tonight."

"Oh." She turned back to the radio. She twisted the dial. Nine, static. Ten, static. Eleven, static. Twelve, static. Thirteen. Silence. Then...

"...ado are you there? Sado!" Lin's voice crackled from the box.

"Move." He pulled Lena from the table and jumped into the seat. "What's happening?" He pushed down on the microphone.

More silence. "Sado! This is Lin. We can't find Talia." She panted. "They've found the entrance. It's just..."

There was a pause. Lena clawed at his arm. "...About thirty of us left in Old Brin. It's only a matter of time."

"Lin." He spoke firmly, directly to her. "I need you, Circ, and Joseph to get to the capital. Hide in the market. Instructions will follow. Lena and I are on our way. We act tonight."

Her voice flickered in and out of static. "What about the others?"

He hesitated. "On the back of the radio is an orange trigger. Disengage the safety. Flip the switch. You'll have ten minutes." The airwaves fizzled for a few moments. "Do you understand?" More crackling. "Lin!"

"But... the others."

"Lin, you of all people know that the Council will mulch the others either way. This is the only way you get something out of the deal."

She hesitated.

"Keep control. Do you understand?"

"Yes." The radio sighed and then there was only the hush of white noise. He looked over to Lena. Six months had gone by since she'd first come to him, but she still carried the same weight on her shoulders, and soon it could be more. Could her knees hold it? Had her training made a difference? He knew it didn't matter if she failed. It only meant that a new plan would be made and a new day would dawn. It only mattered if she succeeded.

She gazed mutely at him.

"Are you ready?"

The room lingered for a moment unsure to whom he was talking. Lena placed a hand on his shoulder. He looked down and noticed his own hand shaking.

"Are *you*?" she whispered.

XXIV.

A road of snakeskin. Oily. Scaled. Twisting, spiraling, slithering. On either side a chasm sprawled without end. Even in its emptiness the gravity of the void was overwhelming. L'appel du vide. It called to her. The silence whispered sweet nothings with lips on her ear. She tasted of orange zest and cinnamon.

Lena's foot took a step. She followed it. Platelets of translucent emerald shifted under her weight. For a brief moment she could see an earthy flesh beating between the tiles, but just as quickly it vanished.

"How odd," she thought, "to be a giraffe's spot." As she walked, months passed. Days became decades. Each footstep wrote a new tale of the beginning and the end. She was alone, no matter the author.

Behind her trailed a flipbook of her past, each page standing lightly in her faded footprints. Below her, beneath the path, stood colossal structures, holding up the serpent's spine. Their faces were set in stone, yet she knew them to be soft. She couldn't keep them hidden forever in the back corner of her mind.

Her eyes opened briefly to feel a sudden lurch, then they closed again.

Her foot hung over the precipice. A thud rippled through her torso and threatened her balance. She opened the door on her chest and from it her heart leapt. It tumbled through the air and disappeared into the haze. She felt lighter. Powerful. Ineffable.

Who was she? Her body moved robotically and turned from the edge. Gears twisted and sputtered, her feet thromped the ground as she continued down the path. Her mind fought and struggled to be free, but she watched as her hand turned the key in her ear.

Clunk! It locked. She was trapped in her body. Behind her burned the pages of her flipbook. She threw herself against her inner walls. The world shook and twisted and tears flowed from her eyes, down her chin, and onto the snake's back. They burrowed through the scales and bled onto its flesh and as they seared it, the roar of lightning echoed through her path and she was thrown free. Plummeting, plummeting, plummeting, then thump!

Lena awoke with a start. The plane rattled around her. Outside, a storm pattered the windows with rain. The "fasten seatbelt" sign glowed orange. She huffed and stood. Her knees wobbled. Her mouth tasted stale. Citrus and spice lingered from their last meal of toast and jam.

Darkness engulfed the cabin, whether from the weather or the night, she was unsure. They'd boarded during the morning, that was certain.

She made her way up to the cabin. The only light came from the dashboard's tap-panels. Their glow illuminated Sado's face in harsh shadows and gentle amber.

"How long have I been out?" she asked, sitting down in the co-pilot's seat. She spun around once in it and stopped. Since the call with Lin, Sado had been silent. Serious. She slouched her shoulders and hoped he hadn't noticed her spin. She knew he had, though. He saw everything.

"Don't slouch." He stared ahead, flipping through an assortment of screens with flickering maps and telemetry.

She sighed and pushed her shoulders back.

Through the beaded haze she could make out a pulsing red. It faded in and out of the drizzle, keeping itself to their right. She motioned to Sado and he nodded. The same blip echoed on the screen in front of him. Slowly, the plane banked toward the glow and the dot became a line. As the line resolved into two stripes, illuminating a small runway, Lena could make out the silhouette of a dome. She squinted. Lightning flashed, and in its aftermath a labyrinthine network of floating cities burned into her retina. She closed her eyes and projected its complexity onto her eyelids. Next to her she could hear Sado's breath adjust, synchronizing with the blinking lights and the rest of his world.

"Why isn't the nursery lit up?"

Sado didn't answer. Lena's question lingered in the air, and a taste of worry painted the wall's palates. He flipped a switch and walked out of the cabin. The craft proceeded to land itself, and Lena wondered if it ever had been told what a good job it did. She sighed and added that to her mental to-do list. "How unappreciative some people are."

Rain continued to pelt them as Lena followed Sado from the plane. She'd never been on the roof of the world before, but it felt the same as the world she'd left six months ago. Detached and cold. Inside were millions of warm bodies. It contained the people she cared for, the people she didn't know, and the people who thought her dead.

She had a job to do now. Lead Sado to Durin. If she could do that, then she would have a secret. Possibly the biggest, most important secret ever to be kept. She could feel her hands sweating inside her exosuit. Her heart beat against the strap that was tightened across her chest. The sword clung to her back. *Get caught. Escape. Kidnap Durin. Let Sado in. Keep it secret.* She gulped. *Easy peasy.*

She watched as Sado climbed down through a hatch and disappeared. *If you won't talk to me, at least tell me where you're going.* Behind her, the blinking runway shut its eyes for good. Everything has its bedtime.

The goggles she'd put on splashed the world with a dull green, and she stepped onto the ladder that led her into Old Brin. For a time, only her breath and Sado's footsteps kept her company. The metallic walls seemed lifeless to her now, and she bit back tears. They walked past street signs and tattered billboards, yet nothing spoke to her. Her body pushed her forward, and she focused on Sado's footsteps. Where had her world's life gone? The outside sensors of her suit read low O₂ levels, and she could see a slow-moving particulate vapor flowing in the opposite direction of her path.

Ahead of her, Sado stopped. In front of him stood an open entrance. Its door was lying several yards inside the chamber, derailed and limp. Sado turned and walked past her in the direction they'd come from. Her feet threatened to follow him, but she forced herself forward to the doorway. What she saw made her shrink to the floor.

In front of her rested a slaughtered forest. A dusting of bodies and trees covered the moonlit nursery. Ash lingered in the remnant air, until it joined the miasmic flow that led from the room. The ambience of Old Brin was now a burial ground.

Lena felt a hand touch her shoulder. "Many of these were the Council's men, not our own. Let's hope that there were some fortunate enough to make it out. Let's hope Lin and the others made it to the capital. Else this is all for naught." He turned and walked away, his footsteps slow and fading.

"No," her voice shook, "all of these are our bodies." *Just sheep following sheep.*

The blended ash of human and nature brushed against her nylon shell and she let out a cry of helplessness. Her suit protected her and detached her from the world. All she wanted was to help share their pain, to feel the lost memories of the many lives that faded against her, but she couldn't. She was confined in her man-made defenses.

She scratched and pulled at her exterior, feeling the fabric bury under her fingernails, but still, she remained trapped. Safe and helpless.

When she finally managed to move, she found Sado waiting for her at the entrance to Brin. He helped her remove her exosuit and when her hands were free, she wiped away her tears.

They passed unnoticed through Brin. The streets shone with day-lights. Even after six months, the city was still full with the distracted motion of hundreds of artists who had flocked to the city's walls to repaint. Lena watched as the people worked as one, pouring their energy to recreate the art that they'd lost. She felt nauseous. She had done this to them. It had been her idea to remove the paint, to destroy centuries of creativity, love, and passion for her ideal world.

My ideal world, her head ached. *These people have spent their lives on these walls. And I tore them down.* How could she have been so naïve? So selfish?

I thought I was being clever. I thought I had found the solution, but really, I was taking the easy way out. Forcing radical change on people to match my dream. Not inspiring them to dream my dream. This whole time I've seen them as just breathers. Layer-less.

"What have we done, Sado? We've stolen these people's foundations."

Sado kept moving, the sound of his voice trailing behind him. "Their foundations were flawed. We're setting them free."

Lena felt her nails press into her palms, her hands clenched into tiny fists. She could feel the weight of the sword pulling down on her shoulder. She shook her head. "That's not for us to decide."

She continued walking, letting the sounds of crying scratch at her mind. She wondered if her home was still her home, but there was no time to check. There was only time to move.

Kardel was a different form of chaos. Its Councilman had settled on leaving the city's murals bare in favor of the view of the outside world. Time there was different. The true night's darkness told the city to sleep, while the dancing of rain against the dome exterior brought the city's population to its edge. Families watched and applauded at claps of thunder. She could feel their happiness and their fear. She wished she could join them, but she had to press onwards. Even as these people celebrated their new world, she knew it was with heavy hearts. This new world had been thrust upon them. The choice had not been theirs.

When they'd made it to Racine it became clear to her that the world was in dispute with itself. Each city's Councilman had his own plan for the city, and Racine, being the city of cities, had a hundred different plans. Lights lit half the city, while the moon lit the rest. Trails of paint led to alleyways where brawls were being started and broken. For some, the fear of losing the sound of rain overthrew their fear of asphyxiation. A siren blared the words, "Limit to limit; fuel to fuel; create to create." The doors of the capitol stood ajar.

"Remember," Sado said, his stare washing over the crowd of people at the market, "Just go in and get caught. They'll take you to the White Laboratory. From there, take the stairs three stories down, go through the Water Way, and Durin's door will be at the end of the corridor. Simple." He forced a laugh.

"Can't I come with you to find the others first?"

Sado kneeled down and enfolded her hands in his. Their eyes met. She couldn't remember if he'd ever dropped to her level before.

"Lena, our plan rests on the fact that they don't know my face. If you come with me, they'll see me and know. You must go. Stick to the plan. Be brave." The tremor in his voice made her question if he'd already given up. "Make Tulu proud. Make your dad proud." He squeezed her hands lightly and walked away, leaving her shivering in front of the capitol. The portrait of Durin stared down at her.

She glided back into the memory of a cycle several weeks after her dad's death.

The classroom door slid closed as she stepped through it. Thirty little faces turned to her with pity in their eyes. They could only sympathize. No one really knew how she felt. The world told her to release her emotions. Express turmoil through art. But these feelings didn't belong to the world. They were hers, and she wanted to keep them. They were all she had left. The teacher, a fragile man at the time, asked her how she wanted to "articulate her anger." She laughed. All she wanted to do was wallow in it. She wanted to plant herself in a hole of her emotions, and when she was ready, she would grow into a new self. But people would never give others time for that. They would want to be part of the struggle, so that they could grow too, without having to understand the pain.

Lena looked to the capitol. She balled her hand into a fist. "Today," she said to no one, "I'm alone. No one holds me up." She bit the side of her cheek. In her dad's voice she whispered, "Go get 'em," and walked towards the door.

The entrance slid back and forth, jammed by a small cylinder at its base. A voice repeated, "Stand clear of the closing door," but it sounded strained, like it had been repeating itself for a phase.

Lena inspected the object to find a small flashlight. As she stepped through the arch, she picked it up. The door slid closed with a "thank you." She eyed the flashlight quizzically and flicked it on. A purple hue coated the wall, and her eyes flared. *A fire-sword!*

She illuminated the walls with it but saw nothing except for the light's faint glow. She wasn't quite sure what she'd been expecting. A small hope for invisible directions, maybe, but that too had faded quickly. She tucked the fire-sword in her back pocket. Someone had wanted her to have it.

Now, to just get caught. Her mind frowned. The halls were deserted. She cleared her throat. "Hello?" The word disappeared down the tube and around the corner. It didn't return. Her footsteps clanked as she walked. She passed an office labeled "Kardel Administration," but its lights were faded grey.

Each tunnel seemed to trifurcate every few yards, and by the fifth turn she knew she was successfully lost. She opened a door to reveal a room full of doors piled atop each other. She closed it, and from behind it heard a soft squeak. When she opened it again, the room had disappeared and was replaced by a series of stairs. Her head shook from side to side with wide eyes. *A labyrinth only conquerable by a collective memory.*

She followed the hill of steps that went up and down and back up again, and by the time she'd reached the staircase's pinnacle, she wasn't entirely sure she was still in the city, let alone the capitol. She sat and exhaled, her breath matching the light breeze of the vent on her neck.

She shifted her weight against the metal grate, allowing it to scratch her back. A tingle shot up her spine. This had happened before. She turned and looked at the paneling. On it was engraved "Maddington 375". She gave it a warm smile. Her dad had shown her this vent-covering model. He'd said it had the most convenient panel because it could be removed without any tools. It only required torsion, which meant under regular strains it was secure. It breathed at her again and tickled her nose. "Pshhhhh," it whispered in her ear.

Her mind buzzed. Was it talking to her? Would it be rude not to answer it? "Hi, Maddington 375, er…Maddi." She spoke softly, trying not to alarm it. "I know you don't recognize me, but I'm not going to hurt you. I'm just taking a rest."

It paused for a moment. "Whisssssp, whisssp, whisssp," it exhaled, singing through her hair.

She exhaled a faint smile. At least she'd have a friendly vent to keep her company. Maybe it knew where everyone was? "Pardon me, Maddi, but I was wondering. Do you know where everyone is? I'm a bit lost."

Its silver gridded lips lay silent as it contemplated the question. Back behind its paneling, Lena noticed a faint glow she'd overlooked before. The vent's passageway was lit just enough for her to see that it was no more than a foot wide, but its depth appeared indefinite.

"Well?" She was feeling impatient.

It grumbled. "Sssssomewhere in Old Brin?"

The words made Lena shiver. Now, she'd never really spoken with vents, as they'd always been a bit airy to her, but she assumed, similar to walls, that they weren't meant to speak human. After all, that's what humans spoke, and if vents spoke it, then what would humans speak? She pressed her ear against its cover.

On a faint wisp it sighed, "No."

Lena's eyes opened wide. That was a person speaking. Maybe two people. Possibly even a room of people. She climbed to her knees and contorted her lips, inspecting the vent. How had he opened these again? Pull and twist? She pulled at the vent's mouth and attempted to rotate it. It didn't budge. Its breath stopped and the words vanished. She had to get closer. She scratched her head.

Twist and pull! Her dad's words resonated in her head, and as its lips came off with a thwunk. She patted them and laid the cover in the hall.

"Let us meet another day. Farewell Maddi!"

Lena pushed her body through the narrow shaft, her hands pulling from the front while her feet pushed from the back. Her belly slid along the metal, and she could feel its chill through her shirt. She tried to force herself around a corner, but her knees were stuck. She scowled and looked ahead.

The light had been coming from another opening. Its mouth lay six feet from her, but she couldn't budge. She cupped her hands around her ears and directed them towards the light.

An older woman's voice spoke with high, scratchy tones. "Well, I think that we've wasted too many resources scraping Old Brin. Clearly, he's not there."

"Resources?" an older gentleman bellowed. "People! He burned his own people and ours alive. As much as I support the people's right to tear down the murals, this violence has to stop!"

The woman chortled. "What you're allowing the citizens of Kardel to do is blasphemous. I mean really, letting terrorist plots reshape your city?"

"The people want it. Am I not supposed to represent the people?"

A chorus of dissonance echoed after this statement. Lena counted ten, maybe twelve different voices, either applauding or guffawing at his words.

The woman tapped her nails on something metal and the room quieted. "The people don't know what they want. That is why we are here. To show them."

There was a sharp digital tone and Lena heard the room's occupants shift uncomfortably. The woman stopped talking. There were footsteps, a click, and the tone ceased. Then a voice sounded. One she'd heard countless times. One hidden behind a still face.

"I was not informed that there was a Council meeting tonight," Durin scorned.

Lena pushed her neck forward as far as it would go, which was not much further than it already was. Oh, if only she were a giraffe.

The woman spoke with a hesitation in her voice. "We didn't see it necessary to disturb you. We were only discussing the updates on the search for the Outcry's leader. If anything had come about, we certainly would have informed you."

The speakers crackled. "You mean, if something such as the ruin of an entire platoon had occurred?"

The only response was breathing. The aligned oscillations of the twelve Council members. Lena followed their breaths, so as not to be heard.

"I see," Durin continued. "Well then, let me be the first to tell you that while you all have sat idly discussing an uneventful search, my guards have taken captive the terrorist leader."

Lena gasped. He had to be bluffing. How could they have found him? She clawed at her side, trying to keep herself from screaming.

"He was discovered outside of the capitol near the market."

The counselor from Kardel interrupted. "But how can we be sure it's him? We've found no trace of who this leader is."

"As was discussed when the incident over Kardel occurred, we had an inside member of the Outcry come forward. Since then, we've had her keep us updated on any movements of this 'Sado' character that she became aware of."

Lena could feel her chest heaving. She flailed, trying to push herself closer to the screen. *It can't be true. It can't be over.*

She twisted and kicked. Her foot hit something hard and the vent twanged violently. The room hushed just as she heard a yelp from behind her. She strained her neck to look back as a hand grasped her ankle. The scream she'd been holding back leapt from her mouth and reverberated through the capitol. The hand pulled her from her perch as her ears rang from her own echoes.

Before she had time to struggle, a needle pricked her ankle and the world faded. Her last sight was of three men in grey uniforms, one of which was clutching his hand and whimpering. He looked familiar, like someone she had bitten before. In that moment she laughed and cried.

For what it was worth, her plan had worked. She had been caught.

XXV.

Two people talked from a world away. Their voices were quiet, masked in a muffled haze of distance. Lena could feel herself waking from a dreamless sleep, or maybe a state of unconsciousness. Whatever drug they'd slipped her, it had felt familiar. Almost as if her body had been adjusting to it. Her eyelids remained closed, but she felt her cornea rub against them, shifting left, right, down, up, without pattern. As her mind got closer to her body, the voices became clearer. They were in the same room with her. Only her mind had been a world away.

Against her wrists, the tattered softness of leather restrained her arms from motion. She rotated her ankle slightly and found that her legs were free. *Possible resource,* she noted. She'd need to get her shoes off, though. Toes were the key to everything. She took another breath. It had occurred to her that if she synchronized with the world, she could hide. *Well*, she thought, *at least I would stick out less.*

The men were talking of gambling. Betting about memories, or reconstruction, or the plasticity of youth. She wasn't sure what that last part meant. They were using phrases like synaptogenesis, amygdala reactivity, and pruning. She wished she knew how flowers fit into this discussion, but she didn't have time to find out. Her eyes flicked open; a crystallization of sleep parted with her lashes.

"Hello." Her throat was drier than she expected it to be, causing the word to sound wispy.

The room hushed and turned to her. Its walls were grey, its equipment was grey, and even the lights seemed to emit greyness. The only white part about the lab was the men's coats. She sighed. If they hadn't taken her to the white room, then she was up a tube without a tank.

"She's awake," the younger of the two piped up. His anxiety was sapid, like powdered latex.

"Astute observation," Lena and the older man mocked in unison. They glanced at each other for but a moment with the hint of a grin. Lena liked this man already. He turned away to pick up a clipboard, leaving her smiling at the observer. His eyes were framed, two portraits mirrored about the bridge of his nose. Lena's head throbbed as the hint of a memory ended before it began. She winced at the pain. *What just happened?* She bit her cheek.

The spectacled man walked to the screen beating on her right and tapped on it. His nametag glinted in the grey: Dr. Vendin.

"Duke, how do I look through the history on this? I think I just saw a spike."

Duke glanced over, flicking a small needle. A bead of liquid leapt from its tip. "Nonsense. She's had no external stimuli to elicit an irregular response. Check your prescription." He turned back.

Vendin scoffed and shook his head, tapping the screen through a series of menus. His finger ran along the rim of his glasses, adjusting their focus and color. Disgruntled, he began to walk back across the room but tripped and stumbled, catching himself.

"Who took her shoes off?" Lena blinked at the question, wide-eyed, oblivious.

"Don't bother me with trivialities." Duke turned, syringe in hand, and walked towards Lena.

She knew she only had moments. It wouldn't be difficult to escape. Toe the latch and unhook the strap, flip the machine and grab her sword. She eyed it propped against the wall next to her flashlight. But what was the point? She didn't know where she was. If they had Sado, they had the Outcry. And what was there waiting for her, other than an empty home and a world full of empty people?

She saw her dad standing before her. He didn't say anything, just smiled. She was showing him a dance she had made for show-and-tell. Her teacher had said, "Too much physicality." "Too much breathing." "A waste of air." Her dad just turned on the music.

She refocused and found herself back in the room. The glint of her blade pointed at the men in white, who stood backed into a corner. Her bare feet balanced atop the remnants of the toppled machine. Her chair sat empty behind her, watching as her chest lifted up and down in deep rhythm.

No, she thought, *not empty people. Only different.* She hadn't told her body what to do. She'd only let it do it, and it wanted to live, to fight. "Where is Durin?" She exhaled.

Vendin stepped towards her. His hands shook in front of him. "Now, if we can be calm about this, how about you put down your stick and we talk?"

She watched as Duke sidestepped to the corner of her vision. He still held the needle in his hand. *Foolish.*

In a breath, she wrapped the sword above her head and brought it down in front of him. The blade slid through the syringe's glass, leaving its base in his hand and its tip spinning on the floor. A translucence dripped from the sword's center of percussion to a puddle atop the doctor's foot. He stepped back with a hiccup.

"Dr. Vendin?" She trained the sword towards the man in glasses. His head nodded and his body jittered.

"Sit down." Lena motioned to the chair behind her. She focused her breathing and concentrated on his footsteps. The unfamiliarity of the control she had over the room threatened to shake her. A tingling rippled through her jaw. Her mind began to recite, *limit to fuel; fuel to create,* but she knew the mantra was useless now. She forced her mouth into a smile. It made Vendin sweat.

He winced as she strapped down his arms and legs to the chair. "I can't have you using your toes, now can I?" She gave him a pat on the head.

Lena eyed Duke. "Let's go." She walked to the door, the sword trailing behind her like a graceful oversized arm. The hallway was empty.

"What do you want with me?" Duke hadn't moved.

Excellent question, she thought. *I haven't the foggiest, but I can't leave you here.* "This isn't a discussion," she retorted, her shoulders firm. *Hah, nice one!* She squinted, half to appear serious and half to hold back the sweat condensing like dew on her forehead.

The two held a momentary staring bout before he conceded and followed her out into the hall. Vendin's whimpering simmered behind them. As the door closed, she turned back, wondering if he would be okay. The question formed on her lips, but before it left them, the lock clicked shut, cutting off his sniffles.

Her words fizzled away as she read the letters etched on the door. "Duke White, PhD."

He turned to her. "How dare you address—"

"Wait," she could feel butterflies fluttering excitedly in her chest. "You're Dr. White?"

"Yes, and I'll have you know that if any harm comes to me—"

"Yes, yes, but this is your lab? White Laboratory?" She squirmed. A smile broke loose and landed on her face.

"Yes, but I—"

Lena brought the sword to his neckline. She stood a foot shorter than him, but she felt so tall that she could see the crown of his head balding. She giggled. "Where are the stairs? The ones that go down."

She watched his forehead ruffle slightly. The way his jaw slightly clenched told her that he was trying to think his way out of this. She flicked her hand, letting the tip of the blade cut off his left collar button. The wing stuck up, making him resemble a ruffled pigeon. "Stairs."

He about-faced and marched down the hall with quivering knees. She followed a few steps behind. The walls avoided eye contact, and she knew why. They were afraid. Afraid of her and who she was becoming. Afraid in the same way that she was. But she didn't have time to comfort them, let alone herself. She'd gone too far to question her actions now, hadn't she?

The doctor stopped in front of a door. They had to have passed by twenty or more, and this one didn't seem any different. Blue paneled and unlabeled with a silver tap-pad. He glanced back, eyed the blade's edge, and then swiped his badge. A soft breeze of unbalanced air pushed past her. The stairs lit as they entered, revealing a three-story zigzag.

It wasn't a long walk down, but the silence made every step feel like a century. When several millennia had passed, they reached the final step. Another tap-pad stood between them and the hall.

"Give me your badge."

Duke paused in front of the door, his hand outstretched ready to swipe. "But don't you—"

She groaned. She was tired of his constant opposition. She pushed the sword past his arm and skated it skywards, cutting through the chain of his badge. As it fell from his hand, she felt her heart sink. Below her blade, pressed into the white of his sleeve, a slow red saturated. It had slid silently atop the surface of his arm, parting each thread like it was running through a field of poppies.

She bit back a cry as he pulled his arm to his chest and screamed. *No, no, no,* she pleaded in her mind. She'd made him bleed. She'd torn his flesh. *It was an accident,* she wanted to say. *I didn't mean to*, were words she never uttered. She couldn't. She'd stolen this man from his home, she'd led him as his captor, and now she'd cut him and would leave him to suffer.

Her arm reached down, and she forced herself not to shake as she picked up the badge. He wouldn't look at her. She wanted him to look into her eyes and see that it was all a misunderstanding, that she wasn't a bad person, that she wanted to help. If he would just look at her, he would understand, and they'd laugh about it, and she wouldn't have to stop her whole body from rattling into pieces. But he didn't look. He collapsed into the bottom of the stairwell and held his arm, and he sobbed.

She swiped the card and the door opened to a quiet hallway. For a moment it was filled with the sound of pain and fear and confusion, and then it was quiet again. The door slid closed and Lena stood on the other side. The sound of his crying repeated over and over again in her head. She walked away down the tube, praying for some noise to distract her from the quiet.

Why had Sado given her this weapon, this responsibility? He had said that in the moment she needed to use it, it would be against those trying to hurt her. But the doctor was no monster. He was just a man doing his job, like anyone else. The tip of her sword dragged along the ground as she rounded a corner. *Like everyone else.*

Lena blinked and stopped as a pair of black, rounded shoes stepped their way into her vision. The well-oiled sheen reflected the overhead lights of the tube. She felt the padded handle of her blade as she tightened her grip.

Shifting her eyes upwards revealed a second pair of feet adorned with earthy-brown soles. She recognized the moccasins immediately. Paxton stood patiently, waiting for her to make eye contact. Next to him, in an ebony suit, towered the man who'd brought her to the capital.

"Mr. Hulten," Paxton's smooth rasp filled the air, "Are you a spiritual man?"

Hulten's lips pursed. "When the occasion calls for it." His body seemed to shift back slightly.

"Well, it appears as if we are seeing a ghost."

The weight of her chest lifted up and down with her breath. She could strike now. She had her weapon. If she acted fast, she could take Hulten down, and maybe that would be enough to scare Paxton. The thought of that made her bite back a laugh. It was uncertain if anything could scare Paxton. "I don't want to hurt you" was all that she could come up with.

Their silence told her that they couldn't even conceptualize her ability to hurt them. She felt like that first pinecone she'd eaten. How a tree egg had managed to ravage her insides while appearing so docile, she still wasn't sure.

Paxton smiled. "Well, if you've made it this far into the capitol, then you must be looking for Durin."

Her body stilled. *Don't let him talk, Lena. Strike now.* Her legs refused. She was her own monument, cast of bone and skin.

He continued. "It's all right." His voice lowered even more. She wondered if some notes he spoke were inaudible, slipping past her eardrums, directly implanting themselves in her mind. "You've done a great job."

Her breath became shallow.

"We're here to lead you to him. Sado instructed us to bring you the rest of the way."

She flinched at the mention of his name. *But how?*

He turned. "He's just this way." His eyes were so honest. She wanted to see them again. Her body wanted to follow him, the back of his head telling her that he trusted her. She glanced up at Hulten, who hadn't turned. His eyes were different. They were less sunken into his face, almost sitting on the surface. There was empathy in them that seemed out of place. She squinted.

Before she had time to react, he struck. In one instant Hulten's fist was at his side, and the next, it was molding with the back of Paxton's head. His body weight extended with his arm, causing Paxton to progress from standing, to tip toes, to kneeling, to collapsing on the ground in a pile of himself.

Her jaw fell. She wanted to watch it all over again, to figure out what she had missed. Hulten turned towards her, and for lack of a better idea, she raised her sword.

"There isn't much time," he whispered, his voice urgent. "I'll deal with Paxton."

She stared at him as he picked up the pile of man from the floor and dragged it past her. When he noticed her stillness, he stopped. "You must go. Now!" His voice quivered. "Durin is never in the same place for long."

Her head nodded, her body moved, and her lips let out a "thank you." Any moment she tried to think about what had just happened was another moment her mind got lost in confusion. *More distractions*. She shook her head and rounded a corner, then stopped and stepped back, remembering. "There's a doctor in the stairwell," she called to Hulten. "He's hurt," she said in a plea. He nodded and continued on. *Now to find Durin*.

She slid the blade into its sheath and set off in a jog. The tube stretched on for miles. Grey floors, grey walls, grey lights. After a time, her mind questioned if she'd taken the wrong path, but there had only ever been one choice: forward.

In near-uniform intervals, a lone door would bar her way. Each time she swiped the stolen badge she would hear a soft voice say "Hello, Dr. White". That, more than the jogging, took her breath away.

Lena picked up her pace into a run. The doors came at a higher frequency. She felt like a hamster on a wheel. Ahead of her, or maybe behind, she could hear a faint scraping of metal. She broke into a sprint and her legs began to feel the strain. The sound got louder, but the source of it eluded her.

In front of her, in the distance, she saw a door sliding closed. She pushed as fast as her legs would carry her, but by the time she got to the entrance there was no one to be found. She muffled a scream into her shirt and kicked the doorway, leaving a dent. She wanted it to be over.

Her feet pushed her forward as her mind reeled her back. *I had to have missed something. Some turn. Some doorway. Some clue.* She followed a cascade of memories until her heart panged at the thought of Ms. Pluck. *"Hishtory,"* her recollection of the teacher's voice echoed.

"Why do we look to our pasht?" Ms. Pluck looked around the room, waiting for a volunteer. Lena sighed the default phrase, "so that we can control our future." Ms. Pluck shook her head, which surprised the students. "Mish Causht, try thinking for yourshelf, inshtead of jusht repeating. Shometimesh, we musht look to the pasht to shee what truly happened. We cannot shee the future, but too often we ashume we know what happened after the fact. But indeed, the pasht ish jusht the future that ish behind ush. We musht look back in order to shee itsh other shide."

Lena stopped, wide-eyed. Another door stood in front of her, no different than any other that she'd passed, but the memory caused her to hesitate. She combed over the doorway. There was no place for anything secret to be hidden. She swiped the badge, and started to walk through, then stopped. Towards the bottom of the frame was a small indent. "No..." escaped her lips. She lifted her foot to the door and pressed it into the dent. It fit. The door was the same. The capitol had been rearranging itself.

She sprinted down the tunnel again, heard the sound of metal grinding, and came upon the door, dent and all. She walked through it, but stopped and turned around, allowing the door to close. Her heart was pounding.

"The past," she said, her voice uncertain. "It's just the future," she swiped the badge, "behind us."

She withdrew her sword and held it out in front of her as she stepped into the passage. The path opened to a corridor of emerald blue. Motion flickered as shadows danced into and out of existence on the floor before her. Her eyes widened. On every side of her appeared an ocean. If it wasn't for the knowledge that her city was floating miles above the earth's surface, she could have believed that she was now in a submerged world. Schools of fish with scales of orange and yellow glimmered about her, suspended in their own liquid existence. She remembered first learning to swim at the cabin, in the frigid waters of the snow-fed lake.

"Where did you all come from?" she thought aloud. Her words sounded muffled. She took another step and realized she was out of the tunnel. Her body had kept her moving, even though the world had tried to distract her.

Lena stepped into a rounded antechamber. Its similarity to the nursery stopped at the fact that it was hemispherical. Where the nursery had clear walls, this room had doors. It was a cul-de-sac of doors. Identical doors. Tall, brown, patterned doors. And in front of each door was a desk with a tap-pad. The same desk, with the same tap-pad, where behind it sat the same empty chair. She sheathed her sword.

"Well then," she sighed.

XXVI.

"They're keeping you here?"

Sado nodded and pulled her into a tighter embrace as they lay there in the small nook of his windowless prison.

Talia nudged her head further into the warmth of his chest. The beat of his heart and the ebb and flow of his breathing moved as one with her own. "You're their prisoner."

"We're all their prisoners."

He felt her scowled response and rebutted with a weak smile.

"Do you think they'll have you stay here?"

"I imagine they'll keep moving me. They won't want me to remain in the same place for long. Wouldn't want the Outcry finding me."

She let out a small laugh. "No, no, just think what that would cause." She ran her finger along his jaw line until it touched his lips.

He kissed her palm and pressed her hand against his cheek. His eyes closed to the touch. "You should probably go back to your post." There was no real force left in his voice, only a tender resignation.

"You think Durin will miss me?" She teased.

"I know he will." His sigh felt cold, and she knew he had already started backing away from her, separating himself, knowing the possibility that it could be the last time they saw each other. Going back to her desk was not what she wanted to do. Sitting, waiting for Lena to arrive.

"Couldn't we just run? We know the way out of the capitol, out of the cities. We could just go." They'd had this conversation before.

She sat up. The two were a world apart. They had been ever since he'd begun training Lena. Ever since he'd taken her in as if she was the daughter that they'd never had. Talia touched her stomach. The daughter that they couldn't have.

She felt his hand rest on her back, the same way he had when she'd been told she couldn't conceive. She remembered the doctor smiling as he said it, his grin practiced and simpering, yet altogether devoid of empathy. He had brought out that bright green pamphlet with "The future is Mothers" emboldened on its cover. It sat on her dresser for months after that. The picture of the perky woman genetically chosen to give birth smiled at her, holding out her baby as an offering. The picture of Esta.

"You need to be there to show Lena the door that leads to Durin's office."

She pulled the marker-marker from her pocket and waved it between her fingers. She felt Sado's weight shift as he sat up. His arms wrapped around her again, and she leaned back into him.

How strange to think that it could all be over soon. Fifteen years ago, when she'd first met Sado, she couldn't even have imagined making it this far. Back then, she was just a secretary, more so a door watcher. Durin's door watcher. No one ever went in and no one ever came out, but she was assured that she was guarding him. The naivety of her excitement only lasted for a year. What once burned as an honor to protect the President eventually smoldered into a tarry residue of apathy.

It wasn't until she'd met Sado that she understood the source of her malaise. He'd told her everything he knew of the world, both inside and out. His transparency tasted sweet against the stale aftertaste of the capital's secrecy. He was honest. He told her about the disparity in the Council and how there were others like him, others who were ready to rejoin the earth. All they needed to do was unite them.

And now he would die for them.

She pushed away his arms and stood. "You're being foolish."

He had hoped that they wouldn't have to go through this again, but she was stubborn, and that's what he loved about her. "If Lena succeeds," his mouth formed the familiar words, "then we have a chance to bring everyone together again. Trust will be restored again in the capital, and we'll be able to start reintegration with the outside world."

"And giving yourself up proves nothing." She avoided his eyes. They were quicksand. She knew if they caught hers, it would be all over.

"You know it's the only way to make both the Outcry and the Council think they've won, to think that they're in control."

"I don't care!" She didn't bother lowering her voice. The walls of the soundproofed room absorbed her anger as fast as she could radiate it. "You're more important than her."

"You know I can't kill Durin."

"And when she fails?"

"If," he emphasized, "she fails, then we'll be in the same place we were a year ago."

"I want her to fail."

"Don't say that."

"If it means keeping you, then I pray for it."

"You're letting your emotions cloud your judgment."

"And you're letting your emotions be led by blind hope." She hit his chest as he pulled her into his arms. Talia could feel herself hyperventilating, tears hot on her cheeks. He was acting like no one would care if he were gone. He had grown so used to being hidden, to being detached.

Behind them they heard a click. The slow progression of gears in torsion pulled back the door, pouring excess light into the dimly lit room. She'd stayed too long, but what did it really matter now?

A flashlight of misty purple shined in on them, casting its holder in silhouette. It clicked off. Framed in light, squinting and quivering, stood the shape of a girl. Lena stepped forward into the room.

Talia turned back to Sado. She cupped her hands around his face and pressed their lips together, the saltiness of her tears mingling with the taste of his kiss. They both let the moment linger, until she felt his release on her slip, letting her know that it was time. She let go.

"If she lives, I'll look after her," Talia whispered to Sado. "I promise."

It took only six footsteps to reach Lena. Only then did Talia think to wipe the dampness from her face. Her voice was weak. "You found the marker okay?" She waved the pen at Lena.

Lena blinked, then nodded. She would understand soon enough.

"I'll be at my desk, then." Talia sighed and looked down to her feet. Her toes felt gripped in tension. "I'll see you when it's over." She wasn't sure to whom she was directing the comment, but she knew it was only meant for one of them. She walked out the door and into the antechamber.

XXVII.

The door slid closed behind Lena. Her body felt light. As if she'd molted and left some hollow replica of herself in the hall. She wondered if that was why she felt nauseous. No more skin to contain her insides. It certainly wasn't pinecones. She hadn't had those in weeks.

The tip of her blade scratched at the floor, whose surface was tiled in painted ceramic. In its fractured assembly, lightning bled in strands of red on a black night. She clenched her calves as her knees threatened to let her fall into the mosaic's chaos.

She had so many questions. Why was Talia embracing Sado? Why was Sado in President Durin's office in the first place? And why was there a knife hurtling towards—

She rotated her sword upwards in front of her as her feet forced her body to sidestep. The two steels met, edge on heel. She redirected its motion into one of the floor's onyx tiles. The tile erupted into a torrent of clay splinters. As she wrapped her eyes towards the blade's origin, another silver-edged tooth bit through the air. She twisted and collapsed to her knees, but the dagger tasted iron. It caressed the lobe of her ear and slipped along the side of her cheek, leaving an invasive heat crawling down her neck. She rolled and pushed herself to standing, speckling the ground with blood. Crimson tears touched her lips. She held her blade steady in front of her, waiting for the next barrage, but the only sound that filled the room was her panting.

The face she'd spent the last six months with smiled sadly at her and walked across the room to a large oak desk. Her eyes followed his movements as he sat behind it in President Durin's chair. In Sado's chair.

Lena's eyes began to tear.

Sado pressed play on a recorder atop the desk. It crackled to life and after a pause, a not so much younger Sado broke through the static.

"Ignorance is not an excuse, it's an offense." He touched another button on the recorder and it shrilled in fast motion. He pressed it again and time resumed its proper procession. A conversation all too familiar to Lena began to replay.

"If you'll listen," the box reiterated, "I have one more thing to tell you."

There was a pause in the sound and Lena rekindled the faint memory of Sado walking out of view that night that he was at her container. His voice continued. "Your father was one of the first members of the Outcry. Back before we even had a name."

"You knew him?" A pause.

"He would have been very proud of who you've become."

The words cut her. Who had she become? She stood, sword in both hands, blood still clotting on the base of her ear. Was it a trap? Was it a trick? Surely she'd taken a wrong turn somewhere, leading her to Sado's prison. Were there drugs still thick in her veins?

The box fizzled again and this time it was a young girl's voice that radiated off the oaken surface. It was tired, and worried, and fading into sleep, but it was familiar. The same voice read bedtime stories to Tulu, sang when no one was around, and sang when everyone was around. A not so much younger, not so less wise Lena yawned through the static. "What's that?" it said. There was a pause and a surprised scream. "Well you have my attention. That was bright."

Past-Sado laughed. "That was a memory marker. It's a very specific flash of light that is used to mark the beginning and end of a sequence of memories, so I can isolate that sequence in your brain. It makes it more precise to wipe clean a segment of your memory."

"But I thought—"

"Now now," the recorder interrupted itself, "do you trust me?" There was a pause again. Lena didn't know what her response would be now, but she knew that six months ago she would have nodded without hesitation. "Good," he continued. "Now tell me, why do you want to join the Outcry?"

Her ears perked. She'd been asked that question before. Or was it after? Time was getting all jumbled up in her grip as if her fingers were made of string. She listened as she explained how the Outcry and the Council needed to come together, how if only Sado could become the faceless leader of both he could bring about change, but this was a different speech than she'd given in the cabin. She spoke slower and without energy. She spoke as if she'd only just witnessed Ms. Pluck's death and had not yet witnessed the outside world's life. Everything she said ended as a question. Skeptical that the words she spoke truly meant anything. And in Sado's voice, there was a quiver, riddled with anxiety.

And then on cue, past-Lena echoed her question about the President. "It's just an old face and a voice. Right?"

The recording hesitated. She didn't remember Sado's pause ruminating for so long. Then static. More noise. Then, in solemnity, he spoke. "I'm Durin."

Lena's knuckles flared white around the sword's handle. The intake of her breath came with a high-pitched squeal, one not replicated on the recording. It would have meant nothing to her then. She imagined herself under the warmth of those covers, getting excited that she had another secret. That's all it would have been to her, something to hold over the heads of giants. What she would give to crawl back into her bed, into the ignorance of an infinite thread count.

The words flowed on as her eyelids dammed the lake welling behind them. She listened as they planned her kidnapping, the erasing of her memories, the fire, the training, and the moment it dawned on her what this was all leading to. She would have to kill Sado.

"I can't." Her voice trembled from the recording.

"You won't know. You'll be made to forget. And when the time comes, you'll realize it's the only way for people to believe."

"Then promise me. Promise you'll play this recording if I make it that far."

Sado's sigh played through the speakers. "I promise."

The voices stopped and only white noise followed.

"Today," Sado spoke in heavy tones, "we see if you're ready." His hand touched his cane. "I gave your father the same chance, you know. And Caldon. But they couldn't do it. They weren't like us, Lena. We understand what it means to have everyone and everything taken from us. To be hidden from the world. We understand what it means not to exist." He twisted the cane's hilt. "When you don't exist, you just become an observer of the world." Sado reached down and stopped the recorder. "And when you're just an observer, you can see how to fix things."

Lena immediately wanted the static to return. It had halted time. It was the sound of life. The sound of crinkled paper. Proof that life still existed in the crumpling of a dead tree. A tree still kicking. Without the static, it was just bodies moving. Sado's cane metamorphosing into a pen, its tip extending to rewrite her existence. Her own blade dividing the air before colliding with clicks and clacks of crackling.

She fell back. She'd forgotten how much heavier he was. Her wrist tinged with an immediate soreness. He swung again. There was youth in his one-handed sword. More whip than blade.

"Plea—"

Steel on steel. His scent of pine touched her tongue and she spat at him.

"Sto—"

He pushed again. Her palms dripped. As did his weary eyes.

Each flick of his cane danced a feather's width closer. She felt the breath of its snap on her throbbing ear.

With a quick twist, she swung at his feet, knocking him off balance. He fell to the ground. She advanced forward, each stab attempting to disarm him and stop this nightmare.

He crawled backwards, parrying each blow, a hint of both sorrow and satisfaction in his expression. His back pressed up against his desk and, in an instant, Lena pinned his sword to the ground.

She was breathless. "Enough. Please," she begged. Her arms quaked as gravity pulled down her blade.

Sado met her eyes. "Limit to fuel."

She stepped back. "I won't hurt you."

"Then," he said, standing up, "I'm sorry. Only one of us can leave this room."

He grabbed his cane and launched forward, twice as fast, his sadness replaced with anger.

Again, their blades met. Her sword felt heavy in both hands. Slow. She was a caged animal, and all she could do was back up. Back back back until she felt her foot kiss the wall. The rest of the room seemed so far away. The glint of the thrown dagger touched her peripheral as her elbow brushed the edge of her cage.

And Sado paused. Only for a moment. Only for the instant it took for him to toss a thread of rope to Lena's feet. She knew it was meant for her to see. It was meant as her distraction. The last blow to say she hadn't grown. That she hadn't learned control of her focus. The thread drifted to the ground. Tattered, twisted, frayed. Cut from the head of a mop, or perhaps the head of a friend. Tulu.

Sado's blade swung into hers and she let go. Her steel clattered to the opposite side of the room, and without its resistance Sado's footing was offset. He stumbled and she fell opposite his motion. She slid and twisted on the ground as Sado regained balance. Her legs pushed her backwards, until she felt the hilt of the embedded knife touch her side.

"Please," she sobbed. He walked towards her. "I can't." Another step. "There must be another way." She quivered. Confirmation that she was just a helpless little girl.

Ten feet away. He pulled his arm back, aligning the tip of his blade with Lena's heart. The edge wouldn't be sharp enough to kill her in a single slash. He wouldn't want her to suffer. To be precise, he'd need to get close.

Six feet away. She recognized the look in his eyes. His mind was somewhere in the distance; his body was only carrying out orders. Her chest throbbed, anticipating the steel's tip penetrating its sanctity. She couldn't kill him. She would be no better than the world she wished to escape.

Three feet away. *Everybody has a secret.* Lena covered her face with her elbow and turned away. The dagger's hilt aligned with her opposite palm. A breath. She twisted back towards Sado. His blade en route to her chest, she dropped her shoulder back, letting the blade pierce through her left arm.

Cold metal burrowed into her muscle. No time to scream. No time to cry. No time to give a name to her wound. She made a mental note as she brought the dagger from behind her back and slipped it into Sado's thigh. A letter delivered through a mail slot.

She screamed. The sword that still lingered in her flesh twisted as Sado fell to the ground. She pulled it free, and the hollow sound of bone on metal echoed through the chamber. Like sword on stone. It clattered across the room.

Both lay in blood. Lena took in deep gulps of air, her teeth clenched. Sado's breathing flickered in shallow sips.

"You're weak," he gasped.

"I... am... sorry," she cried between inhales. The room was spinning.

"The Outcry needs Durin's body. Proof he is dead. Proof that they have control. And the Council needs to believe the Outcry has ended. You know it's the only way. You said it yourself."

She shook her head from side to side. Tears blended with the open wound on her cheek. "It's easy... to just die." From the entrance, Lena heard the door click open. "It's hard to live... and to believe that people... will support each other's dreams." The steps of shoes approached, and she heard the sound of someone picking up a fallen blade. She felt her body start to spasm on the cold clay tiles. "But I have to believe. I have to believe that the layer we see is not the only one. That other layers exist."

There was silence as the footsteps approached Sado. Their sound was soft, like worn leather. Lena waited, unable to move. For a moment Sado's breathing stopped, and then he laughed. Not heavily, or jovially, but she knew it to be his laugh. A day hadn't gone by in the past six months that he hadn't laughed. Today would be the last. "Thank you," he whispered. His breathing ceased. Lena listened, shaking, as the blade fell to the ground. It rocked back and forth, and she remembered sitting, rocking on the cabin's porch, looking out onto a midnight forest. Looking into the unknown. Her vision faded, and with it, the silhouette of jagged brown hair and the sound of footsteps leaving the room.

XXVIII.

Lena watched as needle and thread weaved through the skin on her arm. She sipped real apple juice through a straw. Cookie crumbs sprinkled the desk in front of her.

Talia tied the end of the thread in a knot. The sound of her heels clacked across the room to check the door for a fifth time. The antechamber was still clear.

She stopped at Sado's body. It lay covered beneath a Persian tapestry torn from the wall. Wordlessly, they'd taken it down and placed it over him. Looking into his eyes had momentarily fooled them into thinking he was still there, just drifting behind his lenses on one of his ideas.

"They'll just go on thinking he's alive?" Lena's voice was a whisper.

"That's your choice."

Her cheeks were dry and cracked. When she spoke, she could feel her skin crease and twist. She knew she couldn't just take away the world's leader and leave it leaderless. *One cannot just take,* her words resonated inside her. "How will they know?"

Talia crossed the room and stood behind her. In front of her waited a microphone. She could sense Talia's hand floating inches above her good shoulder, unsure how to make contact. Her instinct was to push it away, but it seemed futile. Anger seemed futile. So instead she raised her own hand and used it to press Talia's hand onto her shoulder. They shared a breath, an uncommon occurrence.

"When you're ready, dial the radio to seventy-point-one." Talia pressed a key into the radio and flipped a toggle that made the radio gurgle like burnt coals. "When you're ready." Talia's words echoed back through the radio in Sado's voice.

Her heart fell an inch and a half.

"Why me?"

She felt a small squeeze on her shoulder. "He saw something in you. He saw that you were both the same, but that also you had something that he didn't have."

"But I was wrong. I've ruined so many people's lives." *It's not right for this world to be founded in blood.*

"Then fix it. Don't make his mistakes."

Lena could feel Talia's hand quivering on her shoulder. She was trying so hard not to show pain by burying Sado in the back of her mind.

Lena turned the dial and watched the numbers count higher in burning red segments. She turned to Talia, whose face was sullen, sunken, and illegible. She knew what Talia was feeling and, for the first time, she could see beneath her layers. She could see Talia. And she was happy to have her by her side. Talia nodded.

Lena turned back and whispered into the microphone. "Joseph?"

It fizzled as she released the button.

A heartbeat.

"Sado!" whispered excitement echoed across the waves. "We all thought—"

"Not now," Lena interrupted. His happiness and her teeth bit at the inside of her cheek. "You're to come collect the body. I'll be gone by the time you've arrived." She sighed. "We've won."

Talia patted her shoulder and switched off the radio.

They didn't talk. Only sat and waited. As much as her body felt inclined, Lena forced her breathing to differ from Talia's. The room didn't breathe, but if it had, Lena would have strayed from it as well. Somewhere, far below her, she imagined a bat inhaling and exhaling with her, most likely upside-down.

She wondered what her dad would say about this predicament she'd gotten herself into, what with posing as the new secret leader of the whole world. Probably something like, *Lena, if you were a boy, I would have named you Dirt.* She smirked. *Always a mess.*

By the time the door slid open, revealing Joseph and the others, Lena had covered her wounds and lay in the small nook of the room where the smell of Sado's pine and soot still lingered. Lin was the first to wrap her arms around her. Lena clenched her teeth to keep herself from screaming at the pressure on her arm, which seemed oddly intentional. Tears of joy, she claimed. Lin wrote that down, and then gave her a quick sad smile. Quick enough that Lena questioned if it had really happened. When she stepped away, the sound of her footsteps rang in Lena's ears, and Lena wondered why they had seemed so familiar.

Circ cleared his throat, and Lena's thoughts went to him. He approached her and ruffled her hair. "Don't see any reason why Sado couldn't have waited for a phase," he grumbled. He turned, shuffled about the room and waited until he thought everyone was distracted to replace his cane with the one that lay near Durin's covered body. Lena watched as he wiped her blood off the sword and onto the tapestry. The secrets he would walk with.

When Lena met Joseph's eyes he seemed immobilized in a teary grin. Lume squirmed in his grasp, waving his banana-length arms in her direction.

"I wasn't sure if I'd see you again," they both thought, but only Joseph said aloud.

She hugged him with her good arm as Lume's feet danced atop her head.

Talia cleared her throat and the room turned.

"It's time," her voice was soft. "Lena, stay and watch Lume. We need to get the body out of here."

As the others packaged Sado into a small box and carried him away, Lena sat Lume atop the desk. He gurgled and puttered, indistinguishable from a radio.

She was alone. And that was how Sado had intended it. But she had inherited a family. Lin, Circ, Joseph, they would be there for her. There would be secrets, but what family doesn't have secrets? And then there was Talia. Whether Lena liked it or not, they were in this together. They shared the same burden. "I'll just have to keep her in line," she winked at Lume.

And the Council? Her brow furrowed. *What can I do?* she thought. *What can I do that Sado couldn't? Tomorrow, the world will begin to pick up its pieces, and they'll be expecting me to have a plan.* She remembered the people sitting around the outskirts of Kardel, watching the storm, and she remembered the artists of Brin rushing to repaint.

There are so many people in this world. So many people that I can't begin to understand. So many opinions, so many gradients of grey. Why does everyone think that life is "yes or no" and "this or that"? Why can't we have a little bit of everything if we're smart about it? Everyone needs to remember that life is precious.

She touched the back of her ear, and a twinge of pain echoed through her body. *We can live together with the world, I know it.* She looked at Lume. "My dad knew we could."

Lume smiled.

"We just need to prove to the world that the earth is ready. And that we're ready." She touched Lume's ear and he laughed. *There's no reason that we can't live in both places, right?* She pursed her lips. "A scout," she said. "An explorer. Like Lady Adele. That's what we need. Before we send the first settlers, we need to show them that all the Snarglops are gone. That it's safe." *That's the plan.*

She sat back in her chair, her throne, and breathed a momentary sigh of relief. For all the uncertainties that she knew were ahead of her, at least she had a semblance of a plan. Her eyes met Lume's. Beside him sat a chessboard, identical to the one in the cabin. Lume picked up a pawn and began to gum it.

Lena's eyes widened. *A girl sits beside me,* the words rekindled in her mind at the shape of the queen. *Her noble steed too.* Beside the marble royalty stood a majestic horse. *You can't win without me.* She exhaled. *And it only seems there are two.* "Can I tell you a secret?" she asked him.

He wiggled. It would be his first secret.

"I finally solved his riddle." She let his hand wrap around her finger. "He thought that he was the king." Her eyes drifted to where Sado's body had once lain. *A king of two worlds.* She turned her head back to Lume; his eyes were a light in the darkness. And she couldn't help but to grin at him as her own eyes welled up. *How foolish we all are.*

Lume smiled and touched her nose. And with all the approval in the world, he nodded to her, or rather he bobbed his head like a melon in the ocean, *assuming,* Lena thought, *that melons float.*

ACKNOWLEDGEMENTS

Well, that's my first book! You read it! Huzzah! There will be two more in the set! My first thanks goes to you, the reader, for doing exactly as your title suggests: reading!

My second thank you is to the exclamation point, for making the prior paragraph possible.

The third and most groveling thank you I owe is to my editor, Lauren Buchsbaum, without whom this book would have mostly been composed of the letters A and H, and exclamation points. Thank you for your amazing generosity, your attention to detail, and your willingness to say, "Brandon, this doesn't make any sense."

I also owe bucket loads of thanks to all my friends and family who I bugged to read early versions of the book and who supplied me with invaluable feedback about it, as well as about the cover art, the layout, and the back description, especially Griffin Pahl, Amanda Brizendine, Faiyam Rahman, Heather Palmer, Dora Miketa, Stephen Keeley, Kevin Huang, Craig Harrison, Derek Crowe, and my grandfather, Duane Morningred.

When the book was still in its infancy, I took it to the amazing group of writers in my writing group out in California, so I want to send my unending thanks to all of them, and in particular thanks to Tom Salameh, Jim Cambra, and Michelle Brooks.

Thank you must also go to all the coffee shops in which this was written and conceived, as well as all the trains and planes, which managed to transport me while giving me the freedom to write. Speaking of which, no thanks goes to my bicycle, which refused to let me write while riding it.

A final thank you to all the people that I'm forgetting to thank. An especial thanks to you because you also have to put up with my amazing ability to forget things!

Yay! Thank you all again,
Brandon Plaster

www.ingramcontent.com/pod-product-compliance
Lightning Source LLC
Chambersburg PA
CBHW052024240626
47153CB00006B/1940